PENGUIN CELEBRATIONS

REGENERATION

Pat Barker was born in 1943. Her books include the highly acclaimed *Regeneration* trilogy, comprising *Regeneration* (1991), which was made into a film of the same name, *The Eye in the Door* (1993), which won the Guardian Fiction Prize, and *The Ghost Road* (1995), which won the Booker Prize, as well as the more recent novels *Another World, Border Crossing* and *Double Vision*. She lives in Durham.

PAT BARKER

—————

REGENERATION

PENGUIN BOOKS

PENGUIN
CELEBRATIONS

For David, and in loving memory of
Dr John Hawkings (1922–1987)

PENGUIN BOOKS

Published by the Penguin Group
Penguin Books Ltd, 80 Strand, London WC2R ORL, England
Penguin Group (USA) Inc., 375 Hudson Street, New York, New York 10014, USA
Penguin Group (Canada), 90 Eglinton Avenue East, Suite 700, Toronto, Ontario, Canada M4P 2Y3
(a division of Pearson Penguin Canada Inc.)
Penguin Ireland, 25 St Stephen's Green, Dublin 2, Ireland
(a division of Penguin Books Ltd)
Penguin Group (Australia), 250 Camberwell Road, Camberwell, Victoria 3124, Australia
(a division of Pearson Australia Group Pty Ltd)
Penguin Books India Pvt Ltd, 11 Community Centre, Panchsheel Park, New Delhi – 110 017, India
Penguin Group (NZ), 67 Apollo Drive, Rosedale, North Shore 0632, New Zealand
(a division of Pearson New Zealand Ltd)
Penguin Books (South Africa) (Pty) Ltd, 24 Sturdee Avenue, Rosebank, Johannesburg 2196, South Africa

Penguin Books Ltd, Registered Offices: 80 Strand, London WC2R ORL, England

www.penguin.com

First published by Viking 1991
Published in Penguin Books 1992
Reissued in this edition 2007

1

The publishers wish to thank the following for permission to reproduce copyright material: George
Sassoon for Siegfried Sassoon's 'The Rear-Guard', 'The General', 'To the Warmongers', the extract
from 'The Death-Bed', the extract from 'The Redeemer', the extract from 'Prelude: The Troops' and
'Death's Brotherhood', all used by permission; and the Estate of Wilfred Owen for extracts from his
'The Next War' and 'Anthem for Doomed Youth', taken from *Wilfred Owen: The Complete Poems and
Fragments*, edited by Jon Stallworthy and published by Chatto & Windus and the Hogarth Press.

Printed in England by Clays Ltd, St Ives plc

ISBN: 978-0-141-03505-5

Part 1

1

Finished with the War
A Soldier's Declaration

I am making this statement as an act of wilful defiance of military authority, because I believe the war is being deliberately prolonged by those who have the power to end it.

I am a soldier, convinced that I am acting on behalf of soldiers. I believe that this war, upon which I entered as a war of defence and liberation, has now become a war of aggression and conquest. I believe that the purposes for which I and my fellow soldiers entered upon this war should have been so clearly stated as to have made it impossible to change them, and that, had this been done, the objects which actuated us would now be attainable by negotiation.

I have seen and endured the suffering of the troops, and I can no longer be a party to prolong these sufferings for ends which I believe to be evil and unjust.

I am not protesting against the conduct of the war, but against the political errors and insincerities for which the fighting men are being sacrificed.

On behalf of those who are suffering now I make this protest against the deception which is being practised on them; also I believe that I may help to destroy the callous complacence with which the majority of those at home regard the continuance of agonies which they do not share, and which they have not sufficient imagination to realize.

S. Sassoon
July 1917

Bryce waited for Rivers to finish reading before he spoke again. 'The "S" stands for "Siegfried". Apparently, he thought that was better left out.'

'And I'm sure he was right.' Rivers folded the paper and ran his fingertips along the edge. 'So they're sending him here?'

Bryce smiled. 'Oh, I think it's rather more specific than that. They're sending him to *you*.'

Rivers got up and walked across to the window. It was a fine day, and many of the patients were in the hospital grounds, watching a game of tennis. He heard the *pok-pok* of rackets, and a cry of frustration as a ball smashed into the net. 'I suppose he is – "shell-shocked"?'

'According to the Board, yes.'

'It just occurs to me that a diagnosis of neurasthenia might not be inconvenient confronted with this.' He held up the Declaration.

'Colonel Langdon chaired the Board. *He* certainly seems to think he is.'

'Langdon doesn't believe in shell-shock.'

Bryce shrugged. 'Perhaps Sassoon was gibbering all over the floor.'

'"Funk, old boy." I know Langdon.' Rivers came back to his chair and sat down. 'He doesn't *sound* as if he's gibbering, does he?'

Bryce said carefully, 'Does it matter what his mental state is? Surely it's better for him to be here than in prison?'

'Better for *him*, perhaps. What about the hospital? Can you imagine what our dear Director of Medical Services is going to say, when he finds out we're sheltering "conchies" as well as cowards, shirkers, scrimshankers and degenerates? We'll just have to hope there's no publicity.'

'There's going to be, I'm afraid. The Declaration's going to be read out in the House of Commons next week.'

'By?'

'Lees-Smith.'

Rivers made a dismissive gesture.

'Yes, well, I know. But it still means the press.'

'And the minister will say that no disciplinary action has been taken, because Mr Sassoon is suffering from a severe mental breakdown, and therefore not responsible for his actions. I'm not sure I'd prefer that to prison.'

'I don't suppose he was offered the choice. Will you take him?'

'You mean I *am* being offered a choice?'

'In view of your case load, yes.'

Rivers took off his glasses and swept his hand down across his eyes. 'I suppose they *have* remembered to send the file?'

Sassoon leant out of the carriage window, still half-expecting to see Graves come pounding along the platform, looking even more dishevelled than usual. But further down the train, doors had already begun to slam, and the platform remained empty.

The whistle blew. Immediately, he saw lines of men with grey muttering faces clambering up the ladders to face the guns. He blinked them away.

The train began to move. Too late for Robert now. *Prisoner arrives without escort*, Sassoon thought, sliding open the carriage door.

By arriving an hour early he'd managed to get a window seat. He began picking his way across to it through the tangle of feet. An elderly vicar, two middle-aged men, both looking as if they'd done rather well out of the war, a young girl and an older woman, obviously travelling together. The train bumped over a point. Everybody rocked and swayed, and Sassoon, stumbling, almost fell into the vicar's lap. He mumbled an apology and sat down. Admiring glances, and not only from the women. Sassoon turned to look out of the window, hunching his shoulder against them all.

After a while he stopped pretending to look at the smoking chimneys of Liverpool's back streets and closed his eyes. He needed to sleep, but instead Robert's face floated in front of him, white and twitching as it had been last Sunday, almost a week ago now, in the lounge of the Exchange Hotel.

For a moment, looking up to find that khaki-clad figure standing just inside the door, he thought he was hallucinating again.

'Robert, what on earth are *you* doing here?' He jumped up and ran across the lounge. 'Thank God you've come.'

'I got myself passed fit.'

'Robert, *no*.'

'What else could I do? After getting *this*.' Graves dug into his tunic pocket and produced a crumpled piece of paper. 'A covering letter would have been nice.'

'I wrote.'

'No, you didn't, Sass. You just sent me this. Couldn't you at least have *talked* about it first?'

'I thought I'd written.'

They sat down, facing each other across a small table. Cold northern light streamed in through the high windows, draining Graves's face of the little colour it had.

'Sass, you've got to give this up.'

'Give it up? You don't think I've come this far, do you, just to give in now?'

'Look, you've made your protest. For what it's worth, I agree with every word of it. But you've had your say. There's no point making a martyr of yourself.'

'The only way I can get publicity is to make them court-martial me.'

'They won't do it.'

'Oh, yes, they will. It's just a matter of hanging on.'

'You're in no state to stand a court-martial.' Graves clasped his clenched fist. 'If I had Russell here now, I'd *shoot* him.'

'It was my idea.'

'Oh, pull the other one. And even if it was, do you think anybody's going to understand it? They'll just say you've got cold feet.'

'Look, Robert, you think exactly as I do about the war, and you *do . . . nothing*. All right, that's your choice. But don't come here lecturing *me* about *cold feet*. This is the hardest thing I've ever done.'

Now, on the train going to Craiglockhart, it still seemed the hardest thing. He shifted in his seat and sighed, looking out over fields of wheat bending to the wind. He remembered the silvery sound of shaken wheat, the shimmer of light on the stalks. He'd have given anything to be out there, away from the stuffiness of the carriage, the itch and constriction of his uniform.

On that Sunday they'd taken the train to Formby and spent the afternoon wandering aimlessly along the beach. A dull, wintry-looking sun cast their shadows far behind them, so that every gesture either of them made was mimicked and magnified.

'They won't *let* you make a martyr of yourself, Sass. You should have accepted the Board.'

The discussion had become repetitive. For perhaps the fourth time, Sassoon said, 'If I hold out long enough, there's nothing else they can do.'

'There's a lot they can do.' Graves seemed to come to a decision. 'As a matter of fact, I've been pulling a few strings on your behalf.'

Sassoon smiled to hide his anger. 'Good. If you've been exercising your usual tact, that ought to get me at least two years.'

'They won't court-martial you.'

In spite of himself, Sassoon began to feel afraid. 'What, then?'

'Shut you up in a lunatic asylum for the rest of the war.'

'And that's the result of your string-pulling, is it? Thanks.'

'No, the result of my string-pulling is to get you another Board. You must take it this time.'

'You can't put people in lunatic asylums just like that. You have to have *reasons*.'

'They've got reasons.'

'Yes, the Declaration. Well, that doesn't prove me insane.'

'And the hallucinations? *The corpses in Piccadilly?*'

A long silence. 'I had rather hoped my letters to you were private.'

'I had to persuade them to give you another Board.'

'They won't court-martial me?'

'No. Not in any circumstances. And if you go on refusing to be boarded, they *will* put you away.'

'You know, Robert, I wouldn't believe this from anybody else. Will you *swear* it's true?'

'Yes.'

'On the Bible?'

Graves held up an imaginary Bible and raised his right hand. 'I swear.'

Their shadows stretched out behind them, black on the white sand. For a moment Sassoon still hesitated. Then, with an odd little gasp, he said, 'All right then, I'll give way.'

In the taxi,· going to Craiglockhart, Sassoon began to feel

frightened. He looked out of the window at the crowded pavements of Princes Street, thinking he was seeing them for the first and last time. He couldn't imagine what awaited him at Craiglockhart, but he didn't for a moment suppose the inmates were let out.

He glanced up and found the taxi-driver watching him in the mirror. All the local people must know the name of the hospital, and what it was for. Sassoon's hand went up to his chest and began pulling at a loose thread where his MC ribbon had been.

For conspicuous gallantry during a raid on the enemy's trenches. He remained for 1½ hours under rifle and bomb fire collecting and bringing in our wounded. Owing to his courage and determination, all the killed and wounded were brought in.

Reading the citation, it seemed to Rivers more extraordinary than ever that Sassoon should have thrown the medal away. Even the most extreme pacifist could hardly be ashamed of a medal awarded for *saving* life. He took his glasses off and rubbed his eyes. He'd been working on the file for over an hour, but, although he was now confident he knew all the facts, he was no closer to an understanding of Sassoon's state of mind. If anything, Graves's evidence to the Board – with its emphasis on hallucinations – seemed to suggest a full-blown psychosis rather than neurasthenia. And yet there was no other evidence for that. Misguided the Declaration might well be, but it was not deluded, illogical or incoherent. Only the throwing away of the medal still struck him as odd. That surely had been the action of a man at the end of his tether.

Well, we've all been there, he thought. The trouble was, he was finding it difficult to examine the evidence impartially. He *wanted* Sassoon to be ill. Admitting this made him pause. He got up and began pacing the floor of his room, from door to window and back again. He'd only ever encountered one similar case, a man who'd refused to go on fighting on religious grounds. Atrocities took place on both sides, he'd said. There was nothing to choose between the British and the Germans.

The case had given rise to heated discussions in the MO's common room – about the freedom of the individual conscience in wartime, and the role of the army psychiatrist in 'treating' a man who refused to fight. Rivers, listening to those arguments, had been left in no doubt of the depth and seriousness of the divisions. The controversy had died down only when the patient proved to be psychotic. That was the crux of the matter. A man like Sassoon would always be trouble, but he'd be a lot less trouble if he were ill.

Rivers was roused from these thoughts by the crunch of tyres on gravel. He reached the window in time to see a taxi draw up, and a man, who from his uniform could only be Sassoon, get out. After paying the driver, Sassoon stood for a moment, looking up at the building. Nobody arriving at Craiglockhart for the first time could fail to be daunted by the sheer gloomy, cavernous bulk of the place. Sassoon lingered on the drive for a full minute after the taxi had driven away, then took a deep breath, squared his shoulders, and ran up the steps.

Rivers turned away from the window, feeling almost ashamed of having witnessed that small, private victory over fear.

2

Light from the window behind Rivers's desk fell directly on to Sassoon's face. Pale skin, purple shadows under the eyes. Apart from that, no obvious signs of nervous disorder. No twitches, jerks, blinks, no repeated ducking to avoid a long-exploded shell. His hands, doing complicated things with cup, saucer, plate, sandwiches, cake, sugar tongs and spoon, were perfectly steady. Rivers raised his own cup to his lips and smiled. One of the nice things about serving afternoon tea to newly arrived patients was that it made so many neurological tests redundant.

So far he hadn't looked at Rivers. He sat with his head slightly averted, a posture that could easily have been taken for arrogance, though Rivers was more inclined to suspect shyness. The voice was slightly slurred, the flow of words sometimes hesitant, sometimes rushed. A disguised stammer, perhaps, but a life-long stammer, Rivers thought, not the recent, self-conscious stammer of the neurasthenic.

'While I remember, Captain Graves rang to say he'll be along some time after dinner. He sent his apologies for missing the train.'

'He *is* still coming?'

'Yes.'

Sassoon looked relieved. 'Do you know, I don't think Graves's caught a train in his life? Unless somebody was there to *put* him on it.'

'We were rather concerned about you.'

'In case the lunatic went missing?'

'I wouldn't put it quite like that.'

'I was all right. I wasn't even surprised, I thought he'd slept in. He's been doing a . . . a lot of rushing round on my behalf recently. You've no idea how much work goes into *rigging* a Medical Board.'

Rivers pushed his spectacles up on to his forehead and

massaged the inner corners of his eyes. 'No, I don't suppose I have. You know this may sound naïve but ... to *me* ... the accusation that a Medical Board has been rigged is quite a serious one.'

'I've no complaints. I was dealt with in a perfectly fair and reasonable way. Probably better than I deserved.'

'What kind of questions did they ask?'

Sassoon smiled. 'Don't you know?'

'I've read the report, if that's what you mean. I'd still like to hear your version.'

'Oh: "Did I object to fighting on religious grounds?" I said I didn't. It was rather amusing, actually. For a moment I thought they were asking me whether I objected to going on a crusade. "Did I think I was qualified to decide when the war should end?" I said I hadn't thought about my qualifications.' He glanced at Rivers. '*Not true*. And then ... then Colonel Langdon asked *said* "Your friend tells us you're very good at bombing. Don't you still dislike the Germans?"'

A long silence. The net curtain behind Rivers's head billowed out in a glimmering arc, and a gust of cool air passed over their faces.

'And what did you say to that?'

'I don't remember.' He sounded impatient now. 'It didn't matter what I said.'

'It matters now.'

'All right.' A faint smile. '*Yes*, I am quite good at bombing. *No*, I do not still dislike the Germans.'

'Does that mean you once did?'

Sassoon looked surprised. For the first time something had been said that contradicted his assumptions. 'Briefly. April and May of last year, to be precise.'

A pause. Rivers waited. After a while Sassoon went on, almost reluctantly. 'A friend of mine had been killed. For a while I used to go out on patrol every night, looking for Germans to kill. Or rather I told myself that's what I was doing. In the end I didn't know whether I was trying to kill them, or just giving them plenty of opportunities to kill me.'

'"Mad Jack."'

Sassoon looked taken aback. 'Graves really *has* talked, hasn't he?'

'It's the kind of thing the Medical Board would need to know.' Rivers hesitated. 'Taking *unnecessary* risks is one of the first signs of a war neurosis.'

'Is it?' Sassoon looked down at his hands. 'I didn't know that.'

'Nightmares and hallucinations come later.'

'What's an "unnecessary risk" anyway? The maddest thing *I* ever did was done under orders.' He looked up, to see if he should continue. 'We were told to go and get the regimental badges off a German corpse. They reckoned he'd been dead two days, so obviously if we got the badges they'd know which battalion was opposite. Full moon, not a cloud in sight, *absolutely mad*, but off we went. Well, we got there – eventually – and what do we find? He's been dead a helluva lot longer than two days, and he's French anyway.'

'So what did you do?'

'Pulled one of his boots off and sent it back to battalion HQ. With quite a bit of his leg left inside.'

Rivers allowed another silence to open up. 'I gather we're not going to talk about nightmares?'

'You're in charge.'

'Ye-es. But then one of the paradoxes of being an army psychiatrist is that you don't actually get very far by *ordering* your patients to be frank.'

'I'll be as frank as you like. I did have nightmares when I first got back from France. I don't have them now.'

'And the hallucinations?'

He found this more difficult. 'It was just that when I woke up, the nightmares didn't always stop. So I used to see . . .' A deep breath. 'Corpses. Men with half their faces shot off, crawling across the floor.'

'And you were awake when this happened?'

'I don't know. I must've been, because I could see the sister.'

'And was this always at night?'

'No. It happened once during the day. I'd been to my club for lunch, and when I came out I sat on a bench, and . . . I suppose I must've nodded off.' He was forcing himself to go on. 'When I woke up, the pavement was covered in corpses. Old ones, new ones, black, green.' His mouth twisted. 'People were treading on their faces.'

Rivers took a deep breath. 'You say you'd just woken up?'

'Yes. I used to sleep quite a bit during the day, because I was afraid to go to sleep at night.'

'When did all this stop?'

'As soon as I left the hospital. The atmosphere in that place was really terrible. There was one man who used to boast about killing German prisoners. You can imagine what living with *him* was like.'

'And the nightmares haven't recurred?'

'No. I do dream, of course, but not about the war. Sometimes a dream seems to go on after I've woken up, so there's a a kind of in-between stage.' He hesitated. 'I don't know whether that's abnormal.'

'I hope not. It happens to me all the time.' Rivers sat back in his chair. 'When you look back now on your time in the hospital, do *you* think you were "shell-shocked"?'

'I don't know. Somebody who came to see me told my uncle he thought I was. As against that, I wrote one or two good poems while I was in there. We-ell . . .' He smiled. '*I* was pleased with them.'

'You don't think it's possible to write a good poem in a state of shock?'

'No, I don't.'

Rivers nodded. 'You may be right. Would it be possible for me to see them?'

'Yes, of course. I'll copy them out.'

Rivers said, 'I'd like to move on now to the . . . thinking behind the Declaration. You say your motives aren't religious?'

'No, not at all.'

'Would you describe yourself as a pacifist?'

'I don't think so. I can't possibly say "*No* war is ever justified", because I haven't thought about it enough. Perhaps some wars are. Perhaps this one was when it started. I just don't think our war aims – *whatever they may be* – and we don't know – justify this level of slaughter.'

'And you say you *have* thought about your qualifications for saying that?'

'*Yes*. I'm only too well aware of how it sounds. A *second-lieutenant*, no less, saying "The war must stop". On the other hand, I have *been* there. I'm at least as well qualified as some of the old men you see sitting around in clubs, cackling on about "attrition" and "wastage of manpower" and . . .' His voice became a vicious parody of an old man's voice. '"*Lost heavily in that last scrap.*" You don't talk like that if you've watched them die.'

'No intelligent or sensitive person would talk like that anyway.'

A slightly awkward pause. 'I'm not saying there are no exceptions.'

Rivers laughed. 'The point is you hate civilians, don't you? The "callous", the "complacent", the "unimaginative". Or is "hate" too strong a word?'

'No.'

'So. What you felt for the Germans, rather briefly, in the spring of last year, you now feel for the overwhelming majority of your fellow-countrymen?'

'Yes.'

'You know, I think you were quite right not to say too much to the Board.'

'That wasn't my idea, it was Graves's. He was afraid I'd sound too sane.'

'When you said the Board was "rigged", what did you mean?'

'I meant the decision to send me here, or or somewhere similar, had been taken before I went in.'

'And this had all been fixed by Captain Graves?'

'Yes.' Sassoon leant forward. 'The point is they weren't going to court-martial me. They were just going to lock me up somewhere . . .' He looked round the room. '*Worse* than this.'

Rivers smiled. 'There *are* worse places, believe me.'

'I'm sure there are,' Sassoon said politely.

'They were going to certify you, in fact?'

'I suppose so.'

'Did anybody on the Board say anything to you about this?'

'No, because it was –'

'All fixed beforehand. Yes, I see.'

Sassoon said, 'May I ask you a question?'

'Go ahead'

'Do *you* think I'm mad?'

'No, of course you're not mad. Did you think you were going mad?'

'It crossed my mind. You know when you're brought face to face with the fact that, yes, you did see corpses on the pavement . . .'

'Hallucinations in the half-waking state are surprisingly common, you know. They're not the same thing as psychotic hallucinations. Children have them quite frequently.'

Sassoon had started pulling at a loose thread on the breast of his tunic. Rivers watched him for a while. 'You must've been in agony when you did that.'

Sassoon lowered his hand. 'No-o. *Agony's* lying in a shell-hole with your legs shot off. I was *upset*.' For a moment he looked almost hostile, then he relaxed. 'It was a futile gesture. I'm not particularly proud of it.'

'You threw it in the Mersey, didn't you?'

'Yes. It wasn't heavy enough to sink, so it just' – a glint of amusement – '*bobbed* around. There was a ship sailing past, quite a long way out, in the estuary, and I looked at this little scrap of ribbon floating and I looked at the ship, and I thought that me trying to stop the war was a bit like trying to stop the ship would have been. You know, all they'd've seen from the deck was this little figure jumping up and down, waving its arms, and they wouldn't've known what on earth it was getting so excited about.'

'So you realized *then* that it was futile?'

Sassoon lifted his head. 'It still had to be done. You can't just acquiesce.'

Rivers hesitated. 'Look, I think we've . . . we've got about as far as we can get today. You must be very tired.' He stood up. 'I'll see you tomorrow morning at ten. Oh, and could you ask Captain Graves to see me as soon as he arrives?'

Sassoon stood up. 'You said a bit back you didn't think I was mad.'

'I'm quite sure you're not. As a matter of fact I don't even think you've got a war neurosis.'

Sassoon digested this. 'What have I got, then?'

'You seem to have a very powerful *anti*-war neurosis.'

They looked at each other and laughed. Rivers said, 'You realize, don't you, that it's my duty to . . . to try to change that? I can't pretend to be neutral.'

Sassoon's glance took in both their uniforms. 'No, of course not.'

*

Rivers made a point of sitting next to Bryce at dinner.

'Well,' Bryce said, 'what did you make of him?'

'I can't find anything wrong. He doesn't show any sign of depression, he's not excited –'

'Physically?'

'Nothing.'

'Perhaps he just doesn't want to be killed.'

'Oh, I think he'd be most insulted if you suggested *that*. To be fair, he did have a job lined up in Cambridge, training cadets – so it isn't a question of avoiding being sent back. He could've taken that if he'd wanted to save his skin.'

'Any trace of . . . er . . . religious *enthusiasm*?'

'No, I'm afraid not. I was hoping for that too.'

They looked at each other, amused. 'You know, the curious thing is I don't think he's even a pacifist? It seems to be entirely a matter of of horror at the extent of the slaughter, combined with a feeling of anger that the government won't state its war aims and impose some kind of *limitation* on the whole thing. That, and an absolutely corrosive hatred of civilians. *And* non-combatants in uniform.'

'What an uncomfortable time you must've had.'

'No-o, I rather gather I was seen as an exception.'

Bryce looked amused. 'Did *you* like *him*?'

'Yes, very much. And I found him . . . much more *impressive* than I expected.'

Sassoon, at his table under the window, sat in silence. The men on either side of him stammered so badly that conversation would have been impossible, even if he had wished for it, but he was content to withdraw into his own thoughts.

He remembered the day before Arras, staggering from the outpost trench to the main trench and back again, carrying boxes of trench mortar bombs, passing the same corpses time after time, until their twisted and blackened shapes began to seem like old friends. At one point he'd had to pass two hands sticking up out of a heap of pocked and pitted chalk, like the roots of an overturned tree. No way of telling if they were British or German hands. No way of persuading himself it mattered.

'Do you play golf?'

'I'm sorry?'

'I asked if you played golf.'

Small blue eyes, nibbled gingery moustache, an RAMC badge. He held out his hand. 'Ralph Anderson.'

Sassoon shook hands and introduced himself. 'Yes, I do.'

'What's your handicap?'

Sassoon told him. After all, why not? It seemed an entirely suitable topic for Bedlam.

'Ah, then we might have a game.'

'I'm afraid I haven't brought my clubs.'

'Send for them. Some of the best courses in the country round here.'

Sassoon had opened his mouth to reply when a commotion started near the door. As far as he could tell, somebody seemed to have been sick. At any rate, a thin, yellow-skinned man was on his feet, choking and gagging. A couple of VADs ran across to him, clucking, fussing, flapping ineffectually at his tunic with a napkin, until eventually they had the sense to get him out of the room. The swing doors closed behind them. A moment's silence, and then, as if nothing had happened, the buzz of conversation rose again.

Rivers stood up and pushed his plate away. 'I think I'd better go.'

'Why not wait till you've finished?' Bryce said. 'You eat little enough as it is.'

Rivers patted his midriff. 'Oh, I shan't fade away just yet.'

Whenever Rivers wanted to get to the top floor without being stopped half a dozen times on the way, he used the back staircase. Pipes lined the walls, twisting with the turning of the stair, gurgling from time to time like lengths of human intestine. It was dark, the air stuffy, and sweat began to prickle in the roots of his hair. It was a relief to push the swing door open and come out on to the top corridor, where the air was cool at least, though he never failed to be depressed by the long narrow passage with its double row of brown doors and the absence of natural light. 'Like a trench without the sky' had been one patient's description, and he was afraid it was only too accurate.

Burns was sitting on his bed, while two VADs helped him off with his tunic and shirt. His collar bones and ribs were clearly visible beneath the yellowish skin. The waistband of his breeches gaped.

One of the VADs tugged at it. 'There's room for two in there,' she said, smiling, coaxing. 'Have I to get in with you?' The other VAD's frozen expression warned her of Rivers's presence. 'I'll get this sponged down for you, Captain.'

They hurried past Rivers, bursting into nervous giggles as they reached the end of the corridor.

Burns's arms were goose-pimpled, though the room was not cold. The smell of vomit lingered on his breath. Rivers sat down beside him. He didn't know what to say, and thought it better to say nothing. After a while he felt the bed begin to shake and put his arm round Burns's shoulders. 'It doesn't get any better, does it?' he said.

Burns shook his head. After a while Rivers got up, fetched Burns's coat from the peg behind the door and wrapped it round his shoulders. 'Would it be easier to eat in your own room?'

'A bit. I wouldn't have to worry about upsetting other people.'

Yes, Burns *would* worry about upsetting other people. Perhaps the most distressing feature of his case was the occasional glimpse of the cheerful and likeable young man he must once have been.

Rivers looked down at Burns's forearms, noting that the groove between radius and ulna was even deeper than it had been a week ago. 'Would it help to have a bowl of fruit in your room?' he asked. 'So you could just pick something up when you felt like it?'

'Yes, that might help.'

Rivers got up and walked across to the window. He's agreeing to make me feel useful, he thought. 'All right, I'll get them to send something up.' The shadows of the beech trees had begun to creep across the tennis courts, which were empty now. Rivers turned from the window. 'What kind of night did you have?'

'Not too good.'

'Have you made any progress with what we talked about?'

'Not really.' He looked up at Rivers. 'I can't make myself think about it.'

'No, well, it's early days.'

'You know, the worst thing is . . .' – Burns was scanning Rivers's face – 'that it's a . . . a joke.'

'Yes.'

After leaving Burns, Rivers went up a further short flight of stairs and unlocked the door to the tower. Apart from his own bedroom, this was the only place in Craiglockhart he could hope to be alone for more than a few minutes. The patients weren't allowed out here, in case the hundred-foot drop to the path below should prove too tempting an exit from the war. He rested his arms on the iron balustrade and looked out towards the hills.

Burns. Rivers had become adept at finding bearable aspects to unbearable experiences, but Burns defeated him. What had happened to him was so vile, so disgusting, that Rivers could find no redeeming feature. He'd been thrown into the air by the explosion of a shell and had landed, head-first, on a German corpse, whose gas-filled belly had ruptured on impact. Before Burns lost consciousness, he'd had time to realize that what filled his nose and mouth was decomposing human flesh. Now, whenever he tried to eat, that taste and smell recurred. Nightly, he relived the experience, and from every nightmare he awoke vomiting. Burns on his knees, as Rivers had often seen him, retching up the last ounce of bile, hardly looked like a human being at all. His body seemed to have become merely the skin-and-bone casing for a tormented alimentary canal. His suffering was without purpose or dignity, and yes, Rivers knew *exactly* what Burns meant when he said it was a joke.

Rivers became aware that he was gripping the edge of the parapet and consciously relaxed his hands. Whenever he spent any time with Burns, he found himself plagued by questions that in Cambridge, in peacetime, he might have wanted to pursue, but which in wartime, in an overcrowded hospital, were no use to him at all. Worse than useless, since they drained him of energy that rightly belonged to his patients. In a way, all this had nothing to do with Burns. The sheer extremity of his suffering set him apart from the rest, but the questions were evoked by almost every case.

He looked down and saw a taxi turn into the drive. Perhaps this was the errant Captain Graves arriving at last? Yes, there was Sassoon, too impatient to wait indoors, running down the steps to meet him.

3

Graves, his mouth slightly open, stared up at the massive yellow-grey façade of Craiglockhart. '*My God.*'

Sassoon followed the direction of his gaze. 'That's what I thought.'

Graves picked up his bag and together they went up the steps, through the black and white tiled entrance hall on to the main corridor. Sassoon began to smile. 'Fine prisoner's escort you turned out to be.'

'I know, I'm sorry. God, what a day. Do you know, the train stopped at *every* station?'

'Well, you're here now. Thank God.'

Graves looked sideways at him. 'As bad as that?'

'Hm. So-so.'

'I don't suppose you've seen anybody yet?'

'I've seen Rivers. Which reminds me, he wants to see *you*, but I imagine it'll be all right if you dump your bag first.'

Graves followed Sassoon up the marble staircase to the first floor.

'Here we are.' Sassoon opened a door and stood aside to let Graves enter. 'The guest room. You've even got a lock on your door.'

'You haven't?'

'No. Nor in the bathroom either.'

'Poor old Sass, you'll just have to *fight* the VADs off.' Graves swung his bag on to the nearest chair. 'No, seriously, what's it like?'

'Seriously, it's *awful*. Come on, the sooner you've seen Rivers the sooner we can talk.'

'Sassoon asked me to give you this.'

Rivers took the envelope without comment and placed it unopened on his desk. 'How did you find him?'

The net curtains breathed in the draught from the open window, and a scent of lime trees invaded the room. A sweet smell. Graves, to whom all sweet smells were terrible, wiped the sweat from his upper lip. 'Calmer. I think it's a relief to have things sorted out.'

'I don't know how sorted out they are. You do realize, don't you, that he can walk out of here at any time?'

'He won't do that,' Graves said definitely. 'He'll be all right now. As long as the pacifists leave him alone.'

'I had quite a long talk with him this afternoon, but I don't think I'm quite clear what happened. I suspect there was a lot going on behind the scenes?'

Graves smiled. 'You could say that.'

'What exactly?'

'Sassoon sent me a copy of his Declaration. I was in a convalescent home on the Isle of Wight at the time –'

'He hadn't talked to you about it?'

'No, I haven't seen him since January. I was absolutely horrified. I could see at once it wouldn't do any good, nobody would follow his example. He'd just destroy himself, for no reason.' He stopped. When he spoke again, his voice was very clear and precise. 'Sassoon's the best platoon commander I've ever known. The men worship him – if he wanted German heads on a platter they'd get them. And *he* loves them. Being separated from them would kill him. And that's exactly what a court-martial would've done.'

'He's separated from them here.'

'Yes, but there's a way back. People can accept a breakdown. There's no way back from being a conchie.'

'So you decided he –'

'Had to be stopped? Yes. I wrote to the CO, asking him to get Siegfried another Board. He'd already skipped one. Then I contacted various people I know and managed to persuade them to treat it as a nervous breakdown. That left Siegfried. I knew it was no use writing. I had to see him, so I got myself passed fit and went back to Litherland. He was in a *shocking* state. He'd just thrown his MC into the Mersey. Did he tell you that?'

Rivers hesitated. 'I believe it was in the Board's report.'

'Anyway, it took a long time, but he saw sense in the end.'

'What made him give in, do you think?'

'He just couldn't go on denying he was ill.'

Rivers didn't reply. The silence deepened, like a fall of snow, accumulating second by second, flake by flake, each flake by itself inconsiderable, until everything is transformed.

'No, it wasn't that.' Graves's knobbly, broken-nosed boxer's face twitched. 'I lied to him.'

Rivers's glasses flashed as he lifted his head. 'Yes, I thought perhaps you had.'

'I swore on the Bible they wouldn't court-martial him, but I didn't know that. I think if he'd held out, they might've done.'

'They might. But you know the advantages of treating this as a nervous breakdown would have been quite apparent to the authorities, even without your pointing them out.'

'The fact remains I lied, and he gave in because he believed the lie. He wouldn't have believed it from anybody else.' He paused. 'Do *you* think I was wrong?'

Rivers said gently, 'I think you did the best you could for your friend. Not the best thing for his *cause*, but then the cause is lost anyway. Did you find the Board difficult to convince?'

'Quite. There was one youngish man who was sympathetic. The other two . . . Well. I got the impression they didn't believe in shell-shock at all. As far as they were concerned, it was just cowardice. I made up my mind right from the start they weren't going to think that. I told them about last year when he took a German trench single-handed and got recommended for the VC. I'd like to see *them* do it. And this April. You know, that bombing expedition of his was fantastic. Everybody I've spoken to who was there thinks he should've got the VC for *that*.' He paused. 'I just wanted them to know what kind of man they were dealing with.' He smiled. 'I kept bursting into tears. I think that helped in a way. I could see them thinking, My God, if this one's fit for duty what *can* the other one be like?'

'And you told them that he had hallucinations?'

'Yes.' Graves looked slightly uncomfortable. 'I had to convince them. There were a lot of things I *didn't* tell them. I didn't tell them he'd threatened to kill Lloyd George.'

'And you persuaded him to say nothing?'

'Yes. The last thing we needed was Siegfried talking sense about the war.'

'*Sense?* You mean you agree with him?'

'Well, yes. In *theory*. In *theory* the war should stop tomorrow, but it won't. It'll go on till there isn't a cat or a dog left to enlist.'

'So you agree with his views, but not his actions? Isn't that rather an artificial distinction?'

'No, I don't think it is. The way I see it, when you put the uniform on, in effect you sign a contract. And you don't back out of a contract merely because you've changed your mind. You can still speak up for your principles, you can argue against the ones you're being made to fight for, but in the end you *do the job*. And I think that way you gain more respect. Siegfried isn't going to change people's minds like this. It may be *in him* to change people's minds about the war, but *this* isn't the way to do it.'

Rivers took his clasped hands away from his mouth. 'I couldn't agree with you more.'

'What's infuriating is that basically *he* knows it better than anybody. He's the one who can communicate with the ordinary soldier. It's just that he got taken over by Bertrand Russell and Ottoline Morrell. You know, I used to admire them. I used to think, well, I don't agree with you, but, on the other hand, I can see it takes *courage* . . .' He shook his head. 'Not any more. I know Russell's over military age, Ottoline's a woman, fair enough, neither of them can understand what he's been through, but they *could* see the state he was in, *and they still went ahead*. They were quite prepared to destroy him for the sake of propagating their views. I don't forgive them for it.' He made a visible effort to calm down. 'Anyway, it's over now. But I must say it gave me great pleasure to write to Russell and tell him Sassoon was on his way here, and he could just *bloody well leave him alone* in future.'

'And what about you?' Rivers asked, after a pause. 'Do you think they'll send you back?'

'No, I don't think so. In fact, the battalion doctor told me if he ever found my lungs in France again, he'd shoot me himself. I'm hoping for Palestine.' A pause. 'I'm glad he's here. At least I can go back to Litherland knowing he's safe.'

'I hope he is.' Rivers stood up. 'And now I think I should let you get back to him. He'll need company on his first evening.'

After Graves had gone, Rivers sat for a while resting his eyes, then opened the envelope Graves had given him. Three sheets of paper. On the top sheet, dated the 22nd April, Sassoon had written in pencil, 'I wrote these in hospital ten days after I was wounded.'

> Groping along the tunnel in the gloom
> He winked his tiny torch with whitening glare,
> And bumped his helmet, sniffing the hateful air.
> Tins, boxes, bottles, shapes too vague to know,
> And once, the foul, hunched mattress from a bed;
> And he exploring, fifty feet below
> The rosy dusk of battle overhead.
> He tripped and clutched the walls; saw someone lie
> Humped and asleep, half-covered with a rug;
> He stooped and gave the sleeper's arm a tug.
> 'I'm looking for headquarters.' No reply.
> 'Wake up, you sod!' (For days *he'd* had no sleep.)
> 'I want a guide along this cursed place.'
> He aimed a kick at the unanswering heap;
> And flashed his beam across that livid face
> Horribly glaring up, whose eyes still wore
> The agony that died ten days before
> Whose bloody fingers clutched a hideous wound.
> Gasping, he staggered onward till he found
> Dawn's ghost that filtered down a shafted stair,
> To clammy creatures groping underground,
> Hearing the boom of shells with muffled sound.
> Then with the sweat of horror in his hair,
> He climbed with darkness to the twilight air.

The General

> 'Good morning, good morning!' the General said
> When we met him last week on our way to the line.
> Now the soldiers he smiled at are most of 'em dead,

And we're cursing his staff for incompetent swine.
'He's a cheery old card,' muttered Harry to Jack
As they slogged up to Arras with rifle and pack.

．　．　．

But he did for them both with his plan of attack.

To the Warmongers

I'm back again from hell
With loathsome thoughts to sell;
Secrets of death to tell;
And horrors from the abyss.
Young faces bleared with blood,
Sucked down into the mud,
You shall hear things like this,
Till the tormented slain
Crawl round and once again,
With limbs that twist awry
Moan out their brutish pain,
As the fighters pass them by.

For you our battles shine
With triumph half-divine;
And the glory of the dead
Kindles in each proud eye.
But a curse is on my head,
That shall not be unsaid,
And the wounds in my heart are red,
For I have watched them die.

Rivers knew so little about poetry that he was almost embarrassed at the thought of having to comment on these. But then he reminded himself they'd been given to him as a therapist, not as a literary critic, and from that point of view they were certainly interesting, particularly the last.

Everything about the poem suggested that Sassoon's attitude to his war experience had been the opposite of what one normally encountered. The typical patient, arriving at Craiglockhart, had usually been devoting considerable energy to the task of *forgetting* whatever traumatic events had precipitated his neurosis. Even if the patient recognized that the attempt was hopeless, he had usually been encouraged to persist in it by friends, relatives, even by his previous medical advisers. The horrors he'd experienced, only partially repressed even by day, returned with redoubled force to haunt the nights, giving rise to that most characteristic symptom of war neurosis: the battle nightmare.

Rivers's treatment sometimes consisted simply of encouraging the patient to abandon his hopeless attempt to forget, and advising him instead to spend some part of every day remembering. Neither brooding on the experience, nor trying to pretend it had never happened. Usually, within a week or two of the patient's starting this treatment, the nightmares began to be less frequent and less terrifying.

Sassoon's determination to remember might well account for his early and rapid recovery, though in his case it was motivated less by a desire to save his own sanity than by a determination to convince civilians that the war was mad. Writing the poems had obviously been therapeutic, but then Rivers suspected that writing the Declaration might have been therapeutic too. He thought that Sassoon's poetry and his protest sprang from a single source, and each could be linked to his recovery from that terrible period of nightmares and hallucinations. If that was true, then persuading Sassoon to give in and go back would be a much more complicated and risky business than he had thought, and might well precipitate a relapse.

He sighed and put the poems back in the envelope. Looking at his watch, he saw that it was time to start his rounds. He'd just reached the foot of the main staircase when he saw Captain Campbell, bent double and walking backwards, emerge from the darkened dining room.

'Campbell?'

Campbell spun round. 'Ah, Captain Rivers, just the man.' He came up to Rivers and, speaking in a discreet whisper that was audible the length and breadth of the corridor, as Campbell's discreet whispers tended to be, said, 'That fella they've put in my room.'

'Sassoon. Yes?'

'Don't think he's a German spy, do you?'

Rivers gave the matter careful consideration. 'No, I don't think so. They *never* call themselves "Siegfried".'

Campbell looked astonished. 'No more they do.' He nodded, patted Rivers briskly on the shoulder, and moved off. 'Just thought I'd mention it,' he called back.

'Thank you, Campbell. Much appreciated.'

Rivers stood for a moment at the foot of the stairs, unconsciously shaking his head.

4

'I was walking up the drive at home. My wife was on the lawn having tea with some other ladies, they were all wearing white. As I got closer, my wife stood up and smiled and waved and then her expression changed and all the other ladies began to look at each other. I couldn't understand why, and then I looked down and saw that I was naked.'

'What had you been wearing?'

'Uniform. When I saw how frightened they were, it made *me* frightened. I started to run and I was running through bushes. I was being chased by my father-in-law and two orderlies. Eventually they got me cornered and my father-in-law came towards me, waving a big stick. It had a snake wound round it. He was using it as a kind of flail, and the snake was hissing. I backed away, but they got hold of me and tied me up.'

Rivers detected a slight hesitation. 'What with?'

A pause. In determinedly casual tones Anderson said, 'A pair of lady's corsets. They fastened them round my arms and tied the laces.'

'Like a strait-waistcoat?'

'Yes.'

'Then?'

'Then I was carted off to some kind of carriage. I was thrown inside and the doors banged shut and it was very dark. Like a grave. The first time I looked it was empty, but then the next time you were there. You were wearing a post-mortem apron and gloves.'

It was obvious from his tone that he'd finished. Rivers smiled and said, 'It's a long time since I've worn those.'

'I haven't recently worn corsets.'

'Whose corsets were they?'

'Just corsets. You want me to say my wife's, don't you?'

Rivers was taken back. 'I want you to say –'

'Well, I really don't think they were. I suppose it is *possible* someone might find being locked up in a loony bin a fairly *emasculating* experience?'

'I think most people do.' Though not many said so. 'I want you to say what you think.'

No response.

'You say you woke up vomiting?'

'Yes.'

'I wonder why? I mean I can quite see the sight of me in a post-mortem apron might not be to everybody's taste –'

'I don't know.'

'What was the most frightening thing about the dream?'

'The snake.'

A long silence.

'Do you often dream about snakes?'

'Yes.'

Another long silence. 'Well, go on, then,' Anderson exploded at last. 'That's what you Freudian Johnnies are on about all the time, isn't it? Nudity, snakes, *corsets*. You might at least try to look *grateful*, Rivers. It's a gift.'

'I think if I'd made any association at all with the snake – and after all what possible relevance can my associations have? – it was probably with the one that's crawling up your lapel.'

Anderson looked down at the caduceus badge of the RAMC which he wore on his tunic, and then across at the same badge on Rivers's tunic.

'What the er snake *might* suggest is that medicine is an issue between yourself and your father-in-law?'

'No.'

'Not at all?'

'No.'

Another long silence. Anderson said, 'It depends what you mean by an issue.'

'A subject on which there is habitual disagreement.'

'No. Naturally my time in France has left me with a certain level of distaste for the practice of medicine, but that'll go in time. There's no *issue*. I have a wife and child to support.'

'You're how old?'

'Thirty-six.'

'And your little boy?'

Anderson's expression softened. 'Five.'

'School fees coming up?'

'Yes. I'll be all right once I've had a rest. Basically, I'm paying for last summer. Do you know, at one point we *averaged* ten amputations a day? Every time I was due for leave it was cancelled.' He looked straight at Rivers. 'There's no doubt what the problem is. Tiredness.'

'I still find the vomiting puzzling. Especially since you say you feel no more than a *mild* disinclination for medicine.'

'I didn't say mild, I said temporary.'

'Ah. What in particular do you find difficult?'

'I don't know that there *is* anything *particular*.'

A long silence.

Anderson said, 'I'm going to start timing these silences, Rivers.'

'It's already been done. Some of the younger ones had a sweepstake on it. I'm not supposed to know.'

'Blood.'

'And you attribute this to the ten amputations a day?'

'No, I was all right then. The . . . er . . . problem started later. I wasn't at Étaples when it happened, I'd been moved forward – the 13th CCS. They brought in this lad. He was a Frenchman, he'd escaped from the German lines. Covered in mud. There wasn't an inch of skin showing anywhere. And you know it's not like ordinary mud, it's five, six inches thick. Bleeding. Frantic with pain. No English.' A pause. 'I missed it. I treated the minor wounds and missed the major one.' He gave a short, hissing laugh. 'Not that the minor ones were all that minor. He started to haemorrhage, and . . . there was nothing I could do. I just stood there and watched him bleed to death.' His face twisted. 'It pumped out of him.'

It was a while before either of them stirred. Then Anderson said, 'If you're wondering why that one, I don't know. I've seen many worse deaths.'

'Have you told your family?'

'No. They know I don't like the idea of going back to medicine, but they don't know why.'

'Have you talked to your wife?'

'Now and then. You have to think about the *practicalities*, Rivers. I've devoted all my adult life to medicine. I've no private income to tide me over. And I do have *a wife and a child*.'

'Public health might be a possibility.'

'It doesn't have much . . . *dash* about it, does it?'

'Is that a consideration?'

Anderson hesitated. 'Not with me.'

'Well, we can talk about the practicalities later. You still haven't told me when you said *enough*.'

Anderson smiled. 'You make it sound like a decision. I don't know that lying on the floor in a pool of piss counts as a decision.' He paused. 'The following morning. *On the ward.* I remember them all looking down at me. Awkward situation, really. What do you do when the doctor breaks down?'

At intervals, as Rivers was doing his rounds as orderly officer for the day, he thought about this dream. It was disturbing in many ways. At first he'd been inclined to see the post-mortem apron as expressing no more than a lack of faith in *him*, or, more accurately, in his methods, since obviously any doctor who spends much time so attired is not meeting with uniform success on the wards. This lack of faith he knew to be present. Anderson, in his first interview, had virtually refused treatment, claiming that rest, the endless pursuit of golf balls, was all that he required. He had some knowledge of Freud, though derived mainly from secondary or prejudiced sources, and disliked, or perhaps feared, what he thought he knew. There was no particular reason why Anderson, who was, after all, a surgeon, should be well informed about Freudian therapy, but his misconceptions had resulted in a marked reluctance to reveal his dreams. Yet his dreams could hardly be ignored, if only because they were currently keeping the whole of one floor of the hospital awake. His room-mate, Featherstone, had deteriorated markedly as the result of Anderson's nightly outbursts. Still, that was another problem. As soon as Anderson had revealed that extreme horror of blood, Rivers had begun tentatively to attach another meaning to the post-mortem apron. If Anderson could see no way out of returning to the practice of a profession which must inevitably, even in civilian life, recall the horrors he'd witnessed in France, then perhaps he was desperate enough to have considered suicide? That might account both for the post-mortem apron and for the extreme terror he'd felt on waking. At the moment he didn't know Anderson well enough to be able to say whether suicide was a possibility or not, but it would certainly need to be borne in mind.

The smell of chlorine became stronger as they reached the bottom of the stairs. Sassoon felt Graves hesitate. 'Are you all right?'

'I could do without the smell.'

'Well, let's not bother —'

'No, go on.'

Sassoon pushed the door open. The pool was empty, a green slab between white walls. They began to undress, putting their clothes on one of the benches that lined the end wall.

'What's your room-mate like?' Graves asked.

'All right.'

'Dotty?'

'Not visibly. I gather the subject of German spies is best avoided. Oh, and I've found out why there aren't any locks on the doors. One of them killed himself three weeks ago.'

Graves caught sight of the scar on Sassoon's shoulder and stopped to look at it. It was curiously restful to submit to this scrutiny, which was prolonged, detailed and impersonal, like one small boy examining the scabs on another's knee. 'Oh, *very* neat.'

'Yes, isn't it? The doctors kept telling me how beautiful it was.'

'You were lucky, you know. An inch further down —'

'Not as lucky as you.' Sassoon glanced at the shrapnel wound on Graves's thigh. 'An inch further up —'

'If this is leading up to a joke about ladies' choirs, forget it. I've heard them all.'

Sassoon dived in. A green, silent world, no sound except the bubble of his escaping breath, no feeling, once the shock of cold was over, except the tightening of his chest that at last forced him to the surface, air, noise, light, slopping waves crashing in on him again. He swam to the side and held on. Graves's dark head bobbed purposefully along at the other side of the pool. Sassoon thought, we joke about it, but it happens. There'd been a boy in the hospital, while he was lying there with that neat little hole in his shoulder. The boy – he couldn't have been more than nineteen – had a neat little hole too. Only his was between the legs. The dressings had been terrible to witness, and you had to witness them. No treatment in that overcrowded ward had been private. Twice a day the nurses came in with the creaking trolley, and the boy's eyes followed them up the ward.

Sassoon shut the lid on the memory and dived for Graves's legs. Graves twisted and fought, his head a black rock splintering white foam. 'Lay off,' he gasped at last, pushing Sassoon away. 'Some of us don't have the full complement of lungs.'

The pool was beginning to fill up. After a few more minutes, they climbed out and started to dress. Head muffled in the folds of his shirt, Graves said, 'By the way, I think there's something I ought to tell you. I'm afraid I told Rivers about your plan to assassinate Lloyd George.'

Rivers's round as duty officer ended in the kitchens. Mrs Cooper, her broad arms splashed with fat from giant frying-pans, greeted him with an embattled smile. 'What d' y' think of the beef stew last night, then, sir?'

'I don't believe I've ever tasted anything quite like it.'

Mrs Cooper's smile broadened. 'We do the best we can with the materials available, sir.' Her expression became grim and confiding. 'That beef was *walking*.'

Rivers got to his room a few minutes after ten and found Sassoon waiting, his hair damp, smelling of chlorine. 'I'm sorry I'm late,' Rivers said, unlocking the door. 'I've just been pretending to know something about catering. Come in.' He waved Sassoon to the chair in front of the desk, tossed his cap and cane to one side, and was about to unbuckle his belt when he remembered that the Director of Medical Services was due to visit the hospital some time that day. He sat down behind the desk and drew Sassoon's file towards him. 'Did you sleep well?'

'Very well, thank you.'

'You look rested. I enjoyed meeting Captain Graves.'

'Yes, I gather you found it quite informative.'

'*Ah.*' Rivers paused in the act of opening the file. 'You mean he told me something you'd rather I didn't know?'

'No, not necessarily. Just something I might have preferred to tell you myself.' A moment's silence, then Sassoon burst out, 'What I can't understand is how somebody of Graves's intelligence can can can have such a shaky grasp of of *rhetoric*.'

Rivers smiled. 'You were going to kill Lloyd George rhetorically, were you?'

'I wasn't going to kill him at all. I said I *felt* like killing him, but it was no use, because they'd only shut me up in a lunatic asylum, "like Richard Dadd of glorious memory". There you are, *exact words*.' He looked round the room. 'Though as things have turned out –'

'This is *not* a lunatic asylum. You are *not* locked up.'

'Sorry.'

'What you're really saying is that Graves took you too seriously.'

'It's not just that. It suits him to attribute everything I've done to to to to . . . a state of mental breakdown, because then he doesn't have to ask himself any awkward questions. Like why he agrees with me about the war and does nothing about it.'

Rivers waited a few moments. 'I know Richard Dadd was a painter. What else did he do?'

A short silence. 'He murdered his father.'

Rivers was puzzled by the slight awkwardness. He was used to being adopted as a father figure – he was, after all, thirty years older than the youngest of his patients – but it was rare for it to happen as quickly as this in a man of Sassoon's age. '"Of *glorious* memory"?'

'He . . . er . . . made a list of old men in power who deserved to die, and fortunately – or or otherwise – his father's name headed the list. He carried him for half a mile through Hyde Park and then drowned him in the Serpentine in full view of everybody on the banks. The only reason Graves and I know about him is that we were in trenches with two of his great nephews, Edmund and Julian.' The slight smile faded. 'Now Edmund's dead, and Julian's got a bullet in the throat and can't speak. The other brother was killed too. Gallipoli.'

'Like your brother.'

'Yes.'

'Your father's dead too, isn't he? How old were you when he died?'

'Eight. But I hadn't seen much of him for some time before that. He left home when I was five.'

'Do you remember him?'

'A bit. I remember I used to like being kissed by him because his moustache tickled. My brothers went to the funeral. I didn't – apparently I was too upset. Probably just as well, because they came back terrified. It was a Jewish funeral, you see, and they couldn't understand what was going on. My elder brother said it was two old men in funny hats walking up and down saying jabber-jabber-jabber.'

'You must've felt you'd lost him twice.'

'Yes. We did lose him twice.'

Rivers gazed out of the window. 'What difference would it have made, do you think, if your father had lived?'

A long silence. 'Better education.'

'But you went to Marlborough?'

'Yes, but I was *years* behind everybody else. Mother had this theory we were delicate and our brains shouldn't be taxed. I don't think I ever really caught up. I left Cambridge without taking my degree.'

'And then?'

Sassoon shook his head. 'Nothing much. Hunting, cricket. Writing poems. Not very good poems.'

'Didn't you find it all . . . rather unsatisfying?'

'Yes, but I couldn't seem to see a way out. It was like being three different people, and they all wanted to go different ways.' A slight smile. 'The result was I went nowhere.'

Rivers waited.

'I mean, there was the riding, hunting, cricketing me, and then there was the . . . the other side . . . that was interested in poetry and music, and things like that. And I didn't seem able to . . .' He laced his fingers. 'Knot them together.'

'And the third?'

'I'm sorry?'

'You said three.'

'Did I? I meant two.'

Ah. 'And then the war. You joined up on the first day?'

'Yes, in the ranks. I couldn't wait to get in.'

'Your superior officers wrote glowing reports for the Board. Did you know that?'

A flush of pleasure. 'I think the army's probably the only place I've ever really belonged.'

'And you've cut yourself off from it.'

'Yes, because –'

'I'm not interested in the reasons at the moment. I'm more interested in the result. The effect on you.'

'Isolation, I suppose. I can't talk to anybody.'

'You talk to *me*. Or at least, I think you do.'

'You don't say stupid things.'

Rivers turned his head away. 'I'm pleased about that.'

'Go on, *laugh*. I don't mind.'

'You'd been offered a job in Cambridge, hadn't you? Teaching cadets.'

Sassoon frowned. 'Yes.'

'But you didn't take it?'

'No. It was either prison or France.' He laughed. 'I didn't foresee this.'

Rivers watched him staring round the room. 'You can't bear to be safe, can you?' He waited for a reply. 'Well, you've got twelve weeks of it. *At least*. If you go on refusing to serve, you'll be safe for the rest of the war.'

Two red spots appeared on Sassoon's cheekbones. 'Not *my* choice.'

'I didn't say it was.' Rivers paused. 'You know you reacted then as if I were attacking you, and yet all I did was to point out *the facts*.' He leant forward. 'If you maintain your protest, you can expect to spend the remainder of the war in a state of Complete. Personal. Safety.'

Sassoon shifted in his seat. 'I'm not responsible for other people's decisions.'

'You don't think you might find being safe while other people *die* rather difficult?'

A flash of anger. 'Nobody else in this *stinking* country seems to find it difficult. I expect I'll just learn to live with it. Like everybody else.'

*

36

Burns stood at the window of his room. Rain had blurred the landscape, dissolving sky and hills together in a wash of grey. He loathed wet weather because then everybody stayed indoors, sitting around the patients' common room, talking, in strained or facetious tones, about the war the war the war.

A sharper gust of wind blew rain against the glass. Somehow or other he was going to have to get out. It wasn't forbidden, it was even encouraged, though he himself didn't go out much. He got his coat and went downstairs. On the corridor he met one of the nurses from his ward, who looked surprised to see him wearing his coat, but didn't ask where he was going.

At the main gates he stopped. Because he'd been inside so long, the possibilities seemed endless, though they resolved themselves quickly into two. *Into* Edinburgh, or away. And that was no choice at all: he knew he wasn't up to facing traffic.

For the first few stops the bus was crowded. He sat on the bench seat close to the door of the bus. People smelling of wet wool jerked and swayed against him, bumping his knees, and he tensed, not liking the contact or the smell. But then at every stop more and more people got off until he was almost alone, except for an old man and the clippie. The lanes were narrower now; the trees rushed in on either side. A branch rattled along the windows with a sound like machine-gun fire, and he had to bite his lips to stop himself crying out.

He got off at the next stop, and stood, looking up and down a country lane. He didn't know what to do at first, it was so long since he'd been anywhere alone. Raindrops dripped from the trees, big, splashy, persistent drops, finding the warm place between his collar and his neck. He looked up and down the lane again. Somewhere further along, a wood pigeon cooed monotonously. He crossed over and began climbing the hill between the trees.

Up, up, until his way was barred by a fence whose wire twitched in the wind. A tuft of grey wool had caught on one of the barbs. Burns blinked the rain out of his eyes. He pressed two strands of wire apart and eased himself through, catching his sleeve, and breaking into a sweat as he struggled to free it.

Trembling now, he began to scramble along the edge of the ploughed field, slipping and stumbling, his mud-encumbered boots like lead weights pulling on the muscles of his thighs. His body was cold inside the stiff khaki, except for a burning round the knees where the tight cloth chafed the skin.

He was walking up the slope of a hill, tensing himself against the wind that seemed to be trying to scrape him off its side. As he reached the crest, a fiercer gust snatched his breath. After that he kept his head bent, sometimes stopping to draw a deeper breath through the steeple of his cupped hands. Rain beat on to his head, dripping from the peak of his cap, the small bones of nose and jaw had started to sing. He stopped and looked across the field. The distance had vanished in a veil of rain. He didn't know where he was going, or why, but he thought he ought to take shelter, and began to run clumsily along the brow of a hill towards a distant clump of trees. The mud dragged at him, he had to slow to a walk. Every step was a separate effort, hauling his mud-clogged boots out of the sucking earth. His mind was incapable of making comparisons, but his aching thighs remembered, and he listened for the whine of shells.

When at last he reached the trees, he sat down with his back to the nearest, and for a while did nothing at all, not even wipe away the drops of rain that gathered on the tip of his nose and dripped into his open mouth. Then, blinking, he dragged his wet sleeve across his face.

After a while he got to his feet and began stumbling, almost blindly, between the trees, catching his feet in clumps of bracken. Something brushed against his cheek, and he raised his hand to push it away. His fingers touched slime, and he snatched them back. He turned and saw a dead mole, suspended, apparently, in air, its black fur spiked with blood, its small pink hands folded on its chest.

Looking up, he saw that the tree he stood under was laden with dead animals. Bore them like fruit. A whole branch of moles in various stages of decay, a ferret, a weasel, three magpies, a fox, the fox hanging quite close, its lips curled back from bloodied teeth.

He started to run, but the trees were against him. Branches clipped his face, twigs tore at him, roots tripped him. Once he was sent sprawling, though immediately he was up again, and running, his coat a mess of mud and dead leaves.

Out in the field, splashing along the flooded furrows, he heard Rivers's voice, as distinctly as he sometimes heard it in dreams: *If you run now, you'll never stop.*

He turned and went back, though he knew the voice was only a voice in his head, and that the real Rivers might equally well have said: *Get away from here.* He stood again in front of the tree. Now that he was calmer, he remembered that he'd seen trees like this before. The animals were not nailed to it, as they sometimes were, but tied, by wings or paws or tails. He started to release a magpie, his teeth chattering as a wing came away in his hand. Then the other magpies, the fox, the weasel, the ferret and the moles.

When all the corpses were on the ground, he arranged them in a circle round the tree and sat down within it, his back against the trunk. He felt the roughness of the bark against his knobbly spine. He pressed his hands between his knees and looked around the circle of his companions. Now they could dissolve into the earth as they were meant to do. He felt a great urge to lie down beside them, but his clothes separated him. He got up and started to get undressed. When he'd finished, he looked down at himself. His naked body was white as a root. He cupped his genitals in his hands, not because he was ashamed, but because they looked incongruous, they didn't seem to belong with the rest of him. Then he folded his clothes carefully and put them outside the circle. He sat down again with his back to the tree and looked up through the tracery of branches at grey and scudding clouds.

The sky darkened, the air grew colder, but he didn't mind. It didn't occur to him to move. This was the right place. This was where he had wanted to be.

By late afternoon Burns's absence was giving cause for concern. The nurse who'd seen him walk out, wearing his coat, blamed herself for not stopping him, but nobody else was inclined to blame her. The patients, except for one or two who were known to be high suicide risks, were free to come and go as they pleased. Bryce and Rivers consulted together at intervals during the day, trying to decide at what point they should give in and call the police.

Burns came back at six o'clock, walking up the stairs unobserved, trailing mud, twigs and dead leaves. He was too tired to think. His legs ached; he was faint with hunger yet afraid to think of food.

Sister Duffy caught him just as he was opening the door of his room and bore down upon him, scolding and twittering like the small, dusty brown bird she so much resembled. She made him get undressed then and there and seemed to be proposing to towel him down herself, but he vetoed that. She left him alone but came back a few minutes later, laden with hot-water bottles and extra blankets, still inclined to scold, though when she saw how tired he looked, lying back against the pillows, she checked herself and only said ominously that Dr Rivers had been informed and would be up as soon as he was free.

I suppose I'm for it, Burns thought, but couldn't make the thought real. He folded his arms across his face and almost at once began drifting off to sleep. He was back in the wood, outside the circle now, but able to see himself inside it. His skin was tallow-white against the scurfy bark. A shaft of sunlight filtered through leaves, found one of the magpies, and its feathers shone sapphire, emerald, amethyst. There was no reason to go back, he thought. He could stay here for ever.

When he opened his eyes, Rivers was sitting beside the bed. He'd obviously been there some time, his glasses were in his lap, and one hand covered his eyes. The room was quite dark.

Rivers seemed to feel Burns watching him, because after a few moments he looked up and smiled.

'How long have I been asleep?'

'About an hour.'

'I've worried everybody, haven't I?'

'Never mind that. You're back, that's all that matters.'

All the way back to the hospital Burns had kept asking himself why he was going back. Now, waking up to find Rivers sitting by his bed, unaware of being observed, tired and patient, he realized he'd come back for this.

5

Rivers started his night round early. Sister Rogers was in her room, drinking the first of the many cups of coffee that would see her through the night. 'Second-Lieutenant Prior,' she said, as soon as she saw him.

'Yes, I know, and there's nothing I can do about it.' Prior was a new patient, whose nightmares were so bad that his room-mate was getting no sleep. 'Has he spoken to anybody yet?'

'No, and if you speak to him he just stares straight through you.'

It was unlike Sister Rogers to take a dislike to a patient, but there was no mistaking the animosity in her voice. 'All right,' Rivers said, 'let's have a look at him.'

Prior was lying on his bed, reading. He was a thin, fair-haired young man of twenty-two with high cheekbones, a short, blunt nose and a supercilious expression. He looked up as Rivers came in, but didn't close the book.

'Sister tells me you had a bad night?'

Prior produced an elaborate shrug. Out of the corner of his eye Rivers saw Sister Rogers's lips tighten. 'What did you dream about?'

Prior reached for the notepad and pencil he kept beside his bed and scrawled in block capitals, 'I DON'T REMEMBER.'

'Nothing at all?'

Prior hesitated, then wrote, 'NO.'

'Does he talk in his sleep, sister?'

Rivers was looking at Prior as he asked the question, and thought he detected a flicker of uneasiness.

'Nothing you can get hold of.'

Prior's lips curled, but he couldn't hide the relief.

'Could you get me a teaspoon, sister?' Rivers asked.

While she was out of the room, Prior went on staring at

Rivers. Rivers, trying to keep the meeting from becoming a confrontation, looked around the room. Sister Rogers came back. 'Thank you. Now I just want to have a look at the back of your throat.'

Again the pad came out. 'THERE'S NOTHING PHYSICALY WRONG.'

'Two l's in "physically", Mr Prior. Open wide.'

Rivers drew the end of the teaspoon, not roughly, but firmly, across the back of Prior's throat. Prior choked, his eyes watered, and he tried to push Rivers's hand away.

'There's no area of analgesia,' Rivers said to Sister Rogers.

Prior snatched up the pad. 'IF THAT MEANS IT HURT YES IT DID.'

'I don't think it *hurt*, did it?' Rivers said. 'It may have been uncomfortable.'

'HOW WOULD YOU KNOW?'

Sister Rogers made a clicking noise with her tongue.

'Do you think you could give us ten minutes alone, sister?'

'Yes, of course, doctor.' She glared at Prior. 'I'll be in my room if you need me.'

After she'd gone, Rivers said, 'Why do you always write in block capitals? Because it's less revealing?'

Prior shook his head. He wrote, 'CLEARER.'

'Depends on your handwriting, doesn't it? I know, if I ever lost *my* voice, I'd have to write in capitals. Nobody can read mine.'

Prior offered the pad. Rivers, feeling like a schoolboy playing noughts and crosses, wrote: 'Your file still hasn't arrived.'

'I SEE WHAT YOU MEAN.'

Rivers said, 'Your file still hasn't arrived.'

Another elaborate shrug.

'Well, I'm afraid it's rather more serious than that. If it doesn't show up soon, we're going to have to try to get a history together – like this. And that's not going to be easy.'

'WHY?'

'Why do we have to do it? Because I need to know what's happened to you.'

'I DON'T REMEMBER.'

'No, not at the moment, perhaps, but the memory will start to come back.'

A long silence. At last Prior scribbled something, then turned over on his side to face the wall. Rivers leant across and picked the pad up. Prior had written: 'NO MORE WORDS.'

'I must say it makes Dottyville almost bearable,' Sassoon said, looking up and down the station platform. 'Knowing you don't have to be vomited over at *every* meal. I'd eat out every night if I could afford it.'

'You'll have to spend *some* time in the place, Sass.' No reply. 'At least you've got Rivers.'

'And at least Rivers doesn't pretend there's anything wrong with my nerves.'

Graves started to speak and checked himself. 'I wish I could say the same about mine.'

'What can I say, Robert? Have my bed. *You* live with a herd of lunatics. I'll go back to Liverpool.'

'I hate it when you talk like that. As if everybody who breaks down is inferior. We've all been' – Graves held up his thumb and forefinger – 'that close.'

'I know how close I've been.' A short silence, then he burst out, 'Don't you see, Robert, that's why I hate the place? I'm frightened.'

'Frightened? *You?* You're not frightened.' He craned round to see Sassoon's expression. 'Are you?'

'Evidently not.'

They stood in silence for a minute.

'You ought to be getting back,' Graves said.

'Yes, I think you're right. I don't want to attract attention to myself.' He held out his hand. 'Well. Give everybody my regards. If they still want them.'

Graves took the hand and pulled him into a bear hug. 'Don't be so bloody stupid, Siegfried. You know they do.'

Alone and shivering on the pavement, Sassoon thought about taking a taxi and decided against it. The walk would do him good, and if he hurried he could probably make it back in time. He threaded his way through the crowds on Princes Street. Now that Robert was gone, he hated everybody, giggling girls, portly middle-aged men, women whose eyes settled on his wound stripe like flies. Only the young soldier home on leave, staggering out of a pub, dazed and vacant-eyed, escaped his disgust.

Once he'd left the city behind, he began to relax and swing along as he might have done in France. He remembered the march to Arras behind a limber whose swaying lantern cast huge shadows of striding legs across a white-washed wall. Then . . . No more walls. Ruined buildings. Shelled roads. 'From sunlight to the sunless land.' And for a second he was back there, Armageddon, Golgotha, there were no words, a place of desolation so complete no imagination could have invented it. He thought of Rivers, and what he'd said that morning about finding safety unbearable. Well, Rivers was wrong, people were more corruptible than that. *He* was more corruptible than that. A few days of safety, and all the clear spirit of the trenches was gone. It was still, after all these weeks, pure joy to go to bed in white sheets and know that he would wake. The road smelled of hot tar, moths flickered between the trees, and when at last, turning up the drive into Craiglockhart, he stopped and threw back his head, the stars burst on his upturned face like spray.

A nightly bath had become essential to Rivers, a ritual that divided his meagre spare time from the demands of the hospital. He was already pulling his tunic off as he crossed the bedroom. Naked, he sat on the edge of the bath, waiting for it to fill. The hot tap was shiny; the cold, misted over, dewed with drops of condensed steam. Absent-mindedly, he played with the drops, making them run together to form larger pools. He was thinking about Prior, and the effect he was having on his room-mate, Robinson, and wondering whether it was worse than the effect Anderson was having on Featherstone. In any event, no single room was available. One solution to the Prior problem was to move Robinson into a room at present shared by two patients, although if the overcrowding were not to prove intolerable, the patients would have to be very carefully selected. He was still running through possible combinations as he bathed.

By his bed was the current issue of *Man*, still in its envelope. He hadn't managed even to glance through it yet. And suddenly he was furious with the hospital, and Prior, and overcrowding and the endless permutations of people sharing that were made necessary by nightmares, sleep-walking, the need of some patients for night-lights and others for absolute darkness.

His irritation, groping for an object, fastened on Sassoon. Sassoon made no secret of his belief that anybody who supported the continuation of the war must be actuated by selfish motives, and yet if Rivers had allowed such motives to dominate, he'd have wanted the war to end tonight. Let the next generation cope with the unresolved problem of German militarism, just get me back to Cambridge and *research*. He flicked through the journal, but he was too tired to concentrate, and, after a few minutes, he switched off the light.

Shortly before dawn he woke. Still dazed from sleep, he put his hand to his left arm, expecting to feel blood. The dry cloth of his pyjama sleeve told him he'd been dreaming. He switched on the lamp and lay for a while, recollecting the details of the dream, then picked up a notepad and pencil from his bedside table and began to write.

I was in my room at St John's, sitting at the table in front of the book case. Head was beside me, his left sleeve rolled up, and his eyes closed. The sleeve was rolled up well above his elbow, so that the full length of the incision was revealed. The scar was purple. The tablecloth was spread with various items of equipment: jugs of water, wisps of cotton wool, bristle brushes, compasses, ice cubes, pins.

My task was to map the area of hypersensitivity to pain on Head's forearm. He sat with his eyes closed and his face turned slightly away. Every time I pricked him he cried out and tried to pull his arm away. I was distressed by this and didn't want to go on, but I knew I had to. Head kept on crying out.

The dream changed and I was drawing a map of the protopathic area directly on to his skin. The pen was as painful as the needle had been. Head opened his eyes and said something I didn't catch. It sounded like, 'Why don't *you* try it?' He was holding an object out towards me. I looked down to see what it was, and saw that my own left arm was bare, though I couldn't recall rolling up my sleeve.

The object in Head's hand was a scalpel. I began to ask him to repeat what he'd said, but before I could get the words out, he'd leant forward and brought the scalpel down my arm, in the region of the elbow. The incision, although about six inches long, was so fine that at first there was no blood. After a second, small beads of blood began to appear, and at that point I woke up.

Rivers started to analyse the dream. The manifest content didn't take long. Except for the cutting of his arm, the dream was an unusually accurate reproduction of events that had actually occurred.

Henry Head had been working for some time on the regeneration of nerves after accidental injury, using as his subjects patients in the public wards of London hospitals, before concluding that, if any further progress was to be made, more rigorously controlled tests would have to be done. Rivers had pointed out that these would have to be carried out on a subject who was himself a trained observer, since an extremely high degree of critical awareness would be needed to exclude preconceptions. Head had volunteered himself as the subject of the proposed experiment, and Rivers had assisted at the operation in which Head's radial nerve had been severed and sutured. Then, together, over a period of five years, they had charted the progress of regeneration.

During the early stage of recovery, when the primitive, protopathic sensibility had been restored, but not yet the finely discriminating epicritic sensibility, many of the experiments had been extremely painful. Protopathic sensibility seemed to have an 'all or nothing' quality. The threshold of sensation was high, but, once crossed, the sensations were both abnormally widely diffused and – to use Head's own word – 'extreme'. At times a pinprick would cause severe and prolonged pain. Rivers had often felt distress at the amount of pain he was causing, but it would not, in life, have occurred to him to stop the experiment for that reason, any more than it would have occurred to Head. In the dream, however, the wish to stop the experiment had been prominent.

The latent content was more difficult. Superficially, the dream seemed to support Freud's contention that all dreams were wish fulfilment. Rivers had wished himself back in Cambridge, doing research, and the dream had fulfilled the wish. But that was to ignore the fact that the dream had not been pleasant. The emphasis in the dream had been on the distress he felt at causing pain, and, on waking, the affect had been one of fear and dread. He didn't believe such a dream could be convincingly explained as wish fulfilment, unless, of course, he wished to torture one of his closest friends. No doubt some of Freud's more doctrinaire supporters would have little difficulty with that idea, particularly since the torture took the form of pricking him, but Rivers couldn't accept it. He was more inclined to seek the meaning of the dream in the conflict his dream self had experienced between the duty to continue the experiment and the reluctance to cause further pain.

Rivers was aware, as a constant background to his work, of a conflict between his belief that the war must be fought to a finish, for the sake of the succeeding generations, and his horror that such events as those which had led to Burns's breakdown should be allowed to continue. This conflict, though a constant feature of his life, would certainly have been strengthened by his conversations with Sassoon. He'd been thinking about Sassoon immediately before he went to sleep. But, on thinking it over, Rivers couldn't see that the dream was a likely dramatization of that conflict. The war was hardly an experiment, and it certainly didn't rest with him to decide whether it continued or not.

Recently almost all his dreams had centred on conflicts arising from his treatment of particular patients. In advising them to remember the traumatic events that had led to their being sent here, he was, in effect, inflicting pain, and doing so in pursuit of a treatment that he knew to be still largely experimental. Only in Burns's case had he found it impossible to go on giving this advice, because the suffering involved in Burns's attempts to remember was so extreme. 'Extreme'. The word Head had used to describe the pain he'd experienced during the protopathic stage of regeneration. Certainly in Burns's case, there was a clear conflict between Rivers's desire to continue using a method of treatment he believed in, but knew to be experimental, and his sense that in this particular instance the pain involved in insisting on the method would be too great.

The dream had not merely posed a problem, it had suggested a solution. 'Why don't you try it?' Henry had said. Rivers felt he'd got there first, that the dream lagged behind his waking practice: he was already experimenting on himself. In leading his patients to understand that breakdown was nothing to be ashamed of, that horror and fear were inevitable responses to the trauma of war and were better acknowledged than suppressed, that feelings of tenderness for other men were natural and right, that tears were an acceptable and helpful part of grieving, he was setting himself against the whole tenor of their upbringing. They'd been trained to identify emotional repression. as the essence of manliness. Men who broke down, or cried, or admitted to feeling fear, were sissies, weaklings, failures. Not *men*. And yet he himself was a product of the same system, even perhaps a rather extreme product. Certainly the rigorous repression of emotion and desire had been the constant theme of his adult life. In advising his young patients to abandon the attempt at repression and to let themselves *feel* the pity and terror their war experience inevitably evoked, he was excavating the ground he stood on.

The change he demanded of them – and by implication of himself – was not trivial. Fear, tenderness – these emotions were so despised that they could be admitted into consciousness only at the cost of redefining what it meant to be a man. Not that Rivers's treatment involved any encouragement of weakness or effeminacy. His patients might be encouraged to acknowledge their fears, their horror of the war – but they were still expected to do their duty and return to France. It was Rivers's conviction that those who had learned to know themselves, and to accept their emotions, were less likely to break down again.

In a moment or two an orderly would tap on the door and bring in his tea. He put the notebook and pencil back on the bedside table. Henry would be amused by that dream, he thought. If wish fulfilment had been involved at all, it was surely one of Henry's wishes that had been fulfilled. At the time of the nerve regeneration experiments, they'd done a series of control experiments on the glans penis, and Henry had frequently expressed the desire for a reciprocal application of ice cubes, bristles, near-boiling water and pins.

6

Prior sat with his arms folded over his chest and his head turned slightly away. His eyelids looked raw from lack of sleep.

'When did your voice come back?' Rivers asked.

'In the middle of the night. I woke up shouting and suddenly I realized I could talk. It's happened before.'

A Northern accent, not ungrammatical, but with the vowel sounds distinctly flattened, and the faintest trace of sibilance. Hearing Prior's voice for the first time had the curious effect of making him *look* different. Thinner, more defensive. And, at the same time, a lot tougher. A little, spitting, sharp-boned alley cat.

'It comes and goes?'

'Yes.'

'What makes it go?'

Another shrug from the repertoire. 'When I get upset.'

'And coming here upset you?'

'I'd have preferred somewhere further south.'

So would I. 'What did you do before the war?'

'I was a clerk in a shipping office.'

'Did you like it?'

'No. It was *boring*.' He looked down at his hands and immediately up again. 'What did *you* do?'

Rivers hesitated. 'Research. Teaching.'

'Did *you* like it?'

'Yes, very much. Research more than teaching probably, but . . .' He shrugged. 'I enjoy teaching.'

'I noticed. "Two l's in physically, Mr Prior."'

'What an insufferable thing to say.'

'I thought so.'

'I'm sorry.'

Prior didn't know what to say to that. He looked down at his hands and mumbled, 'Yes, well.'

'By the way, your file arrived this morning.'

Prior smiled. 'So you know all about me, then?'

'Oh, I wouldn't say *that*. What *did* become clear is that you had a spell in the 13th Casualty Clearing Station in . . .' He looked at the file again. 'January. Diagnosed neurasthenic.'

Prior hesitated. 'Ye-es.'

'Deep reflexes abnormal.'

'Yes.'

'But on that occasion no trouble with the voice? Fourteen days later you were back in the line. Fully recovered?'

'I'd stopped doing the can-can, if that's what you mean.'

'Were there any remaining symptoms?'

'Headaches.' He watched Rivers make a note. 'It's hardly a reason to stay out of the trenches, is it? "*Not tonight, Wilhelm. I've got a headache*"?'

'It might be. It rather depends how bad they were.' He waited for a reply, but Prior remained obstinately silent. 'You were back in the 13th CCS in April. This time unable to speak.'

'I've told you, I don't remember.'

'So the loss of memory applies to the later part of your service in France, but the early part – the first six months or so – is comparatively clear?'

'Ye-es.'

Rivers sat back in his chair. 'Would you like to tell me something about that early part?'

'No.'

'But you do remember it?'

'Doesn't mean I want to talk about it.' He looked round the room. 'I don't see why it has to *be* like this anyway.'

'Like what?'

'All the questions from *you*, all the answers from *me*. Why can't it be both ways?'

'Look, Mr Prior, if you went to the doctor with bronchitis and he spent half the consultation time telling you about his lumbago, you would not be pleased. Would you?'

'No, but if I went to my doctor *in despair* it might help to know he at least understood the *meaning* of the word.'

'Are you in despair?'

Prior sighed, ostentatiously impatient.

'You know, I talk to a lot of people who *are* in despair or very close to it, and my experience is that they don't *care* what the doctor feels. That's the whole point about despair, isn't it? That you turn in on yourself.'

'Well, all I can say is I'd rather talk to a real person than a a strip of empathic wallpaper.'

Rivers smiled. 'I like that.'

Prior glared at him.

'If you feel you can't talk about France, would it help to talk about the nightmares?'

'*No.* I don't think talking *helps*. It just churns things up and makes them seem more real.'

'But they are real.'

A short silence. Rivers closed Prior's file. 'All right. Good morning.'

Prior looked at the clock. 'It's only twenty past ten.'

Rivers spread his hands.

'You can't refuse to talk to me.'

'Prior, there are a hundred and sixty-eight patients in this hospital, all of them wanting to get better, none of them getting the attention he deserves. Good morning.'

Prior started to get up, then sat down again. 'You've no right to say I don't want to get better.'

'I didn't say that.'

'You implied it.'

'All right. *Do* you want to get better?'

'Of course.'

'But you're not prepared to co-operate with the treatment.'

'I don't agree with the treatment.'

Deep breath. 'What methods of treatment do you favour?'

'Dr Sanderson was going to try hypnosis.'

'He doesn't mention it in his report.'

'He was. He told me.'

'How did you feel about that?'

'I thought it was a good idea. I mean *you*'re more or less saying: things are real, you've got to face them, but how *can* I face them when I don't know what they are?'

'That's rather an unusual reaction, you know. Generally, when a doctor suggests hypnosis the patient's quite nervous, because he feels he'll be . . . putting himself in somebody else's power. Actually that's not quite true, but it does tend to be the fear.'

'If it's not true, why don't you use it?'

'I do sometimes. In selected cases. As a last resort. In your case, I'd want to know quite a lot about the part of your war service that you *do* remember.'

'All right. What do you want to know?'

Rivers blinked, surprised by the sudden capitulation. 'Well, anything you want to tell me.'

Silence.

'Perhaps you could start with the day before you went into the CCS for the first time. Do you remember what you were doing that day?'

Prior smiled. 'Standing up to my waist in water in a dugout in the middle of No Man's Land being bombed to buggery.'

'Why?'

'Good question. You should pack this in and join the general staff.'

'If there wasn't a reason, there must at least have been a rationale.'

'There was that, all right.' Prior adopted a strangled version of the public school accent. 'The pride of the British Army requires that absolute dominance must be maintained in No Man's Land at all times.' He dropped the accent. 'Which in *practice* means . . . Dugout in the middle of No Man's Land. Right? Every forty-eight hours two platoons crawl out – night-time, of course – relieve the poor bastards inside, and provide the Germans with another forty-eight hours' target practice. Why it's thought they need all this target practice is beyond me. They seem quite accurate enough as it is.' His expression changed. 'It was flooded. You stand the whole time. Most of the time in pitch darkness because the blast kept blowing the candles out. We were packed in so tight we couldn't move. And they just went all out to get us. One shell after the other. I lost two sentries. Direct hit on the steps. Couldn't find a thing.'

'And you had forty-eight hours of that?'

'Fifty. The relieving officer wasn't in a hurry.'

'And when you came out you went straight to the CCS?'

'I didn't go, I was carried.'

A tap on the door. Rivers called out angrily, 'I'm with a patient.'

A short pause as they listened to footsteps fading down the corridor. Prior said, 'I met the relieving officer.'

'In the clearing station?'

'No, here. He walked past me on the top corridor. Poor bastard left his Lewis guns behind. He was lucky not to be court-martialled.'

'Did you speak?'

'We nodded. Look, *you* might like to think it's one big happy family out there, but it's not. They *despise* each other.'

'You mean you despise yourself.'

Prior looked pointedly across Rivers's shoulder. 'It's eleven o'clock.'

'All right. I'll see you tomorrow.'

'I thought of going into Edinburgh tomorrow.'

Rivers looked up. 'At *nine*.'

'I can guess what Graves said. What a fine upstanding man I was until I fell among pacifists. Isn't that right? Russell used me. Russell wrote the Declaration.'

'No, he didn't say that.'

'Good. Because it isn't true.'

'You don't think you were influenced by Russell?'

'No, not particularly. I think I was influenced by my own experience of the front. I am capable of making up my own mind.'

'Was this the first time you'd encountered pacifism?'

'No. Edward Carpenter, before the war.'

'You read him?'

'Read him. Wrote to him.' He smiled slightly. 'I even made the Great Pilgrimage to Chesterfield.'

'You must've been impressed to do that.'

Sassoon hesitated. 'Yes, I . . .'

Watching him, Rivers perceived that he'd led Sassoon unwittingly on to rather intimate territory. He was looking for a way of redirecting the conversation when Sassoon said, 'I read a book of his. *The Intermediate Sex*. I don't know whether you know it?'

'Yes. I've had patients who swore their entire lives had been changed by it.'

'Mine was. At least I don't know about "changed". "Saved", perhaps.'

'As bad as that?'

'At one point, yes. I'd got myself into quite a state.'

Rivers waited.

'I didn't seem able to feel . . . well. Any of the things you're supposed to feel. It got so bad I used to walk all night sometimes. I used to wait till everybody else was in bed, and then I'd just . . . get out and walk. The book was a life-saver. Because I suddenly saw that . . . I wasn't just a freak. That there was a positive side. Have you read it?'

Rivers clasped his hands behind his head. 'Yes. A long time ago now.'

'What did you think?'

'I found it quite difficult. Obviously you have to admire the man's courage, and the way he's . . . opened up the debate. But I don't know that the concept of an intermediate sex is as helpful as people think it is when they first encounter it. In the end nobody wants to be *neuter*. Anyway, the point is Carpenter's pacifism doesn't seem to have made much impression?'

'I don't know if I was aware of it even. I didn't think much about politics. The next time I encountered pacifism was Robert Ross. I met him, oh, I suppose two years ago. He's totally opposed to the war.'

'And that didn't influence you either?'

'No. Obviously it made things easier at a *personal* level. I mean, frankly, any middle-aged man who Believed in The War would . . .' Sassoon skidded to a halt. 'Present company excepted.'

Rivers bowed.

'I didn't even bother showing him the Declaration. I knew he wouldn't go along with it.'

'Why wouldn't he? Out of concern for you?'

'Ye-es. Yes, that certainly, but . . . Ross was a close friend of Wilde's. I suppose he's learnt to keep his head below the parapet.'

'And you haven't.'

'I don't like holes in the ground.'

Rivers began polishing his glasses on his handkerchief. 'You know, I realize Ross's caution probably seems excessive. To you. But I hope you won't be in too much of a hurry to dismiss it. There's nothing more despicable than using a man's private life to discredit his views. But it's very frequently done, even by people in my profession. People you might think wouldn't resort to such tactics. I wouldn't like to see it happen to you.'

'I thought discrediting my views was what you were about?'

Rivers smiled wryly. 'Let's just say I'm fussy about the methods.'

Rivers had kept two hours free of appointments in the late afternoon in order to get on with the backlog of reports. He'd been working for half an hour when Miss Crowe tapped on the door. 'Mr Prior says could he have a word?'

Rivers pulled a face. 'I've seen him once today. Does he say what's wrong?'

'No, this is the father.'

'I didn't even know he was coming.'

She started to close the door. 'I'll tell him you're busy, shall I?'

'No, no, I'll see him.'

Mr Prior came in. He was a big, thick-set man with a ruddy complexion, dark hair sleeked back, and a luxuriant, drooping, reddish-brown moustache. 'I'm sorry to drop on you like this,' he said. 'I thought our Billy had told you we were coming.'

'I think he probably mentioned it. If he did, I'm afraid it slipped my mind.'

Mr Prior looked him shrewdly up and down. '*Nah*. Wasn't your mind it slipped.'

'Well, sit down. How did you find him?'

'Difficult to tell when they won't talk, isn't it?'

'Isn't he talking? He was this morning.'

'Well, he's not now.'

'It does come and go.'

'Oh, I'm sure. Comes when it's convenient and goes when it isn't. What's supposed to be the matter?'

'Physically, nothing.' Two l's, Rivers thought. 'I think

perhaps there's something he's afraid to talk about, so he solves the problem by making it impossible for himself to speak. This is . . . beneath the surface. He doesn't *know* what he's doing.'

'If he doesn't, it'll be the first time.'

Rivers tried a different tack. 'I believe he volunteered, didn't he? The first week of the war.'

'He did. Against my advice, not that *that's* ever counted for much.'

'You didn't want him to go?'

'No I did not. I told him, time enough to do summat for the Empire when the Empire's done summat for you.'

'It is natural for the young to be idealistic.'

'Ideals had nowt to do with it. He was desperate to get out of his job.'

'I think I remember him saying he didn't like it. He was a clerk in a shipping office.'

'That's right, and getting nowhere. Twenty years wearing the arse of your breeches out and then, if you're a good boy and lick all the right places, you get to be supervisor and then you sit on a bigger stool and watch other people wear their breeches out. Didn't suit our Billy. He's ambitious, you know, you mightn't think it to look at him, but he is. His mam drilled that into him. Schooled him in it. She was *determined* he was going to get on.'

Rather unexpectedly, Rivers found himself wanting to leap to Billy Prior's defence. 'She seems to have succeeded.'

Mr Prior snorted. 'She's made a stool-arsed jack on him, if that's what you mean.'

'You make it sound as if you had no say.'

'I didn't. All the years that lad was growing up there was only one time I put my oar in, and that was when there was this lad at school picking on him. He was forever coming in crying. And one day I thought, well, I've had enough of this. So the next time he come in blubbing I give him a backhander and shoved him out the door. There he was, all tears and snot, yelling his bloody head off. He says, he's waiting for us, our Dad. I says, go on, then. You've got to toughen 'em up, you know, in our neighbourhood. If you lie down there's plenty to walk over you.'

'What happened?'

'Got the shit beat out of him. *And* the next day. *And* the next. *But* – and this is our Billy – when he did finally take a tumble to himself and hit the little sod he didn't just hit him, he half bloody murdered him. I had his father coming round, and all sorts. Not but what *he* got short shrift.'

He seemed to have no feeling for his son at all, except contempt. 'You must be proud of his being an officer?'

'Must I? *I'm* not proud. He should've stuck with his own. Except he can't, can he? That's what she's done to him. He's neither fish nor fowl, and she's too bloody daft to see it. But I tell you one person who *does* see it.' He pointed to the ceiling. 'Oh it's all very lovey-dovey on the surface but underneath he doesn't thank her for it.' He stood up. 'Anyway I'd best be getting back. His nibs'll have a fit, when he knows I've seen you. Wheezing badly, isn't he?' He caught Rivers's expression. 'Oh, I see, he wasn't wheezing either? Not what you could call a successful visit.'

'I'm sure it's done him a lot of good. We often find they don't settle till they've seen their families.'

Mr Prior nodded, accepting the reassurance without believing it. 'Any idea how long he'll be here?'

'Twelve weeks. Initially.'

'Hm. He'd get a damn sight more sympathy from me if he had a bullet up his arse. Anyway . . .' He held out his hand. 'It's been nice meeting you. I don't know when we'll be up again.'

Rivers had completed two reports when Miss Crowe put her head round the door again. '*Mrs* Prior.'

They exchanged glances. Rivers threw down his pen, and said, 'Show her in.'

Mrs Prior was a small upright woman, neatly dressed in a dark suit and mauve blouse. 'I won't stay long,' she said, sitting nervously on the edge of the chair. She was playing with her wedding ring, pulling and pushing it over the swollen knuckle. 'I'd like to apologize for my husband. I thought he was just stepping outside for a smoke, otherwise I'd've stopped him.'

A carefully genteel voice. Fading prettiness. Billy Prior had got his build and features from her rather than the father. 'No, I was pleased to see him. How did you find Billy?'

'Wheezing. I've not seen his chest as tight as that since he was a child.'

'I didn't even know he was asthmatic.'

'No, well, it doesn't bother him much. Usually. As a child it was terrible. I used to have to boil kettles in his room. You know, for the steam?'

'You must be very proud of him.'

Her face softened. 'I am. Because *I* know how hard it's been. I can truthfully say he never sat an exam without he was bad with his asthma.'

'Did he like the shipping office?'

Her mouth shaped itself to say 'yes', then, 'No. It was the same docks as his father and I think that was the mistake. You know, his father was earning more as a ganger than Billy was as a clerk, and I think myself there was a little bit of . . . You see the trouble with my husband, the block had to chip. Do you know what I mean? He's never been able to accept that Billy was different. And I think there might have been a little bit of jealousy as well, because he has, he's had a hard life. I don't deny that. A lot harder than it need have been, because *his* mother sent him to work when he was *ten*. And no need for it either, she had two sons working, but there it is. What can you say? He worships her' She was silent for a moment, brooding. 'You know sometimes I think the less you do for them, the better you're thought of.'

'Would you say Billy and his father were close?'

'*No!* And yet, you see, the funny thing is our Billy's . . .' She sought for a way of erasing the tell-tale 'our' from the sentence and, not finding one, gave a little deprecatory laugh. 'All for "the common people", as he calls them. I said, "You mean your father?"' She laughed again. 'Oh, no, he didn't mean his father. I said, "But you know nothing about the common people. You've had nothing to do with them." Do you know what he turned round and said? "Whose fault is that?"'

Miss Crowe tapped on the door. 'Your husband says he's going now, Mrs Prior.'

'Yes, well, I'll have to go. You'll take care of him, won't you?'

She was close to tears. Rivers said, 'We'll do our best.'

58

'I'd be grateful if you wouldn't mention I've been to see you. He's upset enough about his father.'

After she'd gone, Rivers turned to Miss Crowe. 'That was amazing. Do you know, I think they'd have said *anything*?'

'You get married couples like that, sir. One sympathetic word and you're there till midnight. Captain Broadbent's waiting to see you.'

Rivers looked at the pile of papers on his desk and sighed. 'All right, show him in.' The frustration boiled over. 'And do *please try* not to call him "captain". He's no more a captain than I am.'

'You *are* a captain, Captain Rivers.'

Miss Crowe paused at the door to savour the small moment of triumph. Rivers smiled and said, 'All right. But at least try not to *address* him as "captain". It really doesn't help him to have his fantasies confirmed.'

'I'll do my best, sir. Though as long as he's allowed to walk round the hospital with three stars on his sleeve, I don't see that my remembering to call him "mister" is going to make a great deal of difference.' She smiled sweetly and withdrew. A moment later she reappeared. '*Mister* Broadbent, sir.'

'Come in, Mr Broadbent. Sit down.'

It wasn't just the stars. There was also the little matter of the medals, including the Serbian equivalent of the VC awarded to a foreigner for the first and only time in its long and glorious history. And then there were the honorary degrees, though at least he hadn't yet taken to wearing those on his tunic. However, he was doing very good work with the hospital chamber orchestra. 'Well, Broadbent, what can I do for you?'

'I've had some bad news, Dr Rivers,' Broadbent said in his confiding, insinuating way. 'My mother's been taken ill.'

Rivers didn't believe Broadbent's mother was ill. He didn't believe Broadbent had a mother. He thought it entirely possible that Broadbent had been hatched. 'Oh, I *am* sorry.'

'I was hoping for some leave.'

'You'll have to ask the CO about that.'

'I was hoping you might put a word in for me. You see, I don't think Major Bryce *likes* me very much.'

People who'd heard of Broadbent's exploits, but not met

him, were apt to picture a rather florid, swashbuckling, larger-than-life figure. In reality, Broadbent was a limp, etiolated youth, with a pallid complexion and a notably damp handshake, whose constant and bizarre infringements of the hospital rules took up far far too much time. He was quite right in thinking Bryce didn't like him.

'It's not a question of liking or not liking,' Rivers said. 'Is your mother very ill?'

'I'm afraid so, Dr Rivers.'

'Then I'm sure Major Bryce will be sympathetic. But it *is his* decision. Not mine.'

'I just thought . . .' Suddenly Broadbent's voice hardened. 'This is *extremely* bad for my nerves. You know what happens.'

'I hope it doesn't happen this time. Because last time, if you remember, you had to be locked up. Why don't you go to see Major Bryce now?'

'Yes, all right.' Broadbent stood up, reluctantly, and spat, '*Thank* you, sir.'

At least he didn't offer to shake hands.

After dinner a Charlie Chaplin film was shown in the cinema on the first floor. The whole of the ground floor was deserted. Rivers, taking his completed reports along to the office to be typed, saw that a lamp had been left burning in the patients' common room and went in to switch it off.

Prior was sitting beneath the windows at the far end of the room, looking out over the tennis courts, his face and hands bluish in the dim light. Rivers was tempted to withdraw immediately, but then something about the isolation of the small figure under the huge windows made him pause. 'Don't you want to see the film?'

'I couldn't stand the smoke.'

He was wheezing very badly. Rivers went across to the window and sat beside him. Housemartins were weaving to and fro above the tennis courts, feeding on the myriads of tiny insects that were just visible as a golden haze. He watched them cut, wheel, dive – how skilful they were at avoiding collision – and for a moment, under the spell of the flickering birds, the day's work and responsibility fell away. But he couldn't ignore

Prior's breathing, or the whiteness of the knuckles where his left hand gripped the chair. He turned and looked at him, noting the drawn, anxious face. 'It's bad, isn't it?'

'Bit tight.'

Prior was bent forward to help the expansion of his lungs. Looking at him now, Rivers could see the straightness of the shoulders, the surprising breadth of chest in a delicately built man. Once you knew it was obvious. But why nothing on the file?

'I gather you met my father,' Prior gasped. 'Quite a character.'

'He seemed to be a man of strong views.'

Prior's mouth twisted. 'He's a bar-room socialist, if that's what you mean. Beer and revolution go in, *piss* comes out.' He attempted a laugh. 'My mother was quite concerned. "He'll be down there effing and blinding," she said. "Showing us all up."'

'I liked him.'

'Oh, yes, he's very likeable. Outside the house. I've seen him use my mother as a football.' The next breath screeched. 'When I was too little to do anything about it.'

'You know, I think I ought to have a look at that chest.'

Prior managed a ghostly imitation of his usual manner. 'Your room or mine?'

'The sick bay.'

The walk along the corridor to the lift was painfully slow.

'I didn't want you to meet him,' Prior said, as Rivers pressed the button for the second floor.

'No, I know you didn't. I could hardly refuse.'

'I'm not blaming *you*.'

'Is it a question of blame?'

While the nurses made up the bed, Rivers examined Prior. He'd expected Prior to be impossible, but in the event he became strictly impersonal, gazing over Rivers's shoulder as the stethoscope moved across his chest. 'All right, put your jacket on.' Rivers folded the stethoscope. 'I'm surprised you got to France at all with that.'

'They couldn't afford to be fussy.' Prior started the long climb into the bed. 'I won't be moved to another hospital, will I?'

'No, I shouldn't think so. Four doctors, thirty nurses. I think we might manage.'

'Only I don't want to be moved.'

Rivers helped him to pull up the sheets. 'I thought you didn't like it here?'

'Yes, well, you can get used to anything, can't you? Do you think I could have a towel tied to the bed?'

'Yes, of course. Anything you want.'

'Only it helps, you see. Having something to pull on.'

'What was it like in France? The asthma.'

'Better than at home.'

A shout of laughter from below. Charlie Chaplin in full swing. Rivers, following Prior's gaze, saw the single lamp and the deep shadows, and sensed, with a premonitory tightening of his diaphragm, the breath-by-breath agony of the coming night. 'I'll see about the towel,' he said.

He saw Prior settled down for the night. 'I'll be along in the morning,' he said. Then he went to Sister's room next door and left orders he was to be woken at once if Prior got worse.

7

Sassoon woke to the sound of screams and running footsteps. The screams stopped and then a moment or two later started again. He peered at his watch and made out that it was ten past four.

Because of the rubber underlay, a pool of sweat had gathered in the small of his back. The rubbery smell lingered on his skin, a clinical smell that made his body unfamiliar to him. In the next bed Campbell snored, a cacophony of grunts, snorts and whistles. No screams ever woke *him*. On the other hand he himself never screamed, and Sassoon had been at Craiglockhart long enough now to realize how valuable a room-mate that made him.

Fully awake now, he dragged himself to the bottom of the bed, lifted the thin curtain and peered out of the window. Wester Hill, blunt-nosed and brooding, loomed out of the mist. And yesterday, he thought, shivering a little, his statement had been read in the House of Commons. He wondered what would happen next. Whether anything would happen. In any event there was a kind of consolation in knowing it was out of his hands.

He knew he was shivering more with fear than cold, though it was difficult to name the fear. The place, perhaps. The haunted faces, the stammers, the stumbling walks, that indefinable look of being 'mental'. Craiglockhart frightened him more than the front had ever done.

Upstairs whoever-it-was screamed again. He heard women's voices and then, a few minutes afterwards, a man's voice. Rivers, he thought, but he couldn't be sure. Quaking and comfortless, he propped himself up against the iron bedhead and waited for the dawn.

*

Prior hauled himself further up the bed as Rivers came in. He closed the book he'd been reading and put it down on his bedside table. 'I thought it was you,' he said. 'I can tell your footsteps.'

Rivers got a chair and sat down by the bed. 'Did you manage to get back to sleep?'

'Yes. Did you?'

Silence.

'I wasn't being awkward,' Prior said. 'That was *concern*.'

'I didn't, but it doesn't matter. I don't sleep much after four anyway.' He caught the flicker of interest. How quickly Prior pounced on any item of personal information.

'Thanks for showing up.'

'You hated it.'

Prior looked slightly disconcerted, then smiled. 'I don't suppose anybody'd *choose* to be seen in such a state. I don't really see why they had to call you.'

'They were afraid the fear might bring on another attack. Though in fact you seem to be breathing more easily.'

Prior took a trial deep breath. 'Yes, I think I am. Do you know I detect something in myself. I . . .' He stopped. 'No, I don't think I want to tell you what I detect.'

'Oh, go on. Professional curiosity. I want to see if *I've* detected it.'

Prior smiled faintly. 'No, you won't have detected this. I find myself wanting to impress you. Pathetic, isn't it?'

'I don't think it's pathetic. We all care what the people around us think, whether we admit it or not.' He paused. 'Though I'm a bit surprised *my* opinion matters. I mean, to be quite honest, I didn't think you liked me very much.'

'There's a limit to how warm you can feel about wallpaper.'

'Oh, we're back to that again, are we?'

Prior turned away, hunching his shoulders. 'No-o.'

Rivers watched him for a while. 'Why do you think it has to be like that?'

'So that I . . . I'm sorry. So that *the patient* can fantasize freely. So that *the patient* can turn you into whoever he wants you to be. Well, all right. I just think you might consider the possibility that *this* patient might want you to be *you*.'

'All right.'

'All right, what?'

'All right, I'll consider it.'

'I suppose most of them turn you into Daddy, don't they? Well, I'm a bit too old to be sitting on *Daddy*'s knee.'

'Kicking him on the shins every time you meet him isn't generally considered more mature.'

'I *see*. A negative transference. Is *that* what you think we've got?'

'I hope not.' Rivers couldn't altogether conceal his surprise. 'Where did you learn that term?'

'I can *read*.'

'Well, yes, I know, but its —'

'Not popular science? No, but then neither is this.'

He reached for the book beside his bed and held it out to Rivers. Rivers found himself holding a copy of *The Todas*. He stared for a moment at his own name on the spine. He told himself there was no reason why Prior shouldn't read one of his books, or all of them for that matter. There was no rational reason for him to feel uneasy. He handed the book back. 'Wouldn't you prefer something lighter? You are ill, after all.'

Prior leant back against his pillows, his eyes gleaming with amusement. 'Do you know, I *knew* you were going to say that. Now how did I know that?'

'I didn't realize you were interested in anthropology.'

'Why shouldn't I be?'

'No reason.'

Really, Rivers thought, Prior was cuckoo-backed to the point where normal conversation became almost impossible. He was flicking through the book, obviously looking for something in particular. After a minute or so he held it out again, open at the section on sexual morality. 'Do they really go on like that?'

Rivers said, as austerely as he knew how, 'Their sexual lives are conducted along rather different lines from ours.'

'I'll say. They must be bloody knackered. *I* couldn't keep it up, could you?'

'I think my age and your asthma might effectively prevent either of us setting any records.'

'Ah, yes, but I'm only asthmatic *part* of the time.'

'You have to *win*, don't you?'

Prior stared intently at him. 'You know, you do a wonderful imitation of a stuffed shirt. And you're not like that at all, really, are you?'

Rivers took his glasses off and swept his hand across his eyes. '*Mister Prior.*'

'I know, I know, "Tell me about France." All right, what do you want to know? And *please* don't say, "Whatever you want to tell me."'

'All right. How did you fit in?'

Prior's face shut tight. 'You mean, did I encounter any snobbery?'

'Yes.'

'Not more than I have here.'

Their eyes locked. Rivers said, 'But you did encounter it?'

'Yes. It's made perfectly clear when you arrive that some people are more welcome than others. It helps if you've been to the right school. It helps if you hunt, it helps if your shirts are the right colour. Which is a *deep* shade of khaki, by the way.'

In spite of himself Rivers looked down at his shirt.

'Borderline,' said Prior.

'And yours?'

'Not borderline. Nowhere near. Oh, and then there's the seat. *The Seat.* You know, they sent me on a course once. You have to ride round and round this bloody ring with your hands clasped behind your head. No saddle. No stirrups. It was amazing. Do you know, for the first time I realized that somewhere at the back of their . . . *tiny tiny* minds they really do believe the whole thing's going to end in one big glorious *cavalry charge*. "Stormed at with shot and shell,/Boldly they rode and well,/Into the jaws of death,/Into the mouth of hell . . ." And all. That. Rubbish.'

Rivers noticed that Prior's face lit up as he quoted the poem. '*Is* it rubbish?'

'*Yes.* Oh, all right, I was in love with it once. Shall I tell you something about that charge? Just as it was about to start an officer saw three men smoking. He thought that was a bit too casual, so he confiscated their sabres and sent them into the charge unarmed. Two of them were killed. The one who survived was flogged the following day. The military mind doesn't change much, does it? The same mind now orders men to be punished by tying them to a limber.' Prior stretched his arms out. 'Like this. Field punishment No. 1. "Crucifixion." Even at the propaganda level can you imagine anybody being *stupid* enough to order *this*?'

Either the position, or his anger, constricted his breathing. He brought his arms down sharply and rounded his shoulders. Rivers waited for the spasm to pass. 'How was your seat?'

'Sticky. No, that's *good*. It means you don't come off.'

A short silence. Prior said, 'You mustn't make too much of it, you know, the snobbery. I didn't. The only thing that really makes me angry is when people at home say there are no class distinctions at the front. Ball-*ocks*. What you wear, what you eat. Where you sleep. What you carry. The men are pack animals.' He hesitated. 'You know the worst thing? What seemed *to me* the worst thing? I used to go to this café in Amiens and just across the road there was a brothel. The men used to queue out on to the street.' He looked at Rivers. 'They get two minutes.'

'And officers?'

'I don't know. Longer than that.' He looked up. '*I don't pay.*'

Prior was talking so freely Rivers decided to risk applying pressure. 'What were you dreaming about last night?'

'I don't remember.'

Rivers said gently, 'You know, one of the distinguishing characteristics of nightmares is that they are always remembered.'

'Can't've been a nightmare, then, can it?'

'When I arrived you were on the floor over there. Trying to get through the wall.'

'I'm sure it's true, if you say so, but I don't remember. The first thing I remember is you listening to my chest.'

Rivers got up, replaced his chair against the wall and came back to the bed. 'I can't force you to accept treatment if you don't want it. You *do* remember the nightmares. You remember them enough to walk the floor till two or three o'clock every morning rather than go to sleep.'

'I wish the night staff didn't feel obliged to act as *spies*.'

'Now that's just childish, isn't it? You know it's their job.'

Prior refused to look at him.

'All right. I'll see you tomorrow.'

'It isn't fair to say I don't want treatment. I've asked for treatment and you've refused to give it me.'

Rivers looked blank. 'Oh, I see. The hypnosis. I didn't think you were serious.'

'Why shouldn't I be serious? It *is* used to recover lost memory, isn't it?'

'Ye-es.'

'So why won't you do it?'

Rivers started to speak, and stopped.

'I can understand, you know. I'm not stupid.'

'No, I know you're not stupid. It's just that there's . . . there's a certain amount of technical jargon involved. I was just trying to avoid it. Basically, people who've dealt with a horrible experience by splitting it off from the rest of their consciousness sometimes have a general tendency to deal with any kind of unpleasantness in that way, and if they *have*, the tendency is likely to be reinforced by hypnosis. In other words you might be removing one particular symptom – loss of memory – and making the underlying condition worse.'

'But you do do it?'

'If everything else has failed, yes.'

Prior lay back. 'That's all I wanted to know.'

'In your case not everything else *has* failed or even been tried. For example, I'd want to write to your CO. We need a clear picture of the last few days.' Rivers watched Prior's expression carefully, but he was giving nothing away. 'But I'd have to go to the CO with a precise question. You understand that, don't you?'

'*Yes.*'

'There's no point bothering him with a vague inquiry about an unspecified period of time.'

'No, all right'

'So we still need you to remember as much as possible by conventional means. But we can leave it till you're feeling better.'

'No, I want to get on with it.'

'We'll see how you feel tomorrow.'

After leaving Prior, Rivers walked up the back staircase to the tower and stood for a few moments, his hands on the balustrade, looking out across the hills. Prior worried him. The whole business of the demand for hypnosis worried him. At times he felt almost a sense of foreboding in relation to the case, though he wasn't inclined to give it much credence. In his experience, premonitions of disaster were almost invariably proved false, and the road to Calvary entered on with the very lightest of hearts.

MR MACPHERSON With regard to the case of Second Lieutenant Sassoon, immediately he heard of it, he consulted his military advisers, and in response to their inquiries he received the following telegram: A breach of discipline has been committed, but no disciplinary action has been taken, since Second Lieutenant Sassoon has been reported by the Medical Board as not being responsible for his action, as he was suffering from nervous breakdown. When the military authorities saw the letter referred to, they felt that there must be something wrong with an extremely gallant officer who had done excellent work at the front. He hoped hon. members would hesitate long before they made use of a document written by a young man in such a state of mind, nor did he think their action would be appreciated by the friends of the officer. (*Cheers*.)

Rivers folded *The Times* and smiled. 'Really, Siegfried, what did you expect?'

'I don't know. Meanwhile . . .' Sassoon leant across and pointed to the front page.

Rivers read. '"Platts. Killed in action on the 28th April, dearly loved younger son, etc., aged seventeen years and ten months."' He looked up and found Sassoon watching him.

'He wasn't old enough to *enlist*. And nobody gives a damn.'

'Of course they do.'

'Oh, come on, it doesn't even put them off their sausages! Have you ever sat in a club room and *watched* people read the casualty list?'

'You could say that about the breakfast room here. Sensitivity t-to what's going on in France is not best shown by b-bursting

69

into t-tears over the c-casualty list.' He saw Sassoon noticing the stammer and made an effort to speak more calmly. 'The thing for you to do now is face the fact that you're here, and here for at least another eleven weeks. Have you thought what you're going to do?'

'Not really. I'm still out of breath from getting here. Go for walks. Read.'

'Will you be able to write, do you think?'

'Oh, yes. I'll write if I have to sit on the roof to do it.'

'There's no prospect of a room of your own.'

'No, I know that.'

Rivers chose his words carefully. 'Captain Campbell is an extremely nice man.'

'Yes, I've noticed. What's more, his battle plans are saner than Haig's.'

Rivers ignored that. 'One thing I could do is put you up for my club, the Conservative Club. I don't know whether you'd like that? It'd give you an alternative base at least.'

'I would, very much. Thank you.'

'Though I hope you won't exclude the possibility of making friends here.'

Sassoon looked down at the backs of his hands. 'I thought I might send for my golf clubs. There seem to be one or two keen golfers about.'

'Good idea. I'll see you three times a week. It'd better be evenings rather than mornings, I think – especially if you're going to play golf. Tuesdays, Fridays and Sundays?'

'Fine.' He smiled faintly. 'I've got nothing else on.'

'Eight thirty, shall we say? Immediately after dinner.'

Sassoon nodded. 'It's very kind of you.'

'Oh, I don't know about that.' He closed his appointments book and pulled a sheet of paper towards him. 'Now I need to ask a few questions about your physical health. Childhood illnesses, that sort of thing.'

'All right. Why?'

'For the admission report.'

'Oh, I see.'

'I don't usually include any . . . intimate details.'

'Probably just as well. My intimate details disqualify me from military service.'

Rivers looked up and smiled. 'I know.'

After Sassoon had gone, Rivers got a case sheet from the stack on his side table, paused for a few moments to collect his thoughts, and began to write:

Patient joined ranks of the Sussex Yeomanry on Aug. 3rd, 1914. Three months later he had a bad smash while schooling a horse and was laid up for several months. In May 1915 he received a commission in the Royal Welch Fusiliers. He was in France from Nov. 1915 until Aug. 1916, when he was sent home with trench fever. He had received the Military Cross in June 1916. He was on three months' sick leave and returned to France in Feb. 1917. On April 16th, 1917, he was wounded in the right shoulder and was in the surgical wards of the 4th London for four weeks and then at Lady Brassey's Convalescent Home for three weeks. He then understood that he was to be sent to Cambridge to instruct cadets.

From an early stage of his service in France, he had been horrified by the slaughter and had come to doubt whether the continuance of the War was justifiable. When on sick leave in 1916 he was in communication with Bertrand Russell and other pacifists. He had never previously approved of pacifism and does not think he was influenced by this communication. During his second visit to France, his doubts about the justifiability of the War were accentuated; he became perhaps even more doubtful about the way in which the war was being conducted from a military point of view. When he became fit to return to duty, in July of this year, he felt he was unable to do so, and that it was his duty to make some kind of protest. He drew up a statement which he himself regarded as an act of wilful defiance of military authority (see *The Times*, July 31st, 1917). In consequence of this statement he was ordered to attend a Medical Board at Chester about July 16th, but failed to attend. It was arranged that a second Board should be held at Liverpool on July 20th, which he attended, and he was recommended for admission to Craiglockhart War Hospital for special treatment for three months.

The patient is a healthy looking man of good physique. There are no physical signs of any disorder of the Nervous System. He discusses his recent actions and their motives in a perfectly intelligent and rational way, and there is no evidence of any excitement or depression. He recognizes that his view of warfare is tinged by his feelings about the death of friends and of the men who were under his command in France. At the present time he lays special stress on the hopelessness of any decision in the War as it is now being conducted, but he left out any reference to this aspect of his opinions in the statement which he sent to his Commanding Officer and which was read in the House of Commons. His view differs from that of the ordinary pacifist in that he would no longer object to the continuance of the War if he saw any reasonable prospect of a rapid decision.

He had an attack of double pneumonia when 11 years old, and again at 14. He was at Marlborough College, where he strained his heart at football. He was for four terms at Clare College, Cambridge, where he read first Law and then History, but did not care for either subject. He left Cambridge and spent the following years living in the country, devoting his time chiefly to hunting and cricket. He took no interest in Politics. From boyhood he has written verses at different times, and during his convalescence from his riding accident in 1914 he wrote a poem called 'The Old Huntsman', which has recently been published with other poem under that title.

'I gave Broadbent leave,' Bryce said. 'With some trepidation.'
'Yes, he told me he was going to ask you.'
'You know what he's done? Gone off with his room-mate's new breeches. Marsden's furious.'
Ruggles said, 'You mean this guy's running round the hospital bare-assed frightening the VADs?'
'No, he's wearing his other breeches. And your idea of what might frighten a VAD is —'
'Chivalrous,' said Ruggles.
'Naïve,' said Bryce. 'In the extreme.'
'Why is it always your patients, Rivers?' asked Brock.
The MOs were sitting round a table in Bryce's room over coffee, as they did twice a week after dinner. These gatherings were kept deliberately informal, but they served some of the same purposes as a case conference. Since everybody had now

read *The Times* report, Bryce had asked Rivers to say a few words about Sassoon.

Rivers kept it as brief and uncontroversial as possible. While he was speaking, he noticed that Brock was balancing a pencil between the tips of his extremely long bluish fingers. Never a good sign. Rivers liked Brock, but they didn't invariably see eye to eye.

A moment's silence, after Rivers had finished speaking. Then Ruggles asked Bryce if the press had shown any interest. While Bryce was summarizing a conversation he'd had with the *Daily Mail*, Rivers watched Brock, who sat, arms folded across his chest, looking down his long pinched nose at the table. Brock always looked frozen. Even his voice, high, thin and reedy, seemed to echo across arctic wastes. When Bryce had finished, Brock turned to Rivers and said, 'What are you thinking of doing with him?'

'Well, I have been seeing him every day. I'm going to drop that now to three times a week.'

'Isn't that rather a lot? For someone who – according to you – has nothing wrong with him?'

'I shan't be able to persuade him to go back in less than that.'

'Isn't there a case for leaving him alone?'

'No.'

'I mean, simply by *being* here he's discredited. Discredited, disgraced, *apparently* lied to by his best friend? I'd've thought there was a case for letting him be.'

'No, there's no case,' Rivers said. 'He's a mentally and physically healthy man. It's *his* duty to go back, and it's *my* duty to see he does.'

'And you've no doubts about that at all?'

'I don't see the problem. I'm not going to give him electric shocks, or or subcutaneous injections of ether. I'm simply asking him to defend his position. Which he admits was reached largely on emotional grounds.'

'*Grief* at the death of his friends. *Horror* at the slaughter of everybody else's friends. It isn't clear to me why such emotions have to be ignored.'

'I'm not saying they should be ignored. Only that they mustn't be allowed to dominate.'

'The protopathic must know its place?'

Rivers looked taken aback. 'I wouldn't've put it quite like that.'

'Why not? It's your word. And Sassoon does seem to be a remarkably protopathic young man. Doesn't he? I mean from what you say, it's "all or nothing" all the time. Happy warrior one minute. Bitter pacifist the next.'

'Precisely. He's completely inconsistent. And that's all the more reason to get him to *argue* the position –'

'Epicritically.'

'*Rationally.*'

Brock raised his hands and sat back in his chair. 'I hope you don't mind my playing devil's advocate?'

'Good heavens, no. The whole point of these meetings is to protect the patient.'

Brock smiled, one of his rare, thin, unexpectedly charming smiles. 'Is that what I was doing? I thought I was protecting you.'

Part 2

8

Prior had lost weight during his time in sick bay. Watching the light fall on to his face, Rivers noticed how sharp the cheekbones had become.

'Do you mind if I smoke?'

'No, go ahead.' Rivers pushed an ashtray across the desk.

The match flared behind Prior's cupped hands. 'First for three weeks,' he said. 'God, I feel dizzy.'

Rivers tried not to say, but said, 'It's not really a good idea with asthma, you know.'

'You think it might shorten my life? Do you know how long the average officer lasts in France?'

'Yes. Three months. You're not in France.'

Prior dragged on the cigarette and, momentarily, closed his eyes. He looked a bit like the boys you saw on street corners in the East End. That same air of knowing the price of everything. Rivers drew the file towards him. 'We left you in billets at Beauvois.'

'Yes. We were there, oh, I think about four days and then we were rushed back into the line. We attacked the morning of the night we moved up.'

'Date?'

'April the 23rd.'

Rivers looked up. It was unusual for Prior to be so accurate.

'St George's Day. The CO toasted him in the mess. I remember because it was so bloody stupid.'

'You were in the casualty clearing station on the . . .' He glanced at the file. '29th. So that leaves us with six days unaccounted for.'

'Yes, and I'm afraid I can't help you with any of them.'

'Do you remember the attack?'

'Yes. It was exactly like any other attack.'

Rivers waited. Prior looked so hostile that at first Rivers

thought he would refuse to go on, but then he raised the cigarette to his lips, and said, '*All right*. Your watch is brought back by a runner, having been synchronized at headquarters.' A long pause. 'You wait, you try to calm down anybody who's obviously shitting himself or on the verge of throwing up. You hope you won't do either of those things yourself. Then you start the count down: ten, nine, eight . . . so on. You blow the whistle. You climb the ladder. Then you double through a gap in the wire, lie flat, wait for everybody else to get out – those that are left, there's already quite a heavy toll – and then you stand up. And you start walking. *Not* at the double. Normal walking speed.' Prior started to smile. 'In a straight line. Across open country. In broad daylight. Towards a line of machine-guns.' He shook his head. 'Oh, and of course you're being shelled all the way.'

'What did you *feel*?'

Prior tapped the ash off his cigarette. 'You always want to know what I *felt*.'

'Well, yes. You're describing this attack as if it were a – a slightly ridiculous event in –'

'Not "slightly". Slightly, I did not say.'

'All right, an *extremely* ridiculous event – in somebody else's life.'

'Perhaps that's how it felt.'

'Was it?' He gave Prior time to answer. 'I think you're capable of a great deal of detachment, but you'd have to be *inhuman* to be as detached as that.'

'All right. It felt . . .' Prior started to smile again. '*Sexy*.'

Rivers raised a hand to his mouth.

'You see?' Prior said, pointing to the hand. 'You ask me how it felt and when I tell you, you don't believe me.'

Rivers lowered his hand. 'I haven't said I don't believe you. I was waiting for you to go on.'

'You know those men who lurk around in bushes waiting to jump out on unsuspecting ladies and – *er-um* – display their equipment? It felt a bit like that. A bit like I *imagine* that feels. I wouldn't like you to think I had any personal experience.'

'And was that your only feeling?'

'Apart from terror, yes.' He looked amused. 'Shall we get back to "inhuman detachment"?'

'If you like.'

Prior laughed. 'I think it suits us *both* better, don't you?'

Rivers let him continue. This had been Prior's attitude throughout the three weeks they'd spent trying to recover his memories of France. He seemed to be saying, 'All right. You can make me dredge up the horrors, you can make me remember the deaths, but you will never make me feel.' Rivers tried to break down the detachment, to get to the emotion, but he knew that, confronted by the same task, he would have tackled it in exactly the same way as Prior.

'You keep up a kind of chanting. "Not so fast. Steady on the left!" Designed to avoid bunching. Whether it works or not depends on the ground. Where we were, it was absolutely pitted with shell-holes and the lines got broken up straight away. I looked back . . .' He stopped, and reached for another cigarette. 'I looked back and the ground was covered with wounded. Lying on top of each other, writhing. Like fish in a pond that's drying out. I wasn't frightened at all. I just felt this . . . amazing burst of exultation. Then I heard a shell coming. And the next thing I knew I was in the air, *fluttering* down . . .' He waved his fingers in a descending arc. 'I know it can't've *been* like that, but that's what I remember. When I came to, I was in a crater with about half a dozen of the men. I couldn't move. I thought at first I was paralysed, but then I managed to move my feet. I told them to get the brandy out of my pocket, and we passed that round. Then a man appeared on the other side of the crater, right at the rim, and, instead of crawling down, he put his hands to his sides, like this, and *slid* down on his bottom. And suddenly everybody burst out laughing.'

'You say "came to"? Do you know how long you were unconscious?'

'No idea.'

'But you *were* able to speak?'

'Yes, I told them to get the brandy.'

'And then?'

'Then we waited till dark and made a dash for the line. They saw us just as we got to our wire. Two men wounded.'

'There was no talk of sending you to a CCS when you got back?'

'No, I was organizing other people there.' He added bitterly, 'There was no talk of sending anybody anywhere. Normally you go back after heavy losses, but we didn't. They just left us there.'

'And you don't remember anything else?'

'No. And *I have tried.*'

'Yes, I'm sure you have.'

A long silence. 'I suppose you haven't heard from the CO?'

'No, I'd tell you if I had.'

Prior sat brooding for a while. 'Well, I suppose we go on waiting.' He leant forward to stub his cigarette out. 'You know, you once told me I had to win.' He shook his head. 'You're the one who has to win.'

'This may come as a shock, Mr Prior, but I had been rather assuming we were on the same side.'

Prior smiled. 'This may come as a shock, Dr Rivers, but I had been *rather assuming* that we were not.'

Silence. Rivers caught and held a sigh. 'That does make the relationship of doctor and patient rather difficult.'

Prior shrugged. Obviously he didn't think that was *his* problem. 'You think you know what happened, don't you?' Rivers said.

'I've told you I don't remember.'

The antagonism was startling. They might've been back at the beginning, when it had been almost impossible to get a civil word out of him. 'I'm sorry, I didn't make myself clear. I wasn't suggesting you knew, only that you might have a *theory.*'

Prior shook his head. 'No. No theory.'

A short, dark-haired man sidled round the door, blinking in the sudden blaze of sunlight. Sassoon, sitting on the bed, looked up from the golf club he'd been cleaning. 'Yes?'

'I've b-brought these.'

A stammer. Not as bad as some, but bad enough. Sassoon exerted himself to be polite. 'What is it? I can't see.'

Books. *His* book. Five copies, no less. 'My God, a reader.'

'I wondered if you'd b-be k-kind enough to s-sign them?'

'Yes, of course.' Sassoon put the golf club down and reached for his pen. He could have dispatched the job in a few moments, but he sensed that his visitor wanted to talk, and he had after all bought *five* copies. Sassoon was curious. 'Why five? Has the War Office put it on a reading list?'

'They're f-for m-my f-family.'

Oh, dear. Sassoon transferred himself from bed to table and opened the first book. 'What name shall I write?'

'Susan Owen. M-y m-mother.'

Sassoon began to write. Paused. 'Are you . . . quite sure your mother *wants* to be told that "Bert's gone syphilitic?" I had trouble getting them to print that.'

'It w-won't c-come as a sh-shock.'

'Won't it?' One could only speculate on the nature of Mrs Owen's previous acquaintance with Bert.

'I t-tell her everything. In m-my l-letters.'

'Good heavens,' Sassoon said lightly, and turned back to the book.

Owen looked down at the back of Sassoon's neck, where a thin line of khaki was just visible beneath the purple silk of his dressing gown. 'Don't *you?*'

Sassoon opened his mouth and shut it again. 'My brother died at Gallipoli,' he said, at last. 'I think my mother has enough on her plate without any searing revelations from me.'

'I s-suppose she m-must b-be c-concerned about your b-being here.'

'Oh, I don't think so. On the contrary. I believe the thought of my insanity is one of her few consolations.' He glanced up, briefly. 'Better *mad* than a pacifist.' When Owen continued to look blank, he added, 'You do know why I'm here?'

'Yes.'

'And what do you think about that?'

'I agreed with every w-word.'

Sassoon smiled. 'So did my friend Graves.' He opened the next book. 'Who's this one for?'

Owen, feeding the names, would have given anything to say one sentence without stammering. No hope of that – he was far too nervous. Everything about Sassoon intimidated him. His status as a published poet, his height, his good looks, the clipped aristocratic voice, sometimes quick, sometimes halting, but always cold, the bored expression, the way he had of not looking at you when you spoke – shyness, perhaps, but it *seemed* like arrogance. Above all, his reputation for courage. Owen had his own reasons for being sensitive about that.

Sassoon reached the last book. Owen felt the meeting begin to slip away from him. Rather desperately, he said, 'I l-liked "The D-Death B-Bed" b-best.' And suddenly he relaxed. It didn't matter what *this* Sassoon thought about him, since the real Sassoon was in the poems. He quoted, from memory, '"He's young; he hated War, how should he die/When cruel old campaigners win safe through?/But death replied: 'I choose him.' So he went." That's beautiful.'

Sassoon paused in his signing. 'Yes, I – I was quite pleased with that.'

'Oh, and "The Redeemer". "He faced me, reeling in his weariness,/Shouldering his load of planks, so hard to bear./I say that He was Christ, who wrought to bless . . ."' He broke off. 'I've been wanting to write that for three years.'

'Perhaps you should be glad you didn't.'

The light faded from Owen's face. 'Sorry?'

'Well, don't you think it's rather easily said? "I say that He was Christ"?'

'You m-mean you d-didn't m-mean it?'

'Oh, I meant it. The book isn't putting one point of view, it's charting the – the *evolution* of a point of view. That's probably the first poem that even attempts to look at the war realistically. And that one doesn't go nearly far enough.' He paused. 'The fact is Christ isn't on record as having lobbed many Mills bombs.'

'No, I s-see what you m-mean. I've been thinking about that quite a b-bit recently.'

Sassoon scarcely heard him. 'I got so sick of it in the end. All those Calvaries at crossroads just sitting there waiting to be turned into symbols. I knew a man once, Potter his name was. You know the miraculous crucifix stories? *"Shells falling all around, but the figure of Our Lord was spared"*? Well, Potter was so infuriated by them he decided to start a one-man campaign. Whenever he saw an undamaged crucifix, he used it for target practice. You could hear him for miles. "ONE, TWO, THREE, FOUR, Bastard on the Cross, FIRE!" There weren't many miraculous crucifixes in Potter's section of the front.' He hesitated. 'But perhaps I shouldn't be saying this? I mean for all I know, you're –'

'I don't know what I am. But I do know I wouldn't want a f-faith that couldn't face the facts.'

Sassoon became aware that Owen was standing at his elbow, almost like a junior officer. 'Why don't you sit down?' he said, waving him towards the bed. 'And tell me your name. I take it this one's for you?'

'Yes. Wilfred. Wilfred Owen.'

Sassoon blew on his signature and closed the book. 'You say you've been thinking about it?'

Owen looked diffident. 'Yes.'

'To any effect? I mean, did you reach any conclusions?'

'Only that if I were going to call myself a Christian, I'd have to call myself a pacifist as well. I don't think it's possible to c-call yourself a C-Christian and ... and j-just leave out the awkward bits.'

'You'll never make a bishop.'

'No, well, I think I can live with that.'

'And *do* you call yourself a pacifist?'

A long pause. 'No. Do you?'

'No.'

'It's funny, you know, I never thought about it at all in France.'

'No, well, you don't. Too busy, too tired.' Sassoon smiled. 'Too *healthy*.'

'It's not *just* that, though, is it? Sometimes when you're alone, in the trenches, I mean, at night you get the sense of something *ancient*. As if the trenches had always been there. You know one trench we held, it had skulls in the side. You looked back along and ... Like mushrooms. And do you know, it was actually *easier* to believe they were men from Marlborough's army than to to to think they'd been alive two years ago. It's as if all other wars had somehow ... distilled themselves into this war, and that makes it something you ... almost can't challenge. It's like a very deep voice saying, *Run along, little man. Be thankful if you survive.*'

For a moment the nape of Sassoon's neck crawled as it had

the first time Campbell talked about German spies; but this was not madness. 'I had a similar experience. Well, I don't know whether it is similar. I was going up with the rations one night and I saw the limbers against the skyline, and the flares going up. What you see every night. Only I seemed to be seeing it from the future. A hundred years from now they'll still be ploughing up skulls. And I seemed to be in that time and looking back. I think I saw our ghosts.'

Silence. They'd gone further than either of them had intended, and for a moment they didn't know how to get back. Gradually, they stirred, they looked round, at sunlight streaming over beds and chairs, at Sassoon's razor glinting on the washstand, its handle smeared with soap. Sassoon looked at his watch. 'I'm going to be late for golf.'

Immediately Owen stood up. 'Well, thanks for these,' he said, taking the books. He laughed. 'Thanks for writing it.'

Sassoon followed him to the door. 'Did you say you wrote?'

'I didn't, but I do.'

'Poetry?'

'Yes. Nothing in print yet. Oh, which reminds me. I'm editor of the *Hydra*. The hospital magazine? I was wondering if you could let us have something. It needn't be –'

'Yes, I'll look something out.' Sassoon opened the door. 'Give me a few days. You could bring your poems.'

This was said with such determined courtesy and such transparent lack of enthusiasm that Owen burst out laughing. 'No, I –'

'No, I mean it.'

'All right.' Owen was still laughing. 'They are quite short.'

'No, well, it doesn't lend itself to epics, does it?'

'Oh, they're not about the war.' He hesitated. 'I don't write about that.'

'Why ever not?'

'I s-suppose I've always thought of p-poetry as the opposite of all that. The ugliness.' Owen was struggling to articulate a point of view he was abandoning even as he spoke. 'S-Something to to t-take refuge in.'

Sassoon nodded. 'Fair enough.' He added mischievously, 'Though it does seem a bit like having a faith that daren't face the facts.' He saw Owen's expression change. 'Look, it doesn't matter what they're about. Bring them anyway.'

'Yes, I will. Thank you.'

Anderson, following Sassoon into the bar of the golf club, knew he owed him an apology. At the seventeenth hole, afraid he was losing, he'd missed a vital shot and in the heat of the moment had not merely sworn at Sassoon, but actually raised the club and threatened to hit him with it. Sassoon had looked startled, even alarmed, but he'd laughed it off. At the eighteenth hole, he'd been careful to ask Anderson's advice about which iron he should use. Now, he turned to Anderson and said, 'Usual?'

Anderson nodded. The trouble was, Anderson thought, it looked so much like bad sportsmanship, whereas in reality the apology was being delayed, not by any unwillingness on his part to admit he was wrong, but by the extent of the horror he felt at his own behaviour. He'd behaved like a spoilt child. *So do something about it,* he told himself. 'Sorry about that,' he said, nodding towards the course.

''S all right.' Sassoon turned from the bar and smiled. 'We all have bad days.'

'Here's your half-crown.'

Sassoon grinned and pocketed it. He was thinking, as he turned back to the bar, that if the club had landed on his head he would have been far more seriously injured than he'd been at Arras. He conjured Rivers up in his mind and asked, *What was that you were saying about 'safety'? Nothing more dangerous than playing golf with lunatics.* 'Lunatic' was a word Sassoon would never have dared use to Rivers's face, so it gave him an additional pleasure to yell it at his image.

They took their drinks, found a quiet corner, and began their usual inquest on the game. Under cover of the familiar chat, Anderson watched Sassoon – a good-looking, rather blank face, big hands curved round his glass – and thought how little he knew about him. Or wanted to know. It was a matter of tacit agreement that they talked about nothing but golf. Anderson had read the Declaration, but he wouldn't have dreamt of discussing Sassoon's attitude to the war, mainly because some return of intimacy would then have been required. He might have had to disclose his own reasons for being at Craiglockhart. His horror of blood. He had a momentary picture of the way Sassoon's head would have looked if he'd hit him, and his hand tightened on the glass. 'You're still not taking your time,' he said. 'You're rushing your shots.'

There were other reasons too why he didn't want to talk about the war. Inevitably such talk would have strengthened his own doubts, and they were bad enough already. He even dreamt about the bloody war, not just nightmares, he was used to those; he'd dreamt he was speaking at a debate on whether it should go on or not. In his dream he'd spoken in favour of continuing to the point of German collapse, but Rivers's analysis had left him in no doubt as to how far his horror at the whole business went. He felt safe with Rivers, because he knew Rivers shared the horror, and shared too the conviction that, in spite of everything, it had to go on.

'I don't know whether to spend that half-crown or frame it,' Sassoon was saying. 'I don't suppose I'll ever win another.'

That was to make Anderson feel better about losing his temper on the course. Sassoon was a pleasant companion, there was no doubt about that. He was friendly, modest. But the Declaration hadn't been modest. What had chiefly struck Anderson about that was its arrogance, its totally outrageous assumption that everybody who disagreed with him was 'callous'. Do you think I'm callous? he wanted to ask. Do you think *Rivers* is callous? But there was no point getting worked up. Rivers would soon sort him out.

'I shan't be seeing you tomorrow, shall I?' Sassoon was saying. 'Your wife's coming up.'

'No, I'm afraid she's had to cancel. So it's business as usual.' He took Sassoon's empty glass and stood up. 'You can *try* to make it five bob, if you like.'

Prior watched the amber lights winking in his beer. He was sitting in the shadowy corner of a pub in some sleazy district of Edinburgh. He didn't know where he was. He'd walked miles that evening, not admitting even to himself what he was looking for, and gradually the winding, insidious streets had led him deeper and deeper into a neighbourhood where washing hung, grey-white, from stacked balconies, and the smell of steak frying reminded him of home.

Remembering the smell, his stomach rumbled. He'd had nothing to eat all evening, except a packet of peanuts. Crumbs of salt still clung to his lips, stinging the cracks where the skin had dried during his asthma attack. It was worth it, though, just to sit quietly, to listen to voices that didn't stammer, to have his eyes freed from the ache of khaki.

No theory. He'd lied to Rivers about that. It was a point of honour with him to lie to Rivers at least once during every meeting. He drained his glass and went out into the night.

A little way down the street was a café. He'd passed it on his way to the pub and been tempted to go in, but the door had opened and the breath of hot, damp, dirty, dishwater-smelling air had decided him against it. Now, though, he was too hungry to care. He went in, noticing how the inner windows dripped from condensation, how the damp air insinuated itself into the spaces between his uniform and his skin. A short silence fell. Nobody in an officer's uniform was likely to be inconspicuous or welcome here. He would eat something, fish and chips, quickly and then go.

A group of women was sitting at the next table. Three of them were young, one older, thirty-five, forty perhaps, with blackened stumps for teeth. As far as he could make out from the conversation her name was Lizzie, and the others were Madge, the blonde, pretty one, Betty, who was dark and thin, and Sarah, who had her back to him. Since they all had a slightly yellow tinge to their skin, he assumed they were munitions workers. Munition*ettes*, as the newspapers liked to call them. Lizzie was keeping the younger girls entertained with a string of stories.

'There's this lass and she's a bit simple and she lived next door to a pro – well you know what a pro is.' Lizzie glanced at him and lowered her voice. 'So she's standing at the door this day, and the pro's coming up the street, you know, *dressed to death*. So she says, "Eeh," she says, "you're always lovely dressed." She says, "You've got beautiful clothes." And she says, "I *love* your hats." So the pro says, "Well, why don't you get yourself down the town like I do?" She says, "If a man winks at you, wink back and go with him and let him have what he wants and charge him 7/6. And go to R & K Modes and get yourself a hat." So the next day the pro's coming up the street again. "Hello." "Hello." She says, "D' y' *get* a hat?" She says, "*Nah*." "Well, did you not do as I told you?" She says, "Why of course I did." She says, "I went down the town and there was a man winked at us and I winked back. He says, 'Howay over the Moor.'" So she says, "I gans over the Moor with him," she says, "and I let him have what he wanted. He says, 'How much is that?' I says, '7/6.' He says, 'Hadaway and shite,' and when I come back he'd gone." '

The girls shrieked with laughter. He looked at them again. The one called Madge was very pretty, but there was no hope of winkling her out of the group, and he thought he might as well be moving on. As soon as his meal arrived, he began stuffing limp chips and thickly battered fish into his mouth, wiping the grease away on the back of his hand.

'You'll get hiccups.'

He looked up. It was Sarah, the one who'd been sitting with her back to him. 'You'll have to give us a surprise, then, won't you?'

'Drop me key down your back if you like.'

'That's nose bleeds, Sarah,' Betty said.

'She knows what it is,' said Lizzie.

Madge said, 'Hiccups, you're supposed to drink from the other side of the cup.'

She and Prior stared at each other across the table.

'But it's a con, isn't it?' he said. 'You can't do it.'

''Course you can.'

'Go on, then, let's see you.'

She dipped her small, straight nose into her cup, lapped, spluttered and came up laughing and wiping her chin. Betty, obviously jealous, gave her a dig in the ribs. 'Hey up you, you're gonna gerrus slung out.'

The café owner was eyeing them from behind the till, slowly polishing a glass on a distinctly grubby-looking tea towel. The girls went back to their tea, bursting into minor explosions of giggles, their shoulders shaking, while Prior turned back and finished his meal. He was aware of Sarah beside him. She had very heavy, very thick, dark-brown hair, but all over the surface, in a kind of halo, were other hairs, auburn, copper, chestnut. He'd never seen hair like that before. He looked at her, and she turned around and stared at him, a cool, amused stare from greenish eyes. He said, 'Would you like a drink?'

She looked at her cup.

'No, I meant a proper drink.'

'Pubs round here don't let women in.'

'Isn't there a hotel?'

'Well, there's the Cumberland, but . . .'

The other women looked at each other. Lizzie said, 'Howay, lasses, I think our Sarah's clicked.'

The three of them got up, said a good-natured 'goodnight' and tripped out of the café, only bursting into giggles again after they'd reached the pavement.

'Shall we go, then?' said Prior.

Sarah looked at him. 'Aye, all right.'

Outside, she turned to him. 'I still don't know your name.'

'Prior,' he said automatically.

She burst out laughing. 'Don't you lot *have* Christian names?'

'Billy.' He wanted to say, and I'm not 'you lot'.

'Mine's Sarah. Sarah Lumb.' She held out her hand to him in a direct, almost boyish way. It intrigued him, since nothing else about her was boyish.

'Well, Sarah Lumb, lead on.'

Her preferred drink was port and lemon. Prior was startled at the rate she knocked them back. A flush spread across her cheeks in a different place from the rouge, so that she looked as if her face had slid out of focus. She worked in a factory, she said, making detonators. Twelve-hour shifts, six days a week, but she liked the work, she said, and it was well paid. 'Fifty bob a week.'

'I suppose that's something.'

'Too bloody right it is. I was earning ten bob before the war.'

He thought what the detonators she made could do to flesh and bone, and his mind bulged as a memory threatened to surface. 'You're not Scottish, though, are you?'

'No, Geordie. Well, what *you*'d call Geordie.'

'Did your dad come up looking for work?'

'No, they're still down there. I'm in lodgings down the road.'

Ah, he thought.

'"*Ah*," he thinks.' She looked at him, amused and direct. 'I think you're a bad lad.'

'No, I'm not. Nobody bad could be *that* transparent.'

'That's true.'

'Haven't you got a boyfriend?'

'What do you think?'

'I don't think you'd be sitting here if you had.'

'Oh, I might be one of these two-timing lasses, you never know.' She looked down into her glass. 'No, I haven't got one.'

'Why not? Can't all be blind in Scotland.'

'Perhaps I'm not on the market.'

He didn't know what to make of her, but then he was out of touch with women. They seemed to have changed so much during the war, to have expanded in all kinds of ways, whereas men over the same period had shrunk into a smaller and smaller space.

'I did have one,' she said. 'Loos.'

Odd, he thought, getting up and going to the bar to buy more drinks, that one word should be enough. But then why not? Language ran out on you, in the end, the names were left to say it all. Mons, Loos, Ypres, the Somme. Arras. He paid and carried the drinks back to their table. He thought that he didn't want to hear about the boyfriend, and that he was probably going to anyway. He was right there.

'I was in service at the time. It didn't . . .' Her voice became very brisk. 'It didn't seem to sink in. Then his mate came to see me. You weren't supposed to have followers. "Followers" – that's how old-fashioned she was. Especially *soldiers*. "Oh my *deah*." So anyway he come to the front door and . . .' She waved her hand languidly. 'I sent him away. Then I nipped down the basement and let him in the back.' She took a swig of the port. 'It was *our* gas,' she said, red-lidded. 'Did *you* know that?'

'Yes.'

'Our own bloody gas. After he'd gone, you know, I couldn't believe it. I just walked round and round the table and it was like . . . You know when you get a tune stuck in your head? I just kept on thinking, our gas. Anyway after a bit she come downstairs, and she says, "Where's tea?" I says, "Well, you can see for yourself. It's not ready." *We-ell.* First one thing was said and then another and in the end I did, I let her have it. She says, "You'd be making a great mistake to throw this job away, you know, Sarah." I says, "Oh, aye?" She says, "We don't say 'aye', Sarah, we say 'yes'." I says, "All right," I says, "*'yes'*. But 'aye' or 'yes', it's still ten bob a week and you put it where the monkey put the nuts." Same night I was packing me bags. No testimonial. And you know what that would've meant before the war?' She looked him up and down. 'No, I don't suppose you do. Anyway, I turned up at home and me Mam says, "I've no sympathy, our Sarah," she says. "You should have fixed him while you had the chance," she says. "And made sure of the pension. Our Cynthia had her wits about her," she says. "Why couldn't you?" And of course our Cynthia's sat there. Would you believe *in weeds*? I thought, aw to hell with this. Anyway, a couple of days after, I got on talking to Betty – that's the dark girl you saw me with just now – and we decided to give this a go.'

'I'm glad you did.'

She brooded for a while over her empty glass. 'You know, me Mam says there's no such thing as love between men and women. Love for your bairns, yes. Love for a man? *No.*' She turned to him, almost aggressively. 'What do *you* think?'

'I don't know.'

'Well, that makes two of us, then, 'cause I'm buggered if I do.'

'But you loved –'

'Johnny? I can't remember what he looked like. Sometimes his face pops into me mind, like when I'm thinking about something else, but when I *want* to see it, I can't.' She smiled. 'That's the trouble with port and lemon, isn't it? Truth pours out.'

He took the hint and bought another.

By the time they left the pub she'd drunk enough to need his arm.

'Which way's your lodgings?'

She giggled. 'Won't do you any good,' she said. 'My landlady's a dragon. Fifty times worse than me Mam.'

'Shall we go for a walk, then? I don't fancy saying goodnight, just yet, do you?'

'All right.'

They turned away from the lighted pavements, into the darkness of a side street. He put his arm around her, inching his hand further up until his fingers rested against the curve of her breast. She was tall for a woman, and they fitted together, shoulder and hip. He hardly had to shorten his stride. As they walked, she glanced down frequently at her shoes and stockings, admiring herself. He guessed she more usually wore boots.

They came upon a church with a small churchyard around it. Gravestones leant together at angles in the shadow of the trees, like people gossiping. 'Shall we go in there for a bit?'

He opened the gate for her and they went in, into the darkness under the trees, treading on something soft and crunchy. Pine needles, perhaps. At the church door they turned and followed the path round, till they came to a tall, crumbling, ivy-covered wall. There, in the shadows, he pulled her towards him. He got her jacket and blouse unbuttoned and felt for her breast. The nipple hardened against his palm, and he laughed under his breath. She started to say something, but he covered her mouth with his own, he didn't want her to talk, he didn't want her to tell him things. He would have preferred not even to know her name. Just flesh against flesh in the darkness and then nothing.

'I know what *you* want,' she said, pulling away from him.

Instantly he let her go. '*I* know what I want. What's wrong with *that*? I've never forced anybody.' He turned away from her and sat on a tombstone. 'And I don't go on about it either.'

'Then you're a man in a million.'

'I know.'

'Big-headed bugger.'

'Don't I even get a cuddle?' He patted the tombstone. 'No harm in that.'

She came and sat beside him, and after a while he got his arms around her again. But he didn't feel the same way about it. Now, even as he lowered his head to her breast, he was wondering whether he wanted to play this particular game. Whether it was worth it. He tugged gently at her nipple, and felt her thighs loosen. Instantly, his doubts vanished. He pressed her back on to the tombstone and moved on top of her. Cradling her head on his left arm, he began the complicated business of raising her skirts, pulling down her drawers, unbuttoning his breeches, all while trying to maintain their position on a too-short and sloping tombstone. At the last moment she cried 'No-o-o' and shoved him hard off the tombstone into the long grass. He sat for a while, his back against the stone, picking bits of lichen off his tunic. After a while he yawned and said, 'Short-arsed little buggers, the Scots.'

She looked down at the tombstone, which did seem rather small. 'Oh, I don't know. Everybody was shorter in them days.' You could just make out the word 'Beloved', but everything else was covered in lichen or crumbled away. She traced the word with her fingertip. 'I wonder what they think.'

'Down there? Glad to see a bit of life, I should think. Not that they've seen much.'

She didn't reply. He turned to look at her. Her hair had come down, way past her shoulders, he was glad she didn't wear it short, and there was still that amazing contrast of the dark brown velvety mass and its halo of copper wire. He was being stupid. She'd let him have it in the end, and the more he bellyached about it now, the longer he'd have to wait. He said, 'Come on, one kiss, and I'll walk you home.'

'Hm.'

'No, I mean it.'

He gave her a teasingly chaste kiss, making sure he was the first to pull away. Then he helped her dust down her skirt and walked her back to her lodgings. On the way she insisted they stop in the doorway of a shop, and she crammed her hair up into her hat, with the help of the few hairpins she'd managed to retrieve. 'There'd be eyebrows raised if I went in like this.'

'Can I see you again?'

'You know where I live. Or you will do.'

'I don't know your times off.'

'Sunday.'

'I'll come over on Sunday, then, shall I? If I come mid

morning, we could have a bit to eat in Edinburgh and then go somewhere on the tram.'

She looked doubtful, but the thought of being collected from her lodgings by an officer was too much for her. 'All right.'

They walked on. She stopped outside the door and raised her face. Oh, no, he thought. No fumbling on doorsteps. He lowered his head until his forehead rested against hers. 'Goodnight, Sarah Lumb.'

'Goodnight, Billy Prior.'

After a few paces he turned and looked back. She was standing on the step, watching him walk away. He raised his hand, and she waved slightly. Then he turned and walked briskly on, looking at his watch and thinking, Christ. Even if he found a taxi *immediately* he still couldn't be back at Craiglockhart before the main doors were locked. Oh well, he thought, I'll just have to face it.

9

'Aren't *you* going to start?'

'I imagine Major Bryce has dealt with the matter?'

'You could say. He's confined me to the hospital for a fortnight.'

Rivers made no comment.

'Don't you think that's rather *severe?*'

'It wasn't a simple matter of being late back, was it? Matron says she saw you in town, and you were not wearing your hospital badge.'

'I wasn't wearing the badge because I was looking for a girl. Which – *as you may or may not know* – is not made easier by going around with a badge stuck on your chest saying I AM A LOONY.'

'I gather you also made some rather disrespectful remarks about Matron. Everything from the size of her bosom to the state of her hymen. If you make remarks like that to the CO, what do you *think* is going to happen?'

Prior didn't reply, though a muscle throbbed in his jaw. Rivers looked at the pale, proud, wintry face and thought oh God, it's going to be another one of those.

Prior said, 'Aren't you going to ask me if I got one?'

'One what?'

'Girl. Woman.' When Rivers didn't immediately reply, Prior added, '*Wo-man?*'

'No, I wasn't going to ask.'

'You amaze me. I should've thought that was par for the course.'

Rivers waited.

'*Questions.* On and on and bloody on.'

'Would you like to leave it for today?'

'No.'

'You're sure?'

'Quite sure.'

'All right. We'd got to the time immediately following the April 23rd attack. Have you made any progress beyond that?'

'No.'

'Nothing at all?'

'No.' Prior's hands were gripping the arms of his chair. 'I don't want to talk about this.'

Rivers decided to humour him. 'What do you want to talk about?'

'Something you said earlier on. It's been bothering me ever since. You said officers don't suffer from mutism.'

'It's rare.'

'How many cases?'

'At Craiglockhart? You, and one other. At Maghull, where I was treating private soldiers, it was by far the commonest symptom.'

'Why?'

'I imagine . . . Mutism seems to spring from a conflict between *wanting* to say something, and knowing that if you *do* say it the consequences will be disastrous. So you resolve it by making it physically impossible for yourself to speak. And for the private soldier the consequences of speaking his mind are always going to be far worse than they would be for an officer. What you tend to get in officers is stammering. And it's not just mutism. All the physical symptoms: paralysis, blindness, deafness. They're all common in private soldiers and rare in officers. It's almost as if for the . . . the labouring classes illness *has* to be physical. They can't take their condition seriously unless there's a physical symptom. And there are other differences as well. Officers' dreams tend to be more elaborate. The men's dreams are much more a matter of simple wish fulfilment. You know, they dream they've been sent back to France, but on the day they arrive peace is declared. That sort of thing.'

'I think I'd rather have their dreams than mine.'

'How do you know?' Rivers said. 'You don't remember your dreams.'

'You still haven't said why.'

'I suppose it's just a matter of officers having a more complex mental life.'

Prior reacted as if he'd been stung. 'Are you serious? You honestly believe that that *gaggle* of noodle-brained half-wits down there has a complex mental life? Oh, *Rivers.*'

'I'm not saying it's *universally* true, only that it's *generally* true. Simply as a result of officers receiving a different and, for the most part, more prolonged education.'

'*The public schools.*'

'Yes. The public schools.'

Prior raised his head. 'How do I fit into that?'

'We-ell, it's interesting that you were mute and that you're one of the very few people in the hospital who *doesn't* stammer.'

'It's even more interesting that you do.'

Rivers was taken aback. 'That's d-different.'

'How is it different? Other than that you're on that side of the desk?' He saw Rivers hesitate. 'No, I'm not being awkward. I'm genuinely interested.'

'It's usually thought that neurasthenic stammers arise from the same kind of conflict as mutism, a conflict between wanting to speak and knowing that w-what you've got to say is not acceptable. Lifelong stammerers? Well. Nobody really knows. It may even be genetic.'

Prior smiled. 'Now that is lucky, isn't it? Lucky for you, I mean. Because if your stammer *was* the same as theirs – you might actually have to sit down and work out what it is you've spent fifty years trying not to say.'

'Is that the end of my appointment for the day, Mr Prior?'

Prior smiled.

'You know one day you're going to have to accept the fact that you're in this hospital because you're ill. Not me. Not the CO. Not the kitchen porter. *You.*'

After Prior had gone, Rivers sat for a while, half amused, half irritated. Now that his attention had been drawn to his stammer, it would plague him at intervals throughout the day. Bugger Prior, he thought. To be absolutely accurate, b-b-b-bugger Prior.

Prior had left slightly early, so Rivers had a few minutes before his next appointment. He decided to take a turn in the grounds. The grass was silvery with dew – his footsteps showed up dark along the path he'd come – but here and there the ground was beginning to steam. He sat on a bench under the trees, and watched two patients carrying scythes come round the corner of the building and run down the grassy slope that divided the gravel drive from the tennis courts. They looked, Rivers thought, almost comically symbolic: Time and Death invading the Arcadian scene. Nothing symbolic about the scythes, though. The blades over their shoulders glinted a wicked blue-grey. You could only wonder at an administration that confiscated cut-throat razors and then issued the patients with these. They set to work cutting the long grass by the hedges. There was a great deal of laughter and clumsiness at first, and a not a few false starts, before their bodies bent into the rhythm of the task. Moths, disturbed from their daytime sleep, flickered all around them.

One took off his Sam Browne belt and then tunic, shirt and tie, casting them carelessly aside, and then went back to his scything, his dangling braces describing wide arcs around him as he swung the blade. His body was very pale, with a line round the neck, dividing white from reddish brown. The tunic had landed on the hedge, one sleeve raised as if beckoning. The other flung down his scythe and did the same. Work went more quickly now. Soon there was a gratifyingly large area of mown grass for them to look back on. They stood leaning on the scythes, admiring their work, and then one of them dived into the cut grass, winnowing his way through it, obviously excited by it in the way dogs sometimes are. He lay on his back, panting. The other man came across, said, 'Silly bugger,' and started kicking the grass all over him.

Rivers turned and saw Patterson – the Head of Office Administration – making his way at a steady pace down the slope to deliver the inevitable reprimand. King's regulations. No officer must appear in public with any garment missing. Patterson spoke to them, then turned away. Slowly, they reached for their uniforms, pulled khaki shirts and tunics on to sweating bodies, buckled belts. It had to be done, though it seemed to Rivers that the scything went more slowly after that, and there was less laughter, which seemed a pity.

That night Rivers worked late, compiling lists of men to be boarded at the end of August. This was the most difficult task of any month, since it involved deciding which patients were fit to return to duty. In theory, the decision to return a man to service was taken by the Board, but since his recommendations were rarely, if ever, questioned, in practice his report determined the outcome. He was beginning to work on the first of these reports when there was a tap on the door. He called, 'Come in!'

Prior came into the room.

'Good evening,' Rivers said.

'Good evening. I came to say I'm sorry about this morning.'

The day had been so horrific in so many ways – culminating in a three-hour meeting of the hospital management committee – that Rivers had to grope for the memory. He said. 'That's all right.'

'It was stupid. Going on like that.'

'Oh, I don't know. We just caught each other at a bad moment.'

Prior lingered a few feet away from the desk. 'Why don't you sit down?' Rivers said.

'You must be tired.'

'Tired of paperwork.'

Prior's glance took in the list of names. 'The Boards.'

'The Boards.' He glanced at Prior. 'Not you this time.'

'Not enough progress.'

Rivers didn't immediately reply. He was watching Prior, noticing the pallor, the circles round the eyes. He had shadows under the shadows now. 'You have made progress. You've recovered almost all your memory *and* you no longer lose your voice.'

'You must wish I did.'

Rivers smiled. 'Don't exaggerate, Mr Prior. We both know if you *really* wanted to be offensive, you could do a hundred times better than you did this morning.' He waited for a reply. 'Couldn't you?'

Prior produced a curious rippling motion – half shrug, half flounce – and turned away. After a moment he looked sideways at Rivers. 'I did once think of asking you if you ever fucked any of your headhunters.'

'What stopped you?'

'I thought it was your business.'

Rivers pretended to consider the matter. 'That's true.'

'There's no point trying to be offensive, is there, if *that's* the only response you get?'

'You don't really want to be. You've always made a lot of *noise* about stepping over the line, but you've never actually done it.' Rivers smiled. 'Except just now, of course. And that was incredibly indirect.'

A short silence. Prior said, 'I wish I could go out. No, it's all right, I'm not asking. I'm just saying I wish I could. The nightmares get worse when I'm stuck indoors.' He waited. 'This is where you ask about the nightmares and I say I don't remember.'

'I know.'

Prior smiled. 'You never believed me, did you?'

'Should I have done?'

'No.'

'Do you want to talk about them now?'

'I can't. Look, they're just . . .' He laughed. '"*Standard issue battle nightmares. Potty officers for the use of.*" Nothing you won't have heard a hundred times before.'

'Except?'

'Except nothing.'

A long silence.

'Except that *sometimes* they get muddled up with sex. So I wake up, and . . .' He risked a glance at Rivers. When he spoke again, his voice was casual. 'It makes it really quite impossible to *like* oneself. I've actually woken up once or twice and wondered whether there was any point going on.'

And you might well do it, Rivers thought.

'That's why I was so furious when they got you up in the middle of the night.'

Easy to hand out the usual reassurances about the effects on young men of a celibate life, but not particularly helpful. Prior was becoming unmistakably depressed. It was doing him no good to wait for his CO's letter, which might anyway turn out to contain nothing of any great moment. 'We could try hypnosis now, if you liked.'

'Now?'

'Yes, why not? It's the time we're least likely to be interrupted.'

Prior's eyes flickered round the room. He licked his lips. 'It's odd, isn't it? When you said most people were frightened, I didn't believe you.'

'What frightens them,' Rivers said carefully, 'is the belief that they're putting themselves completely in the therapist's power. That he can make them do anything, even things they'd normally consider ridiculous or even immoral. But that isn't true, you remain your*self* throughout. Not that I shall be trying to make you do anything ridiculous or immoral.' He smiled. 'In spite of being the terror of the South Seas.'

Prior laughed, but his face tightened again immediately.

'We can leave it, if you like,' Rivers said gently.

Deep breath. 'No. I can't pester you for it and then turn it down.'

'If it turns out to be . . .' Rivers groped for a sufficiently bland word. '*Distressing,* I'll give you something to make you sleep. I mean, you won't have to face up to the full implications tonight.'

'All right. What do we do?'

'You relax. Sit back in the chair. That's right. Shoulders. Come on, like this. Now your hands. Let the wrists go. Comfortable? I want you to look at this pen. No, don't raise your head. Raise your eyes. That's right. Keep your eyes fixed on the pen. I'm going to count down from ten. By the time I get to zero, you'll be in a light sleep. All right?'

Prior nodded. He looked profoundly sceptical. Like most bloody-minded people he assumed he would be a poor subject for hypnosis. Rivers thought he'd be very easy. 'Ten . . . Nine . . . Eight . . . Seven . . . Your eyelids are heavy now. Don't fight it, let them close. Six . . . Five . . . Four . . . Three . . . Two . . .'

He woke to a dugout smell of wet sandbags and stale farts. He curled his toes inside his wet boots and felt the creak and sag of chicken wire as he turned towards the table. The usual jumble: paper, bottles, mugs, the black-boxed field telephone, a couple of revolvers – all lit by a single candle stuck to the wood in a pool of its own grease. A barely perceptible thinning of the darkness around the gas curtain told him it must be nearly dawn. And sure enough, a few minutes later Sanderson lifted the curtain and shouted, 'Stand-to!' The bulky forms on the other bunks stirred, groaned, groped for revolvers. Soon they were all trying to climb out of the dugout, difficult because rain and recent near-hits had turned the steps into a muddy slide. All along the trench men were crawling out of funk holes. He clumped along the duckboards to his position, smelling the green, ratty, decomposing smell, stretching the muscles of his face into a smile whenever the men looked up. Then an hour of standing, stiff and shivery, watching dawn grow.

He had first trench watch. He gulped a mug of chlorine-tasting tea, and then started walking along to the outermost position on their left. A smell of bacon frying. In the third fire bay he found Sawdon and Towers crouched over a small fire made out of shredded sandbags and candle ends, coaxing the flames. He stopped to chat for a few minutes, and Towers, blinking under the green mushroom helmet, looked up and offered him tea. A quiet day, he thought, walking on. Not like the last few days, when the bombardment had gone on for seventy hours, and they'd stood-to five times expecting a German counter-attack. Damage from that bombardment was everywhere: crumbling parapets, flooded saps, dugouts with gagged mouths.

He'd gone, perhaps, three fire bays along when he heard the whoop of a shell, and, spinning round, saw the scrawl of dusty brown smoke already drifting away. He thought it'd gone clear over, but then he heard a cry and, feeling sick in his stomach, he ran back. Logan was there already. It must have been Logan's cry he heard, for nothing in that devastation could have had a voice. A conical black hole, still smoking, had been driven into the side of the trench. Of the kettle, the frying-pan, the carefully tended fire, there was no sign, and not much of Sawdon and Towers either, or not much that was recognizable.

There was a pile of sandbags and shovels close by, stacked against the parapet by a returning work party. He reached for a shovel. Logan picked up a sandbag and held it open, and he began shovelling soil, flesh and splinters of blackened bone into the bag. As he shovelled, he retched. He felt something jar against his teeth and saw that Logan was offering him a rum bottle. He forced down bile and rum together. Logan kept his face averted as the shovelling went on. He was swearing under his breath, steadily, blasphemously, obscenely, inventively. Somebody came running. 'Don't stand there gawping, man,' Logan said. 'Go and get some lime.'

They'd almost finished when Prior shifted his position on the duckboards, glanced down, and found himself staring into an eye. Delicately, like somebody selecting a particularly choice morsel from a plate, he put his thumb and forefinger down through the duckboards. His fingers touched the smooth surface and slid before they managed to get a hold. He got it out, transferred it to the palm of his hand, and held it out towards Logan. He could see his hand was shaking, but the shaking didn't seem to be anything to do with him. 'What am I supposed to do with this gob-stopper?' He saw Logan blink and knew he was afraid. At last Logan reached out, grasped his shaking wrist, and tipped the eye into the bag. 'Williams and me'll do the rest, sir. You go on back now.'

He shook his head. They spread the lime together, sprinkling it thickly along the firestep, throwing shovelfuls at a bad patch of wall. When at last they stood back, beating the white dust from the skirts of their tunics, he wanted to say something casual, something that would prove he was all right, but a numbness had spread all over the lower half of his face.

Back in the dugout he watched people's lips move and was filled with admiration for them. There was a sense of joy in watching them, of elation almost. How complex those movements were, how amazing the glimpses of teeth and tongue, the movement of muscles in the jaw. He ran his tongue along the edges of his teeth, curved it back, stroked the ridged palate, flexed his lips, felt the pull of skin and the stretching of muscles in his throat. All present and correct, but how they combined together to make sounds he had no idea.

It was Logan who took him to the casualty clearing station. Normally it would have been his servant, but Logan asked if he could go. They thumped and splodged along cheerfully enough, or at least Prior was cheerful. He felt as if nothing could ever touch him again. When a shell whined across, he didn't flinch, though he knew the Germans had an accurate fix on both communication trenches. They marched from stinking mud to dryish duckboards, and the bare landscape he sensed beyond the tangles of rusty wire gradually changed to fields. Clumps of brilliant yellow cabbage weed, whose smell mimics gas so accurately that men tremble, hung over the final trench.

In the clearing station he sat down, Logan beside him. Lying on the floor was a young man wounded in the back who seemed hardly to know that they were there. From time to time he moaned, 'I'm cold, I'm cold,' but when the doctor came in, he shook his head and said there was nothing he could do. 'There's no need for you to stay,' he said to Logan. 'He'll be all right.' So they shook hands and parted. He sat down on the bench again and tried to think back over the events that had brought him there, but found he could remember very little about them. Two of his men were dead, he remembered that. Nothing else. Like the speechlessness, it seemed natural. He sat on the bench, his clasped hands dangling between his legs, and thought of nothing.

Rivers watched the play of emotions on Prior's face as he fitted the recovered memory into his past. He was unprepared for what happened next.

'*Is that all?*' Prior said.

He seemed to be beside himself with rage.

'I don't know about *all*,' Rivers said. 'I'd've thought that was a traumatic experience by any standards.'

Prior almost spat at him. 'It was *nothing*.'

He put his head in his hands, at first, it seemed, in bewilderment, but then after a few moments he began to cry. Rivers waited a while, then walked round the desk and offered his handkerchief. Instead of taking it, Prior seized Rivers by the arms, and began butting him in the chest, hard enough to hurt. This was not an attack, Rivers realized, though it felt like one. It was the closest Prior could come to asking for physical contact. Rivers was reminded of a nanny goat on his brother's farm, being lifted almost off her feet by the suckling kid. Rivers held Prior's shoulders, and after a while the butting stopped. Prior raised his blind and slobbery face. 'Sorry about that.'

'That's all right.' He waited for Prior to wipe his face, then asked, 'What did you think happened?'

'I didn't know.'

'Yes, you did. You *thought* you knew.'

'I knew two of my men had been killed. I thought . . .' He stopped. 'I thought it must've been my fault. We were in the same trenches we'd been in when I first arrived. The line's terrible there. It winds in and out of brick stacks. A lot of the trenches face the wrong way. Even in daylight with a compass and a map you can get lost. At night . . . I'd been there about a week, I suppose, when a man took out patrol to see if a particular dugout was occupied at night. Compasses don't work, there's too much metal about. He'd been crawling round in circles for God knows how long, when he came upon what he thought was a German wiring party. He ordered his men to open fire. Well, all hell was let loose. Then after a while somebody realized there were British voices shouting on both sides. Five men killed. Eleven injured. I looked at his face as he sat in the dugout and he was . . . You could have done *that* and he wouldn't've blinked. Before I'd always thought the worst thing would be if you were wounded and left out there, but when I saw his face I thought, no. This is the worst thing. And then when I couldn't remember anything except that two of my men had been killed, I thought it had to be something like that.' He looked up. 'I couldn't see what else I'd need to forget.'

'Then you must be relieved.'

'Relieved?'

'You did your duty. You've nothing to reproach yourself with. You even finished cleaning the trench.'

'I've cleaned up dozens of trenches. I don't see why that would make me break down.'

'You're thinking of breakdown as a reaction to a single traumatic event, but it's not like that. It's more a matter of . . . *erosion*. Weeks and months of stress in a situation where you can't get away from it.' He smiled. 'I'm sorry to sound so impersonal. I know how you hate being "the patient".'

'I don't mind in the least. I just want to understand why it happened. You see what I find so difficult is . . . I don't think of myself as the kind of person who breaks down. And yet time and time again I'm brought up hard against the fact that I *did*.'

'I don't know that there is "a kind of person who breaks

down". I imagine most of us could if the pressure were bad enough. I know I could.'

Prior gazed round the room in mock amazement. 'Did the wallpaper speak?'

Rivers smiled. 'I'll tell them to give you a sleeping tablet.'

At the door Prior turned. 'He had very blue eyes, you know. Towers. We used to call him the Hun.'

After making sure Prior got his sleeping tablet, Rivers went upstairs to his own room and began to undress. He tugged at his tie, and as he did so caught sight of himself in the looking-glass. He pulled down his right lid to reveal a dingy and blood-shot white. *What am I supposed to do with this gob-stopper?* He released the lid. *No need to think about that.* If he went on feeling like this, he'd have to see Bryce and arrange to take some leave. It'd reached the point where he woke up in the morning feeling almost as exhausted as he had done when he went to bed. He sat on the edge of the bath and began to take his boots off. *Ye will surely say unto me this proverb. Physician, heal thyself.* One of his father's favourite texts. Sitting, bored and fidgety, in the family pew, Rivers had never thought it an odd choice, though now he wondered why it cropped up as frequently as it did. Fathers remain opaque to their sons, he thought, largely because the sons find it so hard to believe that there's anything in the father worth seeing. Until he's dead, and it's too late. Mercifully, doctors are also opaque to their patients. Unless the patient happens to be Prior.

Rivers finished undressing and got into the bath. He lay back, eyes closed, feeling the hot water start to unravel the knots in his neck and shoulders. Not that Prior was the only patient to have found him ... Well. Rather less than opaque. He remembered John Layard, and as always the memory was painful, because his treatment of Layard had ended in failure. He told himself there was no real resemblance between Layard and Prior. What made Prior more difficult was the constant *probing*. Layard had never probed. But then Layard hadn't thought he needed to probe. Layard had thought he knew.

Lying with his eyes closed like this, Rivers could imagine himself back in St John's, hearing Layard's footsteps coming across the court. What was it he'd said? 'I don't see you as a *father*, you know.' Looking up from the rug in front of the fire. Laughing. 'More a sort of . . . *male mother*.' He *was* like Prior. The same immensely shrewd eyes. X-ray eyes. The same outrageous frankness.

Why should he remember that? It was because of that ridiculous image of the nanny goat that had flashed into his mind while Prior was butting him in the stomach. He disliked the term 'male mother'. He thought he could remember disliking it even at the time. He distrusted the implication that nurturing, even when done by a man, remains female, as if the ability were in some way borrowed, or even stolen, from women – a sort of moral equivalent of the *couvade*. If that were true, then there was really very little hope.

He could see why Layard might use the term. Layard's relationship with his father had been difficult, and he was a young man, without any personal experience of fathering. Though fathering, like mothering, takes many forms beyond the biological. Rivers had often been touched by the way in which young men, some of them not yet twenty, spoke about feeling like fathers to their men. Though when you looked at what they *did*. Worrying about socks, boots, blisters, food, hot drinks. And that perpetually harried expression of theirs. Rivers had only ever seen that look in one other place: in the public wards of hospitals, on the faces of women who were bringing up large families on very low incomes, women who, in their early thirties, could easily be taken for fifty or more. It was the look of people who are totally responsible for lives they have no power to save.

One of the paradoxes of the war – one of the many – was that this most brutal of conflicts should set up a relationship between officers and men that was . . . domestic. Caring. As Layard would undoubtedly have said, maternal. And that wasn't the only trick the war had played. Mobilization. The Great Adventure. They'd been *mobilized* into holes in the ground so constricted they could hardly move. And the Great Adventure – the real life equivalent of all the adventure stories they'd devoured as boys – consisted of crouching in a dugout, waiting to be killed. The war that had promised so much in the way of 'manly' activity had actually delivered 'feminine' passivity, and on a scale that their mothers and sisters had scarcely known. No wonder they broke down.

In bed, he switched off the light and opened the curtains. Rain, silvery in the moonlight, streaked the glass, blurring the vista of tennis courts and trees, gathering, at the lower edge of the pane, into a long puddle that bulged and overflowed. Somebody, on the floor below, screamed. Rivers pulled the curtains to, and settled down to sleep, wishing, not for the first time, that he was young enough for France.

10

Sarah watched the grey trickle of tea creep up the sides of her cup. The tea-lady looked at it, doubtfully. 'That strong enough for you, love?'

'It'll do. Long as it's warm and wet.'

'My God,' Betty Hargreave said. 'Virgin's pee. I can't drink that.'

Madge nudged Sarah sharply in the ribs. 'No, well, it wouldn't be very appropriate, would it?'

'Hey up, you'll make us spill it.'

They went to the far end of the top trestle table and squeezed on to the bench. 'Come on, move your bums along,' Madge said. 'Let two little 'uns in.'

Lizzie collected her Woodbines and matches, and shuffled along. 'What happened to your young man, then, Sarah?'

'Didn't bloody show up, did he? I was sat an hour on Sunday all dolled up and nowhere to go.'

'*Aw,*' Lizzie said.

'Probably just as well,' said Madge. 'At least now you know what he was after.'

'I knew what he was after. I just want to know why he's not still after it.'

'Didn't get it, then?' Betty said, bringing her cup to the table.

'No, he bloody did not.'

'He was good-looking, though, wasn't he?' said Madge.

'All right, I suppose.'

Betty laughed. 'Better fish in the sea, eh, Sarah?'

'Aye, and they can stop there 'n' all. Not interested.'

A whoop of incredulity. Sarah buried her nose in her cup and then, as soon as she felt their attention had been withdrawn, looked at the window. You couldn't really see what it was like outside because the glass was frosted, but here and there raindrops clung to the panes, each with its crescent moon of silver. She wished she was outside and could feel the rain on her face. It would have been nice to have gone to the seaside yesterday, she thought. Bugger him, why didn't he show up?

The others were talking about Lizzie's husband, who'd thrown her into a state of shock by announcing, in his last letter, that he was hoping to come home on leave soon.

'I haven't had a wink of sleep since,' said Lizzie.

'You're getting yourself into a state about nothing,' Betty said. 'First of all he mightn't get it, and second, they sometimes only give them a few days. Ten to one, he'll get no further than London.'

'Aye, and he'll be pissed as a newt.'

'Well, better pissed down there than up here.'

'Don't you want to see him?' asked Sarah.

'I do not. I've seen enough of him to last me a lifetime. Aye, I know what you're thinking. You think I'm hard, don't you? Well I *am* hard and so would you be.' Lizzie's yellow face showed two bright spots of colour on the cheekbones. 'Do you know what happened on August 4th 1914?'

Sarah opened her mouth.

'I'll tell you what happened. *Peace* broke out. The only little bit of peace *I*'ve ever had. No, I don't want him back. I don't want him back on leave. I don't want him back when it's over. As far as I'm concerned the Kaiser can keep him.' She lowered her chin, brooding. 'I'll tell you what I'm going to do. I'm going to get meself some false teeth, and I'm going to have a bloody good time.'

'Yes, well, you want to,' said Betty.

'She's been on about them teeth as long as I've known her.' said Madge. 'You want to stop talking about it, and go and do it. You can afford it. All this won't last, you know.' She jerked her thumb at the room full of overall-clad women. 'It's too good to last.'

'It's not the money that bothers me.'

'He'd give you gas,' said Madge. 'You're never going to look anything while you've got them in your mouth. And you're never going to feel right either for the simple reason you're swallowing all the corruption.'

'Yeh, I know. I will go.'

'Time, ladies,' the supervisor said. 'Time.'

'Eeh, it never is,' said Lizzie. 'Do you know, I'm bloody sure they fix that clock!'

'Three hours down,' said Sarah. 'Nine to go.'

All over the room yellow-skinned women were dragging themselves to their feet. As they were going up the stairs, Sarah fell into line beside Betty. Lizzie had nipped into the toilet to finish her cigarette.

'You think she's hard, don't you?' said Betty.

'Well, yes, I do a bit. When you think what he's going through.'

'Yes, well. You know when I was a kid we used to live next door to them, and it was thump thump thump half the bloody night, you'd've thought she was coming through the wall. Oh, and you used to see her in the yard next morning, and her face'd be all swelled up. "I fell over the coal scuttle," she used to say. Well that used to get me Mam. "*He* knocks you about," she says, "and *you* go round apologizing for it," she says. "Where's the justice in that?" And mind you, she was right, you know.'

Willard lay face down on his bed, naked. His thighs and buttocks were trenched with purple scars, some just beginning to silver. These injuries had been sustained when his company was retreating across a graveyard under heavy fire, and several tombstone fragments had become embedded in his flesh. 'You want to try it,' he said. 'Lying two months on your belly in a hospital bed with *Requiescat in Pace* stuck up your arse.'

This remark was ostensibly addressed to the orderly, so Rivers was able to ignore it. 'They've healed well,' he said, moving down the bed.

Willard looked across his shoulder. 'The flesh wounds have. There's still the injury to the spine.'

'Let's have you on your back.'

The orderly came forward to help, but Willard waved him away. His whole upper body was massively powerful, though inevitably running to flab. By heaving and twisting, he could just manage to drag the wasted legs over, though they followed the bulk of his body, passively, like slime trails after a snail. The orderly bent down and straightened his feet.

Rivers waited until Willard was covered up, then nodded to the orderly to leave. After the door had closed, he said, 'There was no injury to the spine.'

Willard lay back against the pillows, his jaw stubbornly set.

'If you believe your spine was damaged, how do you account for the fact that so many doctors have examined you and told you that it isn't?' He watched Willard's face closely. 'Do you think they're all incompetent? *All* of them? Or do you think they're in some kind of conspiracy to convince you you *can* walk when in fact you can't?'

Willard raised himself on to one elbow. It was extraordinary the impression he created, that mixture of immobility and power. Like a bull seal dragging itself across rocks. 'You think I'm malingering.'

'I know you're not.'

'But you've just said I am.'

'No.'

'If there's no injury to the spine, then why can't I walk?'

'I think you know why.'

Willard gave a short, hissing laugh. 'I know what you want me to say. I can't walk because I don't want to go back.' He glared at Rivers. 'Well, I won't say it. It would be tantamount to an admission of cowardice.'

Rivers picked up his cap and cane. 'Not in my book.' He was aware of Willard watching him. 'It's true paralysis occurs because a man wants to save his life. He doesn't want to go forward, and take part in some hopeless attack. *But neither is he prepared to run away.*' He smiled. 'Paralysis is no use to a coward, Mr Willard. A coward needs his legs.'

Willard didn't reply, though Rivers thought he detected a slight relaxation of tension. The bone structure of Willard's face was strong almost to the point of brutality, and his eyes were a curious shade of pale blue. There was a sheen on his hair and skin like the gloss on the coat of an animal. He'd been something of an athlete before the war, though Rivers suspected he had never been remarkable for depth of intelligence. 'Your wife's coming to see you this afternoon, isn't she?'

Willard's eyes went to the photograph on his washstand. 'Yes.'

'Why don't you get dressed? There's no reason for you to be in bed. And if you got dressed you could go out into the grounds. It'd be a lot pleasanter for your wife.'

Willard thought about it, reluctant to concede anything that might suggest his illness was not purely physical. 'Yes, all right.'

'Good. I'll send an orderly in to help you with your boots.'

Sassoon arrived at the Conservative Club about ten minutes early. 'Captain Rivers isn't here yet, sir,' the porter said. 'But if you'd like to wait in the morning room, I'm sure he won't be long. Up the stairs and first right.'

The staircase was of twisting marble, almost too imposing for the size of the hall, like a Roman nose on an unprepossessing face. As Sassoon climbed, he passed portraits of Edinburgh worthies of the past, men with white beards and wing collars, whose gold watch-chains and fobs nestled on swelling abdomens. His first thought on entering the morning room was that somebody with a taste for practical jokes had cut the Edinburgh worthies out of their frames and stuck them in chairs all over the room. Everywhere saurian heads and necks peered out of wing armchairs, looking at the young man in the doorway with the automatic approval his uniform evoked, and then – or was he perhaps being oversensitive? – with a slight ambivalence, a growing doubt, as they worked out what the blue badge on his tunic meant. Perhaps it *was* just oversensitivity, for you saw that same look of mingled admiration and apprehension, wherever you went. Old men were often ambivalent about young men in uniform, and rightly so, when you considered how very ambivalent the young men felt about them.

The chairs, which looked uncomfortable, were very comfortable indeed. Sassoon, glad to be away from the boiled cabbage and custard smells of the Craiglockhart dining room, sank back and closed his eyes. Further along, at a table by the window, two old men were nattering about the war. Both had sons at the front, it seemed, or was it only one? No, the other was trapped in England, apparently, on a training course. He listened to the rumble of their voices and felt a well-practised hatred begin to flow. It needed only a slighting remark about the courage of the

German Army to rouse him to real fury, and very soon it came. He was aware of something sexual in this anger. He looked at the cloth straining across their broad backs, at the folds of beef-pink skin that overlapped their collars, and thought, with uncharacteristic crudity, *When did you two last get it up?*

Gordon's death had woken him up, there was no doubt. That moment when he'd come down to breakfast, glanced at the casualty lists and seen Gordon's name had been a turning point of sorts, though he didn't yet know in which direction he would turn. It seemed to him that his first month at Craiglockhart had been spent in a kind of sleep. Too much steam pudding, too much putting little balls into holes. Looking round the room, he knew why he felt sickened by himself, why his fuming against elderly men with sons at the front no longer satisfied him. It was because he'd given in, lapsed, pretended to himself that he was still actively protesting whereas in reality he'd let himself be pacified, sucked into the comforting routine, the uneventfulness of Craiglockhart life. As Rivers had meant him to be.

He got up and began looking at the pictures that lined the walls. The portraits here were not of the professional men and civic dignitaries of the recent past, but of the landed gentry of generations before that, shown, for the most part, either setting off to, or returning from, the hunt. He was obviously not destined to get away from memories of Gordon and hunting today. Walking from picture to picture, he remembered the notebook he'd taken with him into the trenches on his first tour of duty. It had contained nothing but bare details of past hunts, where they'd found, how far he'd run, whether they'd killed. On and on. A terribly meaningless little set of squiggles it would have seemed to anybody else, but for him it had contained the Sussex lanes, the mists, the drizzle, the baying of hounds, clods flying from under the horses' feet, staggering into the house, bones aching, reliving the hunt over dinner, and then, after dinner, shadows on the wall of the old nursery and Gordon's face in the firelight, the scent of logs, the warmth, his whole face feeling numbed and swollen in the heat. His mind switched to his last few hours in France when, already wounded in the shoulder, he'd careered along a German trench, slinging

Mills bombs to left and right, shouting, 'View halloa!' *That* was the moment, he thought. That was when the old Sassoon had cracked wide open and something new had stepped out of the shell. *Bless you, my dear,* Eddie Marsh had written, when he told him about it. *Never take it more seriously than that.* But Eddie had missed the point. Hunting had always been serious. Every bit as serious as war.

'Sorry I'm late,' Rivers said, coming up behind him. 'I meant to be here when you arrived.'

'That's all right. These old codgers've been keeping me amused.' He glanced round quickly. 'I mean the ones on the wall.'

'It is rather a geriatric gathering, isn't it?' Rivers sat down. 'Would you like a drink?' He raised his arm and a white-jacketed, elderly waiter came tottering across. 'Gin and tonic for me, I think. What'll you have, Siegfried?'

'The same, please.'

Rivers's inspection of the menu was confined to identifying which particular variety of poached fish was currently on offer. Sassoon gave the matter more thought. Rivers watched him as he pored over the menu and thought how much easier his life would have been if they'd sent Siegfried somewhere else. It wasn't simply the discomfort of having to express views he was no longer sure he held – though, as a scientist, he did find that acutely uncomfortable. No, it was more than that. Every case posed implicit questions about the individual costs of the war, and never more so than in the run up to a round of Medical Boards, when the MOs had to decide which men were fit to return to duty. This would have been easier if he could have believed, as Lewis Yealland, for example, believed, that men who broke down were degenerates whose weakness would have caused them to break down, eventually, even in civilian life, but Rivers could see no evidence of that. The vast majority of his patients had no record of any mental trouble. And as soon as you accepted that the man's breakdown was a consequence of his war experience rather than of his own innate weakness, then inevitably the war became the issue. And the therapy was a test, not only of the genuineness of the individual's symptoms, but also of the validity of the demands the war was making on him.

Rivers had survived partly by suppressing his awareness of this. But then along came Sassoon and made the justifiability of the war a matter for constant, open debate, and that suppression was no longer possible. At times it seemed to Rivers that all his other patients were the anvil and that Sassoon was the hammer. Inevitably there were times when he resented this. As a civilian, Rivers's life had consisted of asking questions, and devising methods by which truthful answers could be obtained, but there are limits to how many *fundamental* questions you want to ask in a working day that starts before eight am and doesn't end till midnight. All very well for Sassoon. *He* spent *his* days playing golf.

None of this prevented him from watching Sassoon's continued poring over the menu with affection as well as amusement.

Sassoon looked up. 'Am I taking too long?'

'No, take as long as you like.'

'It's almost pre-war standard, isn't it?'

'I hope you're not going to protest?'

'No. You can rely on me to be inconsistent.'

Rivers was not afraid of Sassoon's noticing any change in *him*. Siegfried's introversion was remarkable, even by the normal standards of unhappy young men. His love for his men cut through that self-absorption, but Rivers sometimes wondered whether anything else did. And yet he had so many good qualities. It was rare to find a man in whom courage was the *dominating* characteristic, as malice or laziness or greed might be the ruling characteristic of lesser men.

The dining room was almost empty. They were shown to a table for two by a window that overlooked the club's small, walled garden. A scent of roses, drenched from the morning's rain, drifted in through the open window.

The waiter was very young, sixteen perhaps. Red hair, big freckles splodged over a pale skin, knobbly, pink-knuckled hand clasping the carving knife. With his other hand he lifted the domed lid from the platter to reveal a joint of very red beef. Sassoon smiled. 'That looks nice.'

The boy carved three slices. As he bent to get the warmed plate from the shelf below, it was possible to see the nape of his neck, defenceless under the stiff collar.

'Is that all right, sir?'

'One more, perhaps?'

The boy was looking at Sassoon with undisguised hero-worship. Not surprisingly, Rivers thought. He's dragging out the weeks in this dreary job waiting for his turn to go out. At least they no longer allowed boys of his age to *lie* their way in. He noticed Sassoon smiling to himself.

'What's amusing you?'

'I was thinking about Campbell. Not *our* Campbell. A *much* less engaging man, and ... er ... allegedly sane. He gave lectures – still does, I believe – on "The Spirit of the Bayonet". You know, *"Stick him in the kidneys, it'll go in like a hot knife through butter." "What's the good of six inches of steel sticking out the back of a man's neck? Three inches'll do him. When he croaks, go and find another."* And so on. And you know, the men sit there laughing and cheering and making obscene gestures. *They hate it.*' He smiled. 'I was reminded because that boy was doing so well with the carving knife.'

'Yes, I noticed.'

'Very much the sort of man you'd pick as your servant.'

Rivers said mischievously, 'Not bad-looking either.'

'I'm afraid that has to take second place. You look for skill with the bayonet first because he's always on your left in the attack.'

They ate in silence for a while. Rivers said, 'Have you heard from the friend you were going to write to about Gordon?'

'Yes. It's true apparently, he did die instantly. His father said he had, but they don't always tell parents the truth. I've written too many letters like that myself.'

'It must be some consolation to know he didn't suffer.'

Sassoon's expression hardened. 'I was glad to have it confirmed.' An awkward silence. 'I had some more bad news this morning. Do you remember me talking to you about Julian Dadd? Shot in the throat, two brothers killed? Well, his mental state has worsened apparently. He's in a – what I suppose I ought to call a mental hospital. Given present company. The awful thing is he's got some crazy idea he didn't do well enough. Nobody else thinks so, but apparently there's no arguing with him. He was one of my heroes, you know. I remember looking at him one evening. We'd just come in from inspecting the men's billets – which were lousy as usual, and – he cared. He really cared. And I looked at him and I thought, *I want to be like you.*' He laughed, mocking his hero-worship, but not disowning it. 'Anyway, I suppose I've succeeded, haven't I? Since we're both in the loony-bin.'

The provocation was deliberate. When Rivers didn't rise to it, Sassoon said, 'It makes it quite difficult to go on, you know. When things like this keep happening to people you know and and . . . love. To go on with the protest, I mean.'

Silence.

Sassoon leant forward. '*Wake up*, Rivers. I thought you'd pounce on that.'

'Did you?'

A pause. 'No, I suppose not.'

Rivers dragged his hand down across his eyes. 'I don't feel much like pouncing.'

Rivers left the club an hour later. He'd left Siegfried with Ralph Sampson, the Astronomer Royal of Scotland, whom they'd bumped into after lunch. At first Sassoon had been almost too overawed to speak, but Sampson had soon put paid to that. Rivers had left him chatting away quite happily. Lunch itself had been rather depressing. At one point Siegfried had said, 'I'm beginning to feel used up.' You could understand it. He'd suffered repeated bereavements in the last two years, as first one contemporary then another died. In some ways the experience of these young men paralleled the experience of the very old. They looked back on intense memories and felt lonely because there was nobody left alive who'd been there. That habit of Siegfried's of looking back, the inability to envisage any kind of future, seemed to be getting worse.

Not an easy case, Rivers thought. Not in the usual sense a case at all. He had no idea what the outcome would be, though he thought he could get Siegfried to give in. His love for his men. The need he had to *prove* his courage. By any *rational* standard, he'd already proved it, over and over again, but then the need wasn't altogether rational. Given the strength of that need, it was amazing he'd managed to tolerate being cooped up with 'wash-outs' and 'degenerates' even as long as he had. Putting those forces together and getting him back to France was a task of approximately the same order of difficulty as flicking a stag beetle on to its back. The trouble was Rivers respected Sassoon too much to manipulate him. He had to be *convinced* that going back was the right thing to do.

At the foot of the Craiglockhart drive, Rivers saw Willard and Mrs Willard. For some extraordinary reason Willard had got his wife to push him as far as the gates, despite the downward slope which he must have seen would make the return journey difficult. Now they were marooned.

Rivers greeted Willard, waited for an introduction to his wife, and, when it failed to come, introduced himself. Mrs Willard was extremely young, attractive in the small-breasted, slim-hipped way of modern girls. As they chatted about the deceptive nature of slopes and the awkwardness of wheelchairs, Rivers became aware of Willard's hands clenched on the arms of the chair. He felt Willard's fury at being stranded like this, impotent. Good. The more furious he was the better.

Rivers said to Mrs Willard, 'Here, I'll give you a hand.'

With two of them pushing they made steady progress, though there was one nasty moment near the top, when they struck a muddy patch. But then the wheels bit, and they reached level ground at a cracking pace.

'There you are,' Mrs Willard said, bending over her husband, breathless and laughing. 'Made it.'

Willard's face would have curdled milk.

'Why don't you come in and have a cup of tea?' Rivers suggested.

Mrs Willard looked to her husband for guidance. When none came, she said, 'Yes, that would be lovely.'

'My door's on the left as you go in. I'll just go ahead and arrange things. You'll be all right now?'

'Perfectly, thank you,' said Willard.

Rivers went into the hall, smiling, only to have the smile wiped off his face by the sight of Matron standing immediately inside the entrance. She'd observed the entire incident and evidently disapproved. 'You could have sent an orderly down to push the chair, Captain Rivers.'

Rivers opened his mouth, and shut it again. He reminded himself, not for the first time, that it was absolutely necessary for Matron to win some of their battles.

11

Sassoon was trying to decipher a letter from H. G. Wells when Owen knocked on his door.

'As far as I can make out, he says he's coming to see Rivers.'

Owen looked suitably impressed. 'He must be really worried about you.'

'Oh, it's not *me* he wants to talk about, it's his new book.' Sassoon smiled. 'You don't know many writers, do you?'

'Not many.'

And I, Sassoon thought, am showing off. Which at least was better than moaning about Gordon's death to somebody who had more than enough problems of his own. 'I don't suppose he'll come. They all talk about it, but in the end it's just too far. I sometimes wonder whether that's why they put me here. Whether it was a case of being sent to Rivers or just sent as far away as possible.'

'Probably Rivers. He gets all the awkward ones.' Owen stopped in some confusion. 'Not that you're –'

'Oh, I think I count as awkward. By any standard.' He handed a sheet of paper across. 'For the *Hydra*.'

'May I read it?'

'That's the general idea.'

Owen read, folded the paper and nodded.

To forestall possible effusions, Sassoon said quickly, 'I'm not satisfied with the last three lines, but they'll have to do.'

'I tried yesterday, but you were out.'

'I'd be with Rivers.' He smiled. 'Do you ever feel like strangling Brock?'

'No, I get on rather well with him.'

'I *get on* with Rivers. It's just . . . He picked up something I said at lunchtime about not being able to imagine the future. He doesn't often press, but my God when he does . . .'

'Why did he want you to talk about that?'

'Part of the great campaign to get me back to France. He wants me to put the protest in a longer perspective. You know, "What did you do in the Great War, Siegfried?" Well, I spent three very comfortable years in a loony-bin eating steamed pudding and playing golf. While *other people* – some of them rather close friends – got blown to smithereens. He wants me to admit I won't be able to bear it. What's more, he's probably right.'

'Think of the poems you could write.'

'Not war poems.'

Owen's expression darkened. 'There are other subjects.'

'Yes, of course.'

A slightly awkward pause. 'The trouble is he just knows more than I do. You know, he's very good . . . He tries to behave as if we're equal. But in the end he's a Gold Medallist of the Royal Society, and I left Cambridge without taking a degree. And now and again it shows.'

'That doesn't mean he's right.'

'No, but it does make it very difficult for me to keep my end up in a discussion.'

'Did you talk about after the war?'

'No. I can't, I've no plans. Do *you* know what you're going to do?'

'I'm going to keep pigs.'

'*Pigs?*'

'Yes. People think pigs are dirty, you know, but they're not. They're very clean animals, given half the chance. And it would combine so well with poetry, you see. Actually much better than teaching, because if you're teaching *properly* you're using the same part of your mind. But pig-keeping . . .'

'Perhaps we should go into partnership. It'd shut Rivers up.'

Owen, belatedly aware of being laughed at, blushed and didn't reply.

'No, well, I don't suppose I'd be much use with the pigs, but I may be able to help with the poems.' He nodded at Owen's tunic.

Owen extracted a sheaf of papers. 'I told you they were all short but actually there is one long one. Antaeus and and Hercules.' He handed the papers over. 'Do you know the legend? Antaeus is too strong for Hercules as long as he keeps his feet on mother Earth. But as soon as Hercules lifts him –'

'He's helpless. Yes, it rings a bell.' Sassoon started to read. After a few seconds he looked up. 'Why don't you get yourself a book? There's nothing worse than being watched by the Onlie Begetter.'

'Sorry.' Owen got up and pretended to look at the books on Sassoon's shelf.

At last Sassoon looked up. 'It's very good. Why Antaeus?'

'Oh, it's something Brock's keen on. He thinks we – the patients – are *like* Antaeus in the sense that we've been ungrounded by the war. And the way back to health is to re-establish the link between oneself and the earth, but understanding "earth" to mean society as well as nature. That's why we do surveys and things like that.'

'I thought all the dashing around was to keep your mind off it?'

'No, that's part of the treatment. Ergotherapy.'

'Well, it's an interesting idea. Though I don't know that being stuck in a dugout ever made *me* feel I was losing contact with the earth.'

Owen smiled. 'No, nor me. It does *work*, though.'

Sassoon picked up the next sheet. Craning his neck, Owen could just see the title of the poem. 'That's in your style,' he said.

'Yes. I . . . er . . . *noticed*.'

'No good?'

'Starts and ends well. What happened in the middle?'

'That's quite old, that bit. I wrote that two years ago.'

'They do say if you leave something in a drawer long enough it'll either rot or ripen.'

'The bit at the end . . . About "dirt". Those are the actual words.'

'Yes, and they could do with changing. I've just cut: "You sod" out of a poem. Those were *my* actual words.'

'So it's no good?'

Sassoon hesitated. 'It's not much good *at the moment*. I suppose the thing is, are you interested enough to go on?'

'Ye-es. I have to start somewhere. And I think you're right. It's mad not to write about the war when it's –'

'Such an *experience*.'

They looked at each other and burst out laughing.

'My only doubt is . . . The the *fact* that you admire somebody very much doesn't automatically mean they're a good model. I mean, I admire Wilde, but if I started trying to be witty and elegant and incisive, I'd probably fall flat on my face.'

'Yes, I see that. Well not *that*. I mean I see the point. But I do think I can take something from you.'

'Fair enough.' Sassoon went back to his reading. 'I think you're probably right,' he said, after a while. 'If I do nothing else, I might help you get rid of some of this *mush*.'

'Some of the sonnets are quite early.'

'Puberty?' A long pause. Early sonnets fell like snow. 'Oh, now this is good. "Song of Songs."'

'That's last week.'

'*Is it?* Now you see what I mean about me not being necessarily the right model? *I* couldn't do this. And yet of it's kind it's absolutely perfect.'

Owen sat down. He looked as if his knees had buckled.

'I think that should go in the *Hydra*.'

'No.'

'Why not?'

'a. It's not good enough. b. Editors shouldn't publish their own work.'

'a. I'm a better judge of that than you are. *At the moment*. b. Rubbish. And c.' Sassoon leant across and snatched his own poem back. 'If you don't publish *that*, you can't have this.'

Owen seemed to be contemplating a counter-attack.

'd. I'm bigger than you are.'

'All right, I'll print it.' He took Sassoon's poem back. 'Anonymously.'

'Cheat.' Sassoon was shuffling Owen's papers together. 'Look, why don't you have a go at . . .' He peered at the title. '"The Dead-Beat"? Work at it till you think you've made some progress, then bring it back and we'll have a go at it together. It's not too traumatic, is it? That memory.'

'Good heavens, no.'

'How long do you spend on it? Not that one, I mean generally?'

'Fifteen minutes.' He saw Sassoon's expression change. 'That's *every day*.'

'Good God, man, that's no use. You've got to sweat your guts out. Look, it's like drill. You don't wait till you *feel* like doing it.'

'Well, it's certainly a new approach to the Muse. "Number from the left! Form fours! Right turn!"'

'It works. I'll see you – shall we say Thursday? After dinner.' He opened the door and stood aside to let Owen past. 'And I shall expect to find *both* poems in the *Hydra*.'

12

After Prior had been waiting for perhaps five minutes, the lodging house door opened and Sarah stood there. 'You've got a nerve,' she said, beginning to close the door.

Prior put a finger in the crack. 'I'm here now.'

'Which is more than you were last week. Go on, *shift*.'

'I couldn't come last week. I was so late back they kept me in.'

'Bit strict, aren't they? Your *parents*.'

Too late, he remembered the lies he'd told. He pointed to the blue badge on his tunic. 'Not parents. The CO.'

The door stopped shutting.

'I know it sounds stupid, but it *is* the truth.'

'Oh, all right, I believe you.' Her eyes fell on the badge. 'And if you're getting yourself upset about that, don't bother. I knew anyway.'

'How did you know?' What had he been doing? *Drooling?*

'You don't think you're the only one takes it off, do you? They all do. Betty says she had a young man once, she never saw him wearing it. Mind you, knowing Betty, I shouldn't think she saw him wearing much at all.'

By day, the yellowness of her skin astonished him. It said a lot for her that she was still attractive, that she managed to wear it like a rather dashing accessory.

'There is just one thing,' she said, coming out into the porch. 'If I do go out with you, I want one thing clear at the start. I think you must've got a very wrong impression of me the other night. Knocking all that port back.' She raised her eyes to his face. 'I don't usually drink much at all.'

'I know that. You were gone too quick for somebody that was used to it.'

'Right, then. Long as you know. I'll get me jacket.'

He waited, looking up and down the hot street. A trickle of

sweat had started in his armpits. From deep inside the house came a woman's voice raised in anger.

'Me landlady,' Sarah said, coming back. 'Belgian, married a Scot, the poor sod. I don't think he knew what he was getting. Still, she only charges a shilling for the laundry, and when you think the sheets come off the bed bright yellow you can't complain about that.'

He felt at home with her, with this precise delineation of the cost of everything, which was not materialistic or grasping, but simply a recognition of the boundaries and limitations of life. 'I thought we'd get out of Edinburgh,' he said. 'It's too hot.'

Most of Edinburgh was using this last weekend in August to escape the city, not deterred by a sallow tinge to the sky that suggested the hot, sticky weather might break into thunder before the day was out. The train was packed, but he managed to get her a seat, and stood near by. She smiled up at him, but in this rackety, sweating box it was impossible to talk. He looked at the other passengers. A trio of girls out on a spree, a young mother with a struggling toddler tugging at her blouse, a middle-aged couple whose bodies sagged together. Something about that stale intimacy sharpened his sense of the strangeness, the separateness of Sarah's body. He was so physically aware of her that when the knee of his breeches brushed against her skirt he felt as if the contact had been skin on skin.

A ganglion of rails, the train juddering over points, and then they were slowing, and people were beginning to stir and clutch bags, and jam the aisles. 'Let's wait,' he said.

Sarah pressed against him, briefly, to let the woman and her child past, and then he sat beside her as the train emptied. After a while she reached down and touched his hand.

They took their time walking to the sea. At first he was disappointed, it was so crowded. Men with trousers rolled up to show knobbly legs, handkerchiefs knotted over sweating scalps, women with skirts tucked up to reveal voluminous bloomers, small children screaming as the damp sand was towelled off their legs. Everywhere people swirling their tongues round ice-cream cones, biting into candy-floss, licking rock, sucking fingers, determined to squeeze the last ounce of pleasure from the day. In his khaki, Prior moved among them like a ghost.

Only Sarah connected him to the jostling crowd, and he put his hand around her, clasping her tightly, though at that moment he felt no stirring of desire. He said, 'You wouldn't think there was a war on, would you?'

They walked down to the water's edge. He felt quite callous towards her now, even as he drew her towards him and matched his stride to hers. She belonged with the pleasure-seeking crowds. He both envied and despised her, and was quite coldly determined to *get* her. They owed him something, all of them, and she should pay. He glanced at her. 'Shall we walk along?'

Their linked shadows, dumpy and deformed, stretched across the sand. After a while they came to an outcrop of rock, and, clambering over it, found they'd left the crowded part of the beach behind. Sarah took off her jacket and then, with a great fuss and pleas not to look, her shoes and stockings as well. She paddled at the water's edge, where the waves seethed between her toes.

'I don't suppose you're allowed to take anything off?' she said, looking back at him, teasing.

'Not a thing.'

'Not even your boots?'

'No, but I can wade. I always paddle with me boots on.'

He didn't expect her to understand, or if she did, to admit it, but she turned on him at once. 'Boots have a way of springing a leak.'

'Not mine.'

'Oh, you'd be different, I suppose?'

Until now the air had been so still it scarcely moved against the skin. But now small gusts began to whip up the sand, stinging patches of bare skin. Prior looked back the way they'd come. The sun was past its height. Even the little mounds of worm-casts had each its individual shadow, but what chiefly struck him was the yellowing of the light. It was now positively sulphurous, thick with heat. They seemed to be trapped, fixed, in some element thicker than air. Black figures, like insects, swarmed across the beach, making for the shelter of the town.

Sarah, too, had turned to look back. He said quickly, 'No, don't let's go back. It'll blow over.'

'You think *that's* gunna blow over?'

Reluctantly he said, 'Do you *want* to go back?'

'We'd be drenched before we got there. Anyway, I like storms.'

They stood looking out to sea, while the yellow light deepened. There was no difference now between his skin colour and hers. Suddenly Sarah clutched her head. 'What's happening?'

He could hardly believe what he saw. The coppery wires on the surface of her hair were standing straight up, in a way he had never believed any human hair could do. He pulled his cap off, and winced at the tingling in his scalp.

'What is it?' Sarah said.

'Electricity.'

She burst out laughing.

'No, I mean it.'

Lightning flickered once, illuminating her yellow skin.

'Come on,' Prior said.

He snatched her hand and started to run with her towards the shelter of some bushes. Scrambling up the last slope, he staggered, and would have fallen if he hadn't grabbed a clump of marram grass. He felt a sharp pain, and, bringing his hand up, saw a smear of blood on the palm. Sarah pushed him from behind. They stumbled down the other side of the slope, just as a sudden fierce thickening of rain blinded them, and the first rumblings of thunder came.

A dense thicket of buckthorn offered the only possible shelter. Prior stamped down the nettles and thistles that thronged the gaps, and then held the thorns back for Sarah to crawl inside. He followed her in. They crouched down, the rain scarcely reaching them through the thick roof of thorn, though the wind rocked and beat the bush. Prior looked round. The ground was dry, and very bare, the thorn too thick to allow anything else to grow.

Sarah was feeling her hair. 'Is it all right?'

'It's going down.'

'So's yours.'

He grinned. ''S not surprising. Storm took me mind right off it.'

She laughed, but refused to reply. Prior was remembering

129

childhood games, making dens. An interior like this, so dark, so private, so easily defended, would have been a real find. Mixed with this distinctly childish excitement another excitement was growing. He no longer felt hostile to her, as he'd done back there in the crowd. They seemed to have walked away from all that. It was ages since he'd made love. He felt as he sometimes did coming out of the line, listening to the others talk and sometimes joining in, what they were going to do and how many times they were going to do it, though as far as he knew everybody else's experience was like his own. The first time was almost always a disappointment. Either stuck at half mast or firing before you reached the target. He didn't want to think about Sarah like this.

Sarah rolled over on to her elbow and looked at him. 'This is nice.'

He lay beside her. A few splashes of rain found his upturned face. After a while he touched her hand and felt her fingertips curl round his. Through the thickness in his throat, he said, 'I'm not pushing, but if you wanted to, I'd make sure it was all right.'

After a while he felt her fingers creep across his chest, insinuating themselves between the buttons of his tunic. He kissed her, moving from her lips to her breasts, not looking at her, not opening his eyes, learning her with his tongue, flicking the nipples hard, probing the whorled darkness of her navel, and then on down, down, across the smooth marble of her belly into the coarse and springy turf. His nostrils filled with the scent of rock pools at low tide. He slipped his hands underneath her, and lifted her, until her whole pelvis became a cup from which he drank.

Afterwards they lay in silence, enjoying the peace, until footsteps walking along the coastal path warned them that the storm was over. The buckthorn scattered raindrops over them, as they crawled out on to the grass.

They beat sand and twigs from each other's clothes, then started to walk back along the coastal path.

'What we need is something to warm us up,' Prior said.

'We can't go anywhere looking like this.'

They stopped on the outskirts of the town, and tried more seriously to set themselves to rights. They went to a pub, and leant back against the wooden seat, nudging each other under the table, drunk with their love-making and the storm and the sense of having secrets.

'I can feel your voice through the wood,' Sarah said.

Abruptly, the joy died. Prior became quite suddenly depressed. He pushed his half-finished meal away.

'What is it?'

'Oh, I was remembering a man in my platoon.' He looked at her. 'Do you know, he sent the same letter to his wife every week for two years.'

Sarah felt a chill come over her. She didn't know why she was being told this. 'Why?'

'Why not?'

'How do you know he did?'

'Because I had to censor it. I censored it every week. We read all their letters.'

He could see her not liking this, but she kept her voice light. 'Who reads yours?'

'Nobody.' He looked at her again. 'They rely on our sense of honour. Oh, we're supposed to leave them open so the CO *can* read them if wants to, but it would be thought *frightfully bad form* if he did.' Prior had slipped into his mock public school voice, very familiar to Rivers.

Sarah took it at face value. 'You lot make me sick,' she said, pushing her own plate away. 'I suppose nobody else's *got* a sense of honour?'

He preferred her like this. On the beach, she was only too clearly beginning to think that something had happened that mattered. He wasn't going to admit that. A few grains of sand in the pubic hair, a mingling of smells. Nothing that a prolonged soak in the tub wouldn't wash away. 'Come on,' he said, putting down a tip. 'We'd better be getting back.'

13

Burns paced up and down the waiting room. Rivers had told him he intended to recommend an unconditional discharge, and though he hadn't actually said the Board would accept the recommendation, this had been very strongly implied. So there was nothing to worry about, though when the orderly came and asked him to step inside, his stomach knotted and his hands started to tremble. The Sam Browne belt, bunching the loose fabric round his waist, made him look rather like a scarecrow tied together with string. He got himself into the room somehow, and managed a salute. He couldn't see their faces to begin with, since they sat with their backs to the tall windows, but after Bryce had told him to sit down, his eyes started to become accustomed to the light.

There was a great deal of light, it seemed to him, floods of silver-grey light filtered through white curtains that stirred in the breeze, and the insistent buzzing of an insect, trapped. He fastened his eyes on Rivers, who managed to smile at him without moving a muscle of his face.

Major Paget, the third, external member of the Board, was obviously startled by Burns's appearance, but he asked a few questions for form's sake. Rivers scarcely listened either to the questions or to the answers. The buzzing continued. He scanned the high windows, trying to locate the insect. The noise was unreasonably disturbing.

Paget said, 'How often do you vomit now?'

Rivers got up and went across to the window. He found a bumble bee, between the curtain and the window, batting itself against the glass, fetched a file from the desk and, using it as a barrier, guided the insect into the open air. He watched it fly away. Directly below him, Anderson and Sassoon were setting off for their daily round of golf. Their voices drifted up to him. Rivers turned back into the room to find everybody, Burns included, staring at him in some surprise. He smiled faintly and went back to his seat.

'This is getting to be a habit, isn't it?'

Prior, hands twined round the iron bars of the bedhead, smiled without opening his eyes. 'Not one I enjoy.'

He hadn't regained the weight he'd lost during his last stay in sick bay. The ribs showed clearly through the stretched skin. 'You were lucky to get back. When did it start?'

'On the train. It was jam-packed. Everybody smoking.'

'Lucky the young woman with you kept her head.'

'Poor Sarah. I don't think she's ever had anybody pass out on her before.'

'You realize you won't have the sick bay to yourself this time?' Rivers indicated the other bed. 'Mr Willard.'

'The legless wonder. Yes, we've met.'

'Don't you have any sympathy for anybody else?'

'Are you suggesting I have any for myself?' He watched Rivers fold the stethoscope. 'You know what you were saying about the greater mental complexity of officers? How long do you think it'll take you to convince that particular specimen of *complexity* that it hasn't actually got a broken spine?'

'How's your voice, Mr Prior?'

Prior took a moment to register the direct hit. 'Fine. Problem over, I think. I miss it. I used to enjoy my little Trappist times.'

'Oh, I can believe that. I've often thought how nice it would be to retreat into total silence now and again.'

'What do you mean "how nice it would be"? You do it all the time.'

'I've arranged for a consultant to come and see you. A Dr Eaglesham. He'll be in some time this week.'

'Why?'

'I need a measurement of your vital capacity.'

'Demonstrations twice nightly.'

'The *other* vital capacity. Try to get some rest now. Sister Duffy tells me you had a bad night.'

Rivers had got to the door before Prior called him back. '*Why* do you need it?'

'This is the second time this has happened in six weeks. I

133

don't think we can let you go in front of a Medical Board without drawing their attention to your *physical* condition.'

'If you're thinking of wangling permanent home service, I don't want it.'

'I'm not thinking of "wangling" anything.' Rivers looked down at Prior and his expression softened. 'Look, if this is what happens when you're exposed to cigarette smoke on a train, how would you cope with gas?'

'Well, *obviously*, I'm affected at lower concentrations than anybody else. But then so what? I can be the battalion canary.' A pause. 'I'm not the only one with asthma.'

'No, I'm sure you're not. I'm *told* there are cases of active TB in the trenches. It doesn't mean it's a good idea.'

'I want to go back.'

A long silence.

'You can't talk to anybody here,' Prior said. 'Everybody's either lost somebody, or knows somebody who has. They don't want the truth. It's like letters of condolence. "Dear Mrs Bloggs, Your son had the side of his head blown off by a shell and took five hours to die. We did manage to give him a decent Christian burial. Unfortunately that particular stretch of ground came under heavy bombardment the day after, so George has been back to see us five or six times since then." They don't want that. They want to be told that George – or Johnny – or whatever his name was, died a quick death and was given a decent send off.' He said deliberately, 'Yesterday, at the seaside, I felt as if I came from another planet.'

'You can talk to people here.'

'It's the last thing this lot want to talk about. The point is, I'm better.'

'That's for the Board to decide.'

'You mean, *you*.'

'No-o. The Board. How are the nights? I mean apart from the asthma? I know last night was bad.'

'I just refuse to play this game. I haven't enough *breath* to answer questions you already know the answers to.'

'What's your *subjective* estimate of your nights?'

'Better.'

'Good. That was Sister Duffy's impression too.'

'Oh *well*, then . . .' Prior glowered. 'There's another reason I want to go back. Rather a nasty, selfish little reason, but since you clearly think I'm a nasty selfish little person that won't come as a surprise. When all this is over, people who didn't go to France, or didn't do well in France – people of my generation, I mean – aren't going to count for anything. This is the Club to end all Clubs.'

'And you want to belong.'

'Yes.'

'You already do.'

'I broke down.'

'And that's why you want to go back? You're ambitious, aren't you?'

Prior didn't answer.

'No reason why you shouldn't be. What do you want to do?'

'Politics.' He started back-tracking immediately. 'Of course, it's probably useless. You can't get anywhere in this shitting country without an Oxford or Cambridge degree.'

'Rubbish.'

'Easily said.'

'Not easily said at all. I didn't go to either.'

Prior looked surprised.

'I got typhoid in my last year at school. We couldn't afford Cambridge without the scholarship. No, you can certainly get on without. And things'll be freer after the war. If only because hundreds of thousands of young men have been thrown into contact with the working classes in a way they've never been before. That has to have some impact.'

'Careful, Rivers. You're beginning to sound like a Bolshevik.'

'I'm just trying to give you some faith in your own abilities. And by the way, I do *not* think you are a nasty selfish little person.'

Prior scowled ferociously, probably to hide his pleasure.

'I'll try to be here when Dr Eaglesham comes. Meanwhile, do you think you could try to get on with Willard?'

Rivers had just started shaving when the VAD banged on his door. She gasped something about 'Captain Anderson' and 'blood', and, dreading what he would find, Rivers hurried downstairs to Anderson's room. He found Anderson huddled in a foetal position, in the corner by the window, teeth chattering, a dark stain spreading across the front of his pyjamas. His room-mate, Featherstone, stood by the washstand, razor in hand, looking at him with more irritation than sympathy.

'What happened?' Rivers asked.

'I don't know, he just started screaming.'

Rivers knelt beside Anderson and quickly checked that he wasn't injured. 'Was he asleep?'

'No, he was waiting for the basin.'

Rivers looked at Featherstone. A thin trickle of blood was dribbling down his wet chin. *Ah.* Rivers stood up, and patted him on the arm. 'Bleed elsewhere, Featherstone, there's a good chap.'

Featherstone – not in the best of tempers – strode out of the room. Rivers went across to the basin, rinsed his flannel out, wiped the bowl, gave the slightly blood-stained towel to the VAD and held the door open for her to leave. 'There,' he said, looking across at Anderson. 'All gone.'

Slowly Anderson relaxed, becoming in the process aware of the stain between his legs. Rivers fetched his dressing gown and threw it across to him. 'You'd better wrap this round you, you'll be chilly once the sweating's stopped.' He went back to the washstand. 'Do you mind if I borrow your flannel?'

He wiped the remaining shaving soap from his face, and checked to see he hadn't cut himself when the VAD banged on his door. That would *not* have been helpful. Out of the corner of his eye he saw Anderson pull the coverlet up to hide the wet patch in the bed. When Rivers next looked round, he was sitting on the bed, swinging his legs and doing his best to look casual. Rivers sat down, far enough away for Anderson not to have to worry about the smell. 'Still as bad as that?'

'I suppose it's as bad as it looks.'

And this was the man who was going to return to medicine. 'You know, we're going to have to start talking about what you realistically want to do.'

'We've been through all that.'

'I can get you a month's extension in October. After that –'

'That's all right. I can't stay here for ever.'

Rivers hesitated. 'Is there any sign of your wife managing to get up?'

Mrs Anderson's visit had been much talked of, but had still not occurred.

'No. It's difficult with a child.'

Others managed. Rivers left Anderson to get dressed and went back to his own room to finish shaving. Now that the surge of excitement had worn off, he felt tired and unwell. Quite unfit for work, though the day would have to be got through somehow.

Willard was his first patient. He was following a regime which involved early-morning exercises in the pool, and was wheeled into the room, wet-haired and smelling of chlorine. He started at once. 'I can't share a room with that man.'

Rivers went on kneading Willard's calf muscles.

'Prior.'

'You're not sharing a room with him, are you? You just happen to be in the sick bay at the same time.'

'In *effect* I'm sharing a room.'

'That feels quite a bit firmer. Does it feel firmer to you?'

Willard felt his calf. 'A bit. He wakes up screaming. It's intolerable.'

'No, well, I don't suppose he likes it much either.'

Willard hesitated. 'It's not just that.' He bent towards Rivers. 'He's one of those.'

Rivers looked and felt stunned. 'I really don't think he is, you know. You mustn't take everything Prior says seriously. He likes to tease.'

'He is. You can always tell.'

'Press against the palm of my hand.'

'I don't suppose you'd consider moving him?'

'No. And again. He's ill, Mr Willard. He *needs* the sick bay. If anybody moves out, it'll be *you*.'

Willard was followed by an unscheduled appointment with Featherstone, also demanding a change of room, though with more reason. Nobody could be expected to share with Anderson, he said. The nightmares and vomiting were too bad, and the loss of sleep was beginning to affect his nerves. All of this was true. Rivers listened and sympathized and promised Featherstone a change of room as soon as the September Boards had introduced some leeway into the system. At the moment the hospital was so crowded there was no hope of a room change for anybody.

Next, Lansdowne, an RAMC captain, whose long-standing claustrophobia had been uncovered by his inability to enter dugouts. A particularly testing session. Lansdowne was always demanding, though Rivers didn't mind that, since he felt he was making progress. Then Fothersgill, Sassoon's new room-mate, a fanatical Theosophist. He spoke throughout in mock medieval English – lots of 'Yea verilys' and 'forsooths' – as if his brief exposure to French horrors had frightened him into a sort of terminal facetiousness. He was forty-three, but with his iron-grey hair, monocle and stiff manners he seemed far older. He didn't take long. Basically, he was suffering from being too old for the war, a complaint with which Rivers had a little more sympathy every day.

Then a meeting of the Hospital Management Committee. Fletcher, one of the two patient representatives, was a highly efficient, conscientious man whose stay in France had ended when he'd developed paranoid delusions that the quartermaster was deliberately and systematically depriving the men of food. This delusion he had now transferred to the hospital steward. The meeting went well enough until the standard of hospital catering came under discussion, and then Fletcher's delusions came to the fore. Tempers became heated, and the meeting closed on an acrimonious note. It was an unfortunate incident, since it would certainly fuel the administration's view that patients should take no part in the running of the hospital. Bryce, supported by Rivers, believed that patient participation was essential, even if this meant that Craiglockhart committee meetings sometimes developed a flavour all of their own.

After lunch, Rivers went along to Bryce's room to discuss Broadbent. Broadbent had been to see his sick mother twice in recent months. Towards the end of the second visit a telegram arrived from Broadbent, saying that his mother had passed on, and asking permission to stay for the funeral. Naturally, permission had been granted. In due course Broadbent came back, wearing a black armband, and – rather less explicably – the red tabs of a staff officer. The red tabs disappeared overnight, but the black armband remained. For some days after that Broadbent sat around the patients' common room, pink-eyed and sorrowful, being consoled by the VADs. This happy state of affairs came to a close when Mrs Broadbent arrived, demanding to know why she never heard from her son. Broadbent was now upstairs, in a locked room. It was not easy to see how a court-martial could be avoided.

The rest of the afternoon was spent on a succession of young men. Rivers, by now feeling quite ill, was carried through it only by his perception that some at least were showing signs of improvement. One young man in particular, who'd broken down after finding the mutilated body of his friend, had become dramatically better in the last few weeks.

After dinner, Rivers decided to abandon the paperwork he ought to have been doing and have an early night. No bath tonight, he decided, he was too tired. He got between the sheets and stretched out his legs, thinking he'd never been so glad to be in a bed in his life. After a while he pushed the window further open and lay listening to the rain, a soft hushing sound that seemed to fill the room. Soon, still listening, he drifted off to sleep.

He was woken at two am by a pain in his chest. At first he tried to convince himself it was indigestion, but the leaping and pounding of his heart soon suggested other, more worrying possibilities. He pulled himself up, and concentrated on breathing slowly and quietly.

The wind had risen while he was asleep, and rain pelted the glass. All over the hospital, he knew, men would be lying awake, listening to the rain and the wind, thinking of their battalions sinking deeper into the mud. Bad weather was bad for the nerves. Tomorrow would not be an easy day.

An hour later he would have given anything for tomorrow to arrive. He was getting all the familiar symptoms. Sweating, a constant need to urinate, breathlessness, the sense of blood not flowing but squeezing through veins. The slightest movement caused his heart to pound. He was relieved when dawn came and it was possible to summon the orderly.

Bryce arrived shortly afterwards, brisk and sympathetic. He produced a stethoscope, and told Rivers to take his pyjama jacket off. The stethoscope moved across his chest. He sat up, leant forward and felt the same procession of cold rings across his back. 'What do *you* think's wrong?' Bryce asked, putting the stethoscope away.

'War neurosis,' Rivers said promptly. 'I already stammer and I'm starting to twitch.'

Bryce waited for Rivers to settle back against the pillows. 'I suppose we've all got one of those. Your heartbeat's irregular.'

'Psychosomatic.'

'And, as we keep telling the patients, psychosomatic symptoms are REAL. I think you should take some leave.'

Rivers shook his head. 'No, I –'

'That wasn't a suggestion.'

'Oh. I've got the September reports to do. If I do nothing else, I've got to do those.'

Bryce had started to smile. 'There's never going to be a convenient time, is there? Three weeks starting this weekend.'

A mutinous silence.

'That gives you time to do the reports, provided you don't see patients. All right?' Bryce patted the coverlet and stood up. 'I'll tell Miss Crowe to put a notice up.'

Rivers was going on leave. He hadn't been down to dinner for the past few days, but he was there tonight, Sassoon saw, looking rather better than he'd done recently, though still very tired. The MO's table was the noisiest in the room. Even at this distance you could distinguish Brock's high, reedy voice, MacIntyre's broad Glaswegian, Bryce's Edinburgh, Ruggles's American, and Rivers, who, when he got excited in a discussion, as he often did, sounded rather like a sodawater syphon going off. Nobody, listening to him now, would have thought him capable of those endless silences.

Fothersgill, his long nose twitching fastidiously, had started to complain about the soup. 'Nay, verily,' he said. 'A man knoweth not what manner of thing he eateth.' He laughed as he said it, the laugh of a man who takes small discomforts very seriously indeed. Sassoon, marooned between two particularly bad stammerers, felt no need to take part in the conversation. Instead, he twisted round in his seat and looked for Owen, remembering the last poem he'd been shown. '*Out there, we've walked quite friendly up to Death;/Sat down and eaten with him, cool and bland —/Pardoned his spilling mess-tins in our hand . . .*' Precisely, Sassoon thought. And now we complain about the soup. Or rather, *they* do.

After dinner he went straight to Owen's room. 'Do you mind?' he said. 'I'm on the run from Theosophy.'

Owen was already clearing papers from the chair. 'No, come in.'

'I can't stay in the same room with him.'

'You should ask Rivers for a change.'

'Too late. He goes tomorrow. Anyway, I wouldn't want to bother him. Have you got anything for me?'

'This.'

Sassoon took the sheet and read the whole poem through twice, then returned to the first two lines.

> What minute-bells for these who die so fast?
> – Only the monstrous/solemn anger of our guns.

'I thought "passing" bells,' Owen said.

'Hm. Though if you lose "minute" you realize how weak "fast" is. "Only the monstrous anger . . ."'

'"Solemn"?'

'"Only the solemn anger of our guns." Owen, for God's sake, this is War Office propaganda.'

'No, it's not.'

'Read that line.'

Owen read. 'Well, it certainly isn't meant to be.'

'I suppose what you've got to decide is who are "these"? The British dead? Because if they're *British*, then *our* guns is . . .'

Owen shook his head. 'All the dead.'

'Let's start there.' Sassoon crossed out "our" and pencilled in "the". 'You're sure that's what you want? It isn't a minor change.'

'No, I know. 'If it's "the", it's got to be "monstrous".'

'Agreed.' Sassoon crossed out 'solemn'. 'So:

> What passing-bells for these who die . . . so *fast*?
> – Only the monstrous anger of the guns.

'Well, there's nothing wrong with the second line.'
'"In herds"?'
'Better.'
They worked on the poem for half an hour. The wind had been rising all evening, and the thin curtain billowed in the draught. At one point Sassoon looked up and said, 'What's that noise?'

'The wind.' Owen was trying to find the precise word for the sound of shells, and the wind was a distraction he'd been trying to ignore.

'No, *that*.'
Owen listened. 'I can't hear anything.'
'That tapping.'
Owen listened again. 'No.'
'Must be imagining things.' Sassoon listened again, then said, 'They don't *wail*. They hiss.'
'No, these are going right over.'
'That's right. They hiss.' He looked at Owen. 'I hear hissing.'
'*You* hear tapping.'
The wind went on rising all evening. By the time Sassoon left Owen's room, it was wailing round the building, moaning down chimneys, snapping branches off trees with a crack like rifle fire. All over the decayed hydro, badly fitting windows rattled and thumped, and Sassoon, passing several of his 'fellow breakdowns' in the corridor, thought they looked even more 'mental' than usual.

His own room was empty. He got into bed and lay reading while he waited for Fothersgill to return from his bridge session. As soon as he entered the room, Sassoon rolled over and pretended to be asleep. A tuneless whistling ensued, punctuated by grunts as Fothersgill bent over his shaving mirror and tweezed hairs out of his nostrils.

At last the light was out. Sassoon lay on his back, listening to the roar of wind and rain. Again he heard tapping, a distinct, purposeful sound, quite unlike the random buffeting of the wind. On such a night it was impossible not to think of the battalion. He listened to the surge and rumble of the storm, and his mind filled with memories of his last few weeks in France. He saw his platoon again, and ran through their names – not a particularly difficult feat, since no fewer than eight of them had been called Jones. He recalled his horror at their physique. Many of them were almost incapable of lifting their equipment, let alone of carrying it mile after mile along shelled roads. He'd ended one march pushing two of them in front of him, while a third stumbled along behind, clinging to his belt. None of the three had been more than five feet tall. You put them alongside an officer – almost any officer – and they seemed to be almost a different order of being. And as for their training. One man had arrived in France not knowing how to load a rifle. He saw them now, his little band, sitting on bales of straw in a sun-chinked barn, while he knelt to inspect their raw and blistered feet, and wondered how many of them were still alive.

The windows banged and rattled, and again, in a brief lull, he thought he heard tapping. There were no trees close enough to touch the glass. He supposed there might be rats, but then whoever heard of rats tapping? He tossed and turned, thinking how stupid it was not to be able to sleep here, in safety and comfort, when in France he'd been able to sleep anywhere. If he could sleep on a firestep in drenching rain, surely he could sleep now . . .

He woke to find Orme standing immediately inside the door. He wasn't surprised, he assumed Orme had come to rouse him for his watch. What did surprise him, a little, was that he seemed to be *in bed*. Orme was wearing that very pale coat of his. Once, in 'C' company mess, the CO had said, 'Correct me if I'm wrong, Orme, but I have always assumed that the colour of the British Army uniform is khaki. Not . . . *beige*.' 'Beige' was said in such Lady Bracknellish tones that Sassoon had wanted to laugh. He wanted to laugh now, but his chest muscles didn't seem to work. After a while he remembered that Orme was dead.

This clearly didn't worry Orme, who continued to stand quietly by the door, but Sassoon began to think it ought to worry him. Perhaps if he turned his head it would be all right.

He stared at the window's pale square of light, and when he looked back Orme had gone.

Fothersgill was awake. 'Did you see anybody come in?' Sassoon asked.

'No, nobody's been in.' He turned over and within a few minutes was snoring again.

Sassoon waited for the rhythm to be firmly established, then got out of bed and walked across to the window. The storm had blown itself out, though twigs, leaves and even one or two larger branches, scattered across the tennis courts, bore witness to its power. The palms of his hands were sweating and his mouth was dry.

He needed to talk to Rivers, though he'd have to be careful what he said, since Rivers was a thorough-going rationalist who wouldn't take kindly to tales of the supernatural, and might even decide the symptoms of a war neurosis were manifesting themselves at last. Perhaps they were. Perhaps this was the kind of hallucination he'd had in the 4th London, but no, he didn't believe that. His nocturnal visitors *there* had come trailing gore, pointing to amputations and head wounds, rather like the statues of medieval saints pointing to the instruments of their martyrdom. This had been so restrained. Dignified. And it hadn't followed on from a nightmare either. He thought back, wanting to be sure, because he knew this was the first question Rivers would ask. No, no nightmare. Only that tapping at the window before he went to sleep.

He got dressed and sat on the bed. At last eight o'clock came, and the hospital became noisy as the shifts changed. Sassoon ran downstairs. He felt certain Rivers would go to his office to check the post before he left, and there might just be time for a few words. But when he tapped on the door, a passing orderly said, 'Captain Rivers's gone, sir. He left on the six o'clock train.'

So that was that. Sassoon went slowly upstairs, unable to account for his sense of loss. After all, he'd known Rivers was going. And he was only going for three weeks. Fothersgill was still asleep. Sassoon collected his washbag and went along to the bathroom. He felt almost dazed. As usual he turned to lock the door, and as usual remembered there were no locks. At times like this the lack of privacy was almost intolerable. He filled the basin, and splashed his face and neck. Birds, sounding a little stunned as if they too needed to recover from the night, were beginning, cautiously, to sing. He looked at his face in the glass. In this half-light, against white tiles, it looked scarcely less ghostly than Orme's. A memory tweaked the edges of his mind. Another glass, on the top landing at home, a dark, oval mirror framing the face of a small, pale child. Himself. Five years old, perhaps. Now why did he remember that? Birds had been singing, then, too. Sparrows, twittering in the ivy. A day of shouts and banged doors and tears in rooms he was not allowed to enter. The day his father left home. Or the day he died? No, the day he left. Sassoon smiled, amused at the link he'd discovered, and then stopped smiling. He'd joked once or twice to Rivers about his being his father confessor, but only now, faced with this second abandonment, did he realize how completely Rivers had come to take his father's place. Well, that didn't matter, did it? After all, if it came to substitute fathers, he might do a lot worse. No, it was all right. Slowly, he lathered his face and began to shave.

Part 3

14

'Hymn No. 373.'

With a rustling of paper the maroon-backed hymn books blossomed into white. The congregation struggled to its feet. Children at the front under the watchful eye of Sunday-school teachers, the rest, middle-aged or elderly men, and women. A preliminary wheeze from the organ, then:

> God moves in a mysterious way
> His wonders to perform . . .

Since the Somme, this seemed to have become the nation's most popular hymn. Rivers had lost count of the number of times he'd heard it sung. He lifted his eyes to the flag-draped altar, and then to the east window. A crucifixion. The Virgin and St John on either side, the Holy Ghost descending, God the Father beaming benignly down. Beneath it, and much smaller, Abraham's sacrifice of his son. Behind Abraham was the ram caught in a thicket by his horns and struggling to escape, by far the best thing in the window. You could see the fear. Whereas Abraham, if he regretted having to sacrifice his son at all, was certainly hiding it well and Isaac, bound on a makeshift altar, positively smirked.

Obvious choices for the east window: the two bloody bargains on which a civilization claims to be based. *The* bargain, Rivers thought, looking at Abraham and Isaac. The one on which all patriarchal societies are founded. If you, who are young and strong, will obey me, who am old and weak, even to the extent of being prepared to sacrifice your life, then in the course of time you will peacefully inherit, and be able to exact the same obedience from your sons. Only we're breaking the bargain, Rivers thought. All over northern France, at this very moment, in trenches and dugouts and flooded shell-holes, the inheritors were dying, not one by one, while old men, and women of all ages, gathered together and sang hymns.

Blind unbelief is sure to err,
And scan His works in vain;
He is His own interpreter
And He will make it plain. Amen.

The congregation, having renounced reason, looked rather the happier for it, and sat down to await the sermon. Charles leant towards Rivers and whispered, 'He doesn't usually go on very long.'

That whisper brought back the Sunday mornings of their childhood when they'd drive to church in a pony and trap, and spent the sermon looking up the naughty bits in the Old Testament, a task made easier by the grubby fingerprints of those who had gone before. He remembered Michal's bride-price: an hundred foreskins of the Philistines. As an anthropologist, he still found that fascinating. He remembered the smell of hassocks, and fastened his eyes on the flag-draped altar. They would never come back, those times.

The vicar had reached the top of the pulpit steps. A faint light flashed on his glasses as he made the sign of the cross. 'In the name of the Father and of the Son and of the Holy Ghost . . .'

Charles was busy with a great rehousing of the hens. They were to be transferred from deep litter in the barn to the new coops in Two-acre Field. This was best done after dusk when the hens were drowsy and less likely to rebel. The brothers lingered over tea in the living room, and then went out across the black, sodden, dismal mud of the yard towards the large, low barn. Rivers was wearing a pair of old cord breeches kept up with one of his brother's belts, visible proof that Bertha's strictures on his loss of weight were justified. 'It isn't as if,' she said at every mealtime, piling his plate high, 'you had it to lose.' 'He's all right, Bertha, leave him alone,' Charles always said, though it made no difference. Rivers still staggered away from the table feeling that he'd been force-fed.

Charles carried the hens easily, his arms binding the wings fast to his sides. Rivers, less expert, picked up two birds and set off after him. His fingers dug through the fluffiness into the surprisingly hard quills, and touched clammy flesh. The blood-red combs jiggled as he walked, amber eyes looked up with a kind of bright vacuity. As he tried to nudge the farmyard gate open with his elbow, one of them got its wings free and flapped frantically until he managed to subdue it again. God, I hate hens, he thought.

The chicken farm had been his idea, after Charles came back from the East with malaria. Work in the open air, Rivers had advised. He was paying for it now. As he left the shelter of the hedge and set off across Two-acre Field, a great gust of 'open air' almost lifted him off his feet. He felt responsible for the farm idea, and it wasn't paying. At the moment they were only just breaking even. Mainly it was the effect of the war. Feed was scarce and expensive, male help impossible to get. The last land girl had stayed only long enough to work out the distance to the nearest town, before discovering that some domestic crisis required her immediate return home. But even without the war it might not have been easy. Hens had a curious way of not thriving. They seemed to be subject to a truly phenomenal range of diseases and to take a perverse pleasure in working their way down the list.

It was almost completely dark now, a few faint stars pricking through the clear sky. One hen, weaker than the rest, was being picked on by the others. Its chest was bare of feathers and raw where they'd pecked at it.

'I'll have to get that one out and wring its neck,' Charles said.

'Can't you just isolate her and then put her back in?'

'No. Once they start they never stop.'

They turned and walked back. McTavish, the farm cat, a black, battered tom, met them at the corner of the yard and preceded them across it. A notably morose cat, McTavish, a defect of temperament Rivers attributed to his being perpetually surrounded by forbidden flesh. He was fond of McTavish and slipped him titbits from his plate whenever he thought Bertha wasn't looking.

They moved hens for an hour; slow, tedious work and then, as real darkness set in, went back to the house. Bertha had been baking. An earthenware pot full of bread dough stood by the kitchen range, and the whole firelit room was full of the smell of warm yeast. 'You'll be all right, won't you?' Bertha said, driving a hat pin neatly into her hat, and craning towards the mirror to make sure it was on straight. She and Charles were using Rivers as a chicken-sitter while they enjoyed a rare night out.

'Don't fuss, Bertha,' Charles said.

'There's two loaves in the oven. They'll be done at ten past eight. Turn them out, tap the base. If it sounds hollow, they're done. Do you think you can manage that?'

'He's not a complete idiot, Bertha,' Charles called in from the hall.

Bertha looked doubtful. 'All right, then. Are we off?'

Charles came in wearing his hat and coat.

Rivers said, 'I'll see if I can get those accounts finished, Charles.'

'I wish you would,' Bertha murmured as she went past.

Once they'd gone, Rivers sat in the rocking chair by the fire, and concentrated on not dozing off. He hadn't dared not eat at dinner, and the unaccustomed heavy meal and the firelight were making his eyelids droop. Last spring when he'd been here, boxes of chicks had been put to warm before the fire, and then the room had been full of the pecking and scratching of tiny beaks and feet. He remembered them struggling out of the eggs, how exhausted, wet and miserable they looked, and yet curiously powerful, little Atlases struggling to hold up the world. Now the same chicks were scruffy, bedraggled things running in the coops, and the only sound in the room was the roar of flame.

He stretched out his legs and looked at the account book on the edge of the kitchen table. He had letters he ought to write, the most urgent being one to David Burns, who'd invited him to spend the last few days of his leave at the family's holiday cottage on the Suffolk coast. As far as Rivers could make out, Burns's parents wanted to talk about his future, and although Rivers was not particularly anxious to do this – he found it difficult to envisage any future for Burns – he thought it his duty to accept. And then there was a half-completed letter to Sassoon, but the accounts would have to come first. Ten past eight. He got the loaves from the oven, tipped them out, and tapped the bases. Since he'd never done this before, he had no way of knowing whether this particular sound was 'hollow' or not. He decided they *looked* done, and set them to cool on the tray. Then he fetched the shoe box in which Charles stored his receipts and set to work on finishing the accounts. At intervals as he worked he looked up. The wind which had been blowing a gale all day was beginning to die down. Once he heard an owl hoot from the copse at the other side of Two-acre Field, a cold, shivery sound that made him glad of the fire and the smell of warm bread.

When he'd finished, he took the oil lamp and went along to the front room, intending to have another go at finishing his letter to Siegfried. He put the lamp down on the desk. Ranged at intervals around the walls, big heavy pieces of furniture squatted on their own shadows. Most of them he remembered from his childhood home: Knowles Bank. They were too big to fit into his sisters' cottage, he had no need of them, and so Charles and Bertha had inherited them all. Their presence here in different places, at different angles to the walls and to each other, gave him an odd feeling of slipping back into an out-of-focus version of his childhood.

A cold, unused room. All the farm paperwork was done in the kitchen. He decided to take his letter along and finish it there, but then lingered, fingering the leather of the desk top and looking at the picture that hung above the empty grate. At Knowles Bank it had hung in the same position, above the fireplace, in his father's study. As a picture it could hardly have been more appropriate to his father's dual role as priest and speech therapist, since it showed the Apostles at Pentecost immediately after they had received the gift of tongues. There they sat, each under his own personal flame, rendered in an instant fluent, persuasive and articulate, not merely in their own language but in all known tongues. Rivers remembered the bishop's sermon one Pentecost when he'd explained that the gift of tongues as bestowed upon the Apostles had absolutely nothing to do with 'the gift of tongues' as bestowed regularly every Sunday on uneducated riff-raff in various tin-roofed chapels about the diocese. The gift of Pentecost had made the Apostles *comprehensible* in all known languages. And there they sat still, looking, Rivers couldn't help thinking, most unchristianly smug about it all.

He'd sat with other boys – his father's pupils – underneath that picture for many a long hour, stumbling over the consonants of his own language, remembering to hold down the back of his tongue, project his breath in an even flow, etc., etc. Sometimes his father would walk with him up and down the room, since he believed the measured pace helped to regulate the flow of breath. Rivers hadn't been the star pupil in those classes, not by any means. If anything he'd made rather less progress than the rest, in spite of – or because of? – having his teacher with him all the time. The house was full of stammering boys, any age from ten to nineteen, and at least it meant he was not the only one. It had had another advantage too, he remembered. While the boys were there, the Reverend Charles Dodgson stayed away. Mr Dodgson didn't like boys. As soon as they left at Christmas or in the summer holidays, he arrived, taking lessons every evening after dinner. Rivers, from long exposure to other people's speech impediments, could sum up the main features of a stammer almost as quickly as his father. Dodgson found *m* difficult, and *p* in consonant combinations, particularly in the middle of words, but his arch enemy was hard *c*.

During the day there were boating trips on the river. Dodgson and the four Rivers children, himself, Charles, Ethel and – Dodgson's favourite – Katharine. He'd never enjoyed those trips much, and neither, he thought, had Charles, though probably that was no more than the slight pique of two Victorian schoolboys, finding themselves, for the first time in their lives, not of the preferred sex. Afterwards, during those apparently endless summer evenings, there would be croquet on the lawn, Rivers's father and Dodgson playing, the children watching. There was a photograph of them on the desk, doing just that, he and Charles leaning back against the garden roller, no doubt getting grass stains on their white shirts, the two little girls, his sisters, under the shade of the beech tree. If he tried hard, he could recall the feel of the roller against his shoulder blades, the heat of the sun on the back of his neck.

He had one other memory of Dodgson. One evening he'd

crept close to the open window of his father's study, sat down with his back to the wall and listened to the lesson in progress. Why he'd done this he couldn't now remember, except that it hadn't *felt* like eavesdropping, since he knew nothing private was likely to be said. Perhaps he'd just wanted to hear Dodgson put through the same routine he and the other boys were put through. Perhaps he'd wanted to see him cut down to size. Dodgson had just embarked on the sentence about the careful cat catching the mouse – a simple enough tale, but already, in Dodgson's mouth, threatening to become an epic. Rivers listened to his father's advice, the same advice, basically, that *he* got, though conveyed without that peculiar note of fraught patience. He thought suddenly, this is nonsense. It *doesn't* help to remember to keep your tongue down, it doesn't help to think about the flow of breath. So he'd thought, sweeping away his father's life work in a single minute as twelve-year-old boys are apt to do. He'd raised his head very cautiously above the window sill, and seen his father sitting behind the desk – this desk – his back to the window, clean pink neck showing above clean white collar, broad shoulders straining the cloth of his jacket. He stared at the back of his neck, at the neck of the man whom he had, in a way, just killed, and he didn't feel sad or guilty about it at all. He felt glad.

Later that summer he'd given a talk to the speech therapy group on monkeys. *M* was to him what *c* was to Dodgson, but he was interested in monkeys, and still more interested in Darwin's theory of evolution, which by this time had achieved acceptance in some circles. Knowles Bank was not among them. His father had been furious, not because Rivers had stumbled over every single *m* without exception – though indeed he had – but because he'd dared suggest that Genesis was no more than the creation myth of a Bronze Age people. Dinner that night was a strained occasion. Father angry, mother upset, Charles covertly sympathetic, sisters goggle-eyed and making the most of it, Rivers himself outwardly subdued, inwardly triumphant. For the first time in his life, he'd forced his father to listen to what he had to say, and not merely to the way he'd said it.

And yet, Rivers thought, running his hands across the scarred leather of the desk top, the relationship between father and son is never simple, and never over. Death certainly doesn't end it. In the past year he'd thought more about his father than he'd done since he was a child. Only recently it had occurred to him that if some twelve-year-old boy had crept up to his window at Craiglockhart, as he'd done to his father's window at Knowles Bank, he'd have seen a man sitting at a desk with his back to the window, listening to some patient, with a stammer far worse than Dodgson's, try and fail to reach the end of a sentence. Only that boy would not have been his son.

The unfinished letter to Siegfried lay on the desk. He'd got as far as a comment on the weather, and there the letter had ground to a halt. What he did so easily in conversation, always nudging Siegfried gently in the same direction, and yet always avoiding any suggestion of pressure, was a feat he apparently could not perform on paper. Perhaps he was just too tired. He told himself the letter could wait till morning.

He picked up the lamp, pushed aside the heavy dark red curtains and opened the window. A big dizzy moth flew in, with pale wings and a fat, furry body, and began bumping against the ceiling. He leant out of the window, smelling roses he couldn't see. The wind had fallen completely now, giving way to a breathless hush. Faintly, over dark hedges and starlit fields, came the soft thud-thud of the guns. When he'd first arrived, suffering from the usual medley of physical and neurasthenic symptoms – headaches, dry mouth, pounding heart – he'd confused that sound with the throbbing of blood in his head. Then one night, lying sleepless, he'd heard the water jug vibrating in the bowl, and realized what it was that he kept hearing. Siegfried must have heard it in June when he was at home convalescing from his wound.

Perhaps he'd better write tonight after all. He closed the window, and sat down at the desk. The moth's huge shadow, flickering over the walls and ceiling, darkened the page, as, drawing the pad towards him, he tore off the sheet and started again. *My dear Siegfried* . . .

'What draft is this?'

'Lost count,' Owen said. 'You did tell me to sweat my guts out.'

'Did I really? What an inelegant expression. "What passing-bells for these who die as cattle?" I see we got to the slaughterhouse in the end.' Sassoon read through the poem. When he'd finished, he didn't immediately comment.

'It's better, isn't it?'

'Better? It's *transformed*.' He read it again. 'Though when you look at the *sense* ... You do realize you've completely contradicted yourself, don't you? You start by saying there is no consolation, and then you say there is.'

'Not consolation. Pride in the sacrifice.'

'Isn't that consolation?'

'If it is, it's justifiable. There's a point beyond which –'

'I don't see that.'

'There's a point beyond which you can't press the meaninglessness. Even if the courage is being abused, it's still ...'

Owen leapt up, went to the drawer of his washstand and produced the typescript Sassoon had lent him. He began leafing quickly but carefully through it. Sassoon, watching, thought, he's getting better. No stammer. Quick, decisive movements. The self-confidence to contradict his hero. And the poem had been a revelation.

'Look, you do exactly the same thing,' Owen said, coming across with the sheet he wanted.

> O my brave brown companions, when your souls
> Flock silently away, and the eyeless dead
> Shame the wild beast of battle on the ridge,
> Death will stand grieving in that field of war
> Since your unvanquished hardihood is spent.
> And through some mooned Valhalla there will pass
> Battalions and battalions, scarred from hell;
> The unreturning army that was youth;
> The legions who have suffered and are dust.

'What's that if not pride in the sacrifice?'

'Grief? All right, point taken. I just don't like the idea of ... making it out to be less of a horror than it really is.' He looked down at the page. 'I think you should publish this.'

'You mean in the *Hydra*?'

'No, I mean in the *Nation*. Give me a fair copy and I'll see what I can do. You'll need a different title, though. "Anthem for . . ."' He thought for a moment, crossed one word out, substituted another. 'There you are,' he said, handing the page back, smiling. '"Anthem for *Doomed* Youth."'

The main corridor of the hospital stretched the whole length of the building, with wards opening off on either side. From one of these came an unpleasant smell which Madge said was gangrene, though Sarah didn't believe she knew. Ward Fourteen was overcrowded, the beds packed close together, men sitting up and staring with interest at the two girls hesitating just inside the door. Most of them looked reasonably well and cheerful. The trouble was that with their cropped heads and hospital blue uniforms, they also looked exactly alike.

'I won't recognize him,' Madge said in a frantic whisper.

'Go on,' Sarah said, giving her a shove.

They started to walk up the ward. Madge stared from bed to bed with a dazed look. She really mightn't recognize him at this rate, Sarah thought, but then a voice cried, 'Madge!' A dark-haired man with a gingery moustache was sitting up, waving and looking delighted to see her. Madge walked forward cautiously, located the bandaged left arm, checked to see that the swelling beneath the counterpane was the right length and breadth to consist of two legs. He looked all right. He planted a smacking kiss on Madge's lips, and Sarah looked away in embarrassment, only to realize she was herself the object of amused appreciation from all parts of the ward.

'Eh, look, I've brought you these,' Madge said. 'How are you?'

'I'm all right. Went right through,' he said. 'Just here.' He pointed to his biceps. 'No gangrene, no nothing.'

'You were lucky.'

'I'll say. I'm gunna be in here two weeks they reckon, and then I'll have a bit of leave before I go back.'

'This is Sarah,' Madge said.

'Pleased to meet you.'

They shook hands. Madge was now sitting by the bed, beginning, cautiously, to bask in the admiration of her restored lover and to plan what they would do on his leave. After this had been going on for a while, Sarah began to feel distinctly green and hairy. 'I'll just have a walk round the grounds,' she said. 'It's a bit hot in here.'

'Yeh, all right,' Madge said.

'I'll see you at the main entrance, then. Half an hour?'

They hardly noticed her go. None of these men was badly wounded, and several of them whistled and clicked their tongues as she walked past. The whole atmosphere of the ward was happy. The general air of relief at being out of it was what chiefly came across, though she supposed there must be other wards where the wounds were not so slight.

Outside, in the corridor, she looked up and down, realizing she didn't know in which direction the exit lay. She was surrounded by notices directing people to the pharmacy, the path lab, the X-ray department, everywhere except the way out. She tried walking to her left, but her way was blocked by a large notice saying: THEATRES. NO UNAUTHORIZED PERSONNEL BEYOND THIS POINT. She turned right, and shortly afterwards came to a corridor she thought she recognized, and began to walk along it, but the feeling of familiarity soon vanished. The building was enormous, and seemed to have no plan, no structure to it, at all. To add to the sense of unreality most of the notices referred to its civilian use before the war. Maternity, she read, and then the swing doors banged open to reveal beds full of people who were most unlikely ever to give birth.

Obviously she ought to stop and ask somebody, but then everybody seemed to be in such a hurry, and so grim-faced. At last she found a door that led out to the grounds at the back of the hospital, where the tall chimney of an incinerator dribbled brownish-yellow smoke. Here, a huge tent had been erected and this served as another ward. She glanced into the interior, which was golden in the sunlight filtered through the roof, but the atmosphere was close, stifling, a humming darkness in which the clumsiness of bandages and the itch of healing skin must be almost intolerable.

A constant traffic of nurses and orderlies passed between the tent and the main building, and, feeling herself to be in the way, Sarah looked around for somewhere she could find temporary refuge and not bother anybody. There was a conservatory along the side of the hospital, facing east so that at the moment it caught the full warmth of the sun. Shadowy figures sat inside, and the door was open so she thought she might perhaps sit there.

Once across the threshold she became aware of a silence, a silence caused, she suspected, by her entrance. She was still dazzled by the brightness of the light outside and the relative dimness of the interior, and so she had to blink several times before she saw them, a row of figures in wheelchairs, but figures that were no longer the size and shape of adult men. Trouser legs sewn short; empty sleeves pinned to jackets. One man had lost all his limbs, and his face was so drained, so pale, he seemed to have left his blood in France as well. The blue of the hospital uniform looked garish against his skin. They'd been pushed out here to get the sun, but not right outside, and not at the front of the hospital where their mutilations might have been seen by passers-by. They stared at her, but not as the men had stared on the other ward, smiling, trying to catch her eye. This was a totally blank stare. If it contained anything at all, it was fear. Fear of her looking at the empty trouser legs. Fear of her not looking at them. She stood there, unable to go forward, and unable, for a few crucial moments, to turn back, until a nurse bustled up to her and said, 'Who is it you want to see?'

'I'm just waiting for a friend. It's all right, I'll wait outside.'

She backed out, walking away in the sunlight, feeling their eyes on her, thinking that perhaps if she'd been prepared, if she'd managed to smile, to look normal, it might have been better. But no, she thought, there was nothing she could have done that would have made it better. Simply by being there, by being that inconsequential, infinitely powerful creature: *a pretty girl*, she had made everything worse. Her sense of her own helplessness, her being forced to play the role of Medusa when she meant no harm, merged with the anger she was beginning to feel at their being hidden away like that. If the country demanded that price, then it should bloody well be prepared to look at the result. She strode on through the heat, not caring where she was going, furious with herself, the war ... Everything.

*

Prior took off his clothes, put on the white hospital gown and sat on the bed to await the arrival of the doctor. This was his second visit. The first time he'd seen Eaglesham, the consultant, a big, kindly, grizzled bear of a man who'd said very little but whom he'd trusted at once. He'd raised his eyebrows when Prior blew into the Vitalograph or whatever the machine was called, but he hadn't said what he thought, and Prior had not wanted to ask. It wasn't going to be Eaglesham today, though. A much younger man with a sallow skin and slick dark hair was popping in and out of the other cubicles. Prior looked down at his thin white legs. He didn't see why he had to take all his clothes off. Were they trying to cater for some unforeseen medical emergency in which his lungs had slipped into his pelvis? He didn't like the way the gown fastened at the back. He didn't mind displaying his wares, if he liked the other person and the time seemed right, but he did like the illusion at least that the act was voluntary. He could hear the doctor's voice in the cubicle next door, talking to a man who couldn't complete a sentence without coughing. At last the curtains were pushed aside and the doctor came in, followed by a nurse, clasping a beige file to her bosom. Prior slipped off the robe and stood up to be examined.

'Second-Lieutenant Prior.'

'Mister' he wanted to say. He said, 'Yes.'

'I see there's some question whether you're fit to go back. I mean apart from the state of your *nerves*.'

Prior said nothing at all.

The doctor waited. 'Well, let's have a look at you.'

He moved the stethoscope all over Prior's chest, pressing so hard that at times the stethoscope left overlapping rings on the skin that flushed and faded to white. He thinks I'm shirking, Prior thought, and the idea made him go cold.

'How *are* your nerves?' the doctor said.

'Better.'

'Shell explosion, was it?'

'Not exactly.'

Not one word of what he'd told Rivers would he repeat to this man.

'Do *you* think you're fit?'

'I'm not a doctor.'

The doctor smiled. Contemptuously, it seemed to Prior. 'Keen to get back, are we?'

Prior closed his eyes. He had a picture of himself driving his knee into the man's groin, and the picture was so vivid that for a moment he thought he might have done it, but then he opened his eyes and there was the sallow face, still smiling. He stared at him.

The doctor nodded, almost as if Prior had replied, and then slowly, to avoid any suggestion of backing off, turned and made a brief note on the file. It's all bluff, Prior thought. It's what Eaglesham says that matters.

He was in a torment as he got back into his uniform, reckoning his chances, despising himself for reckoning them. He didn't thank Rivers for any of this. I haven't lied to any of them, he thought. I haven't made things out to be worse than they really are. He finished lacing his puttees and stood up. The nurse came back with a card. 'If you tell them at the appointments desk, three weeks.'

'Yes, all right. Thank you.'

He took the card, but walking down the long corridor afterwards he was tempted not to make the appointment. In the end he did, then put the card away and strode out into the hospital grounds as fast as he could. He thought he might buy himself something from the barrow at the entrance, fruit or sweets, any little treat that might make him feel better. Less contaminated.

He saw her before she saw him, and called out, 'Sarah.' She turned and smiled. He'd thought about her a lot while he'd been in the sick bay, remembering that time on the beach. Illness, once the worst was over, always made him randy. What he'd forgotten, he thought now, looking at the yellow face beneath the aureole of extraordinary hair, was how much he *liked* her.

'What are *you* doing here?' she asked, obviously delighted.

'Having my chest examined.'

'Are you all right?'

'Fine – thanks to you. What are *you* doing here?'

'I'm with Madge. Her fiancé's been wounded.'

'Is he all right?'

'Yes, I think so.' Her face darkened. 'I've just seen some that aren't all right. There's a sort of conservatory round the back. They're all sat in there. Where the rest of us don't have to see them.'

'Bad?'

She nodded. 'You know I used to wonder how I'd go on if Johnny came back like that. You always tell yourself it'd make no difference. Easy said, isn't it?'

He sensed the anger and responded to it immediately. She might not know much about the war, but what she did know she faced honestly. He admired her for that. 'Look, do you have to wait for Madge?' he asked. 'I mean, how long do you think she'll be?'

'Ages, I should think. She was virtually in bed with him when I left.'

'Well, can't you tell her you're going? She can walk back by herself all right, can't she? It's broad daylight.'

She looked at him consideringly. 'Yes, all right.' She started to move away. 'I won't be a minute.'

Left alone, Prior bought two bunches of chrysanthemums, bronze and white, from the barrow near the entrance. They weren't the flowers he would have chosen, but he wanted to give her something. He stood craning his head for the first sight of her. When she arrived, smiling and out of breath, he handed her the flowers, and then, on a sudden impulse, leant across and kissed her. The flowers, crushed between them, released their bitter, autumnal smell.

They were burning leaves on Hampstead Heath where Rivers walked with Ruth Head on the second day of his visit. Acrid smoke drifted across their path and below them London lay in a blue haze. They stopped by one of the ponds, and watched a coot cleave the smooth water. 'You see over there behind those houses?' Ruth said. 'That's the RFC hospital. And then over there – just in that dip there – that's the Big Gun.'

'I'm glad you and Henry don't take refuge in the kitchen every night. Everybody else seems to.'

'Can you imagine Henry cowering under the kitchen table?'

They smiled at each other and walked on.

'Actually the air raids are my guilty secret,' Ruth said.

'You mean you'd rather be under the table?'

'Oh no, quite the opposite. I enjoy them. It's a terrible thing to say, isn't it? All that damage. People killed. And yet every time the siren goes, I feel this immense sense of exhilaration. I'd really like to go out and run about in it.' She laughed, self-deprecatingly. 'I don't of course. But I get this feeling that the . . . the *crust* of everything is starting to crack. Don't you feel that?'

'*Yes.* I'm just not sure we're going to like what's under the crust.'

They started to walk towards Spaniard's Road. Rivers said, 'You know last night I got the distinct impression that Henry was plotting something.'

'About you? If he is, it'll be something to your advantage.'

'You mean you know and you're not going to tell me?'

Ruth laughed. 'That's right.'

By Spaniard's Road, men in blue hospital uniforms sat in wheelchairs, waiting for someone to come and push them away. Ruth was silent for a while after they'd walked past. 'You know there was something I didn't say last night.' She looked up at him. 'I think Sassoon's absolutely right.'

'Oh dear, I was hoping I might be able to introduce you. But if you're going to be a bad moral influence –'

'*Seriously.*'

'All right, seriously. Suppose he *is* right? Does that mean it's a good idea to let him go ahead and destroy himself?'

'Surely it has to be his choice?'

'It *is* his choice.'

Ruth smiled and shook her head.

'Look,' Rivers said, 'I wear the uniform, I take the pay, *I do the job.* I'm not going to apologize for that.'

'I'm not suggesting you should. All the same,' she said, turning to look at him, 'you're tearing yourself in pieces as well as him.'

They walked in silence for a while. Rivers said, 'Is that what Henry thinks?'

Ruth laughed. 'Of course not. You want perception, you go to a novelist, not a psychiatrist.'

'I'm sure you're right.'

'No, you're not. You don't believe a word of it.'

'At any rate, I'm too cowed to disagree.'

That evening, left alone with Henry after dinner, Rivers watched him massage the triangle of skin between the thumb and forefinger of his left hand. 'Does that still bother you?'

'A bit. Cold weather. Do you know, I don't think I'd have the courage to do that now.'

'No, I look back sometimes, and . . . I'm amazed. What are you doing these days?'

'Gross injuries to the spinal cord. We've got a lot of interesting material.' Head's mouth twisted. 'As we call the poor sods.'

Rivers shook his head. He'd seen Head too often on the wards to believe him capable of that particular kind of research-orientated callousness.

'It's an interesting atmosphere,' Head said. 'Dealing with physical trauma and war neurosis in the same hospital. You'd like it.'

'I'm sure I would.' A trace of bitterness. 'I'd like London.'

'There's a job going if you want it.'

'You mean there's a vacancy?'

'No, I mean there's a job *for you* if you want it. I've been asked to sound you out. Psychologist with the Royal Flying Corps. At the Central Hospital, Hampstead.'

'*Ah.* I wondered why Ruth was so keen on the Heath.'

'I imagine you'd find it interesting? Apparently there are some quite striking differences between the rate of breakdown in pilots and in other branches of the service.'

'It sounds marvellous.' He raised his hands and let them drop. 'I just don't see how I can.'

'Why not? You'd be closer to your family, your friends, your research contacts, you'd be able to get back to Cambridge at weekends. And . . . I don't suppose it *matters*, but we'd be able to work together again.'

Rivers buried his face in his hands. 'O-o-o-oh. "Get thee behind me, Satan."'

'I am behind you. I was thinking of giving you a shove.'

'I couldn't leave Bryce.'

Head looked incredulous. 'You mean, your CO?'

'He's in a difficult situation. We're in for a general inspection, and ... it all goes back a long way. Bryce is determined this time he's not going to play their game. He's not going to parade the patients, or polish the bottoms of the frying-pans, or pretend to be anything other than just an extremely busy, overcrowded and I think bloody good hospital.'

'What do they want?'

'They want a barracks. It's got all the makings of a really nasty confrontation. I think Bryce may have to go.'

'Well, I hate to sound harsh, but wouldn't that rather solve the problem? *Your* problem, I mean.'

'If it happened. Meanwhile, I think I can be ... of some use to him.'

'When is this inspection?'

'End of the month.'

'We'd need to know about the job ... Well. Three weeks?'

'I'll think about it.'

'Good. And don't be *too* altruistic, will you? You're isolated up there, it's not good for you.'

'I don't know about isolated. I never have a minute to myself.'

'*Precisely*. Come on, let's find Ruth.'

15

Aldeburgh was the end of the line, but the train, as if reluctant to accept this, produced, as Rivers stepped down on to the platform, an amazing burst of steam. He stood, looking up and down, as the train's hissing subsided into grunts, and the steam cleared. Burns had promised to meet him, but his memory wasn't good, and, faced with the empty platform, Rivers was glad he had the address. But then, just as Rivers was resigning himself to finding the house on his own, Burns appeared, a tall, emaciated figure wearing a coat of stiff herringbone tweed that reached almost to the ground. He'd obviously been running, and was out of breath. 'Hello,' he said. Rivers tried to judge whether Burns looked better or worse. It was hard to tell. His face in the light of the naphtha flares was as expressionless as beaten bronze.

'How are you?' they asked simultaneously, and then laughed.

Rivers decided he should be the one to answer. 'A lot better, thanks.'

'Good,' Burns said. 'It's walking distance,' he added across his shoulder, already striding off. 'We don't need a taxi.'

They came out of the station and began walking downhill, through the quiet cold fringes of the town, past the church, through streets of huddled houses, and out on to the front.

The sea was calm, almost inaudible, a toothless mouth mumbling pebbles in the darkness. Instead of walking along the path, Burns struck out across the shingle and Rivers followed, to where the tide had laid bare a thin strip of sand. The crunch and slither of shingle under their feet blotted out all other sounds. Rivers turned, and saw the bones of Burns's face gleaming in the moonlight. He wondered what he made of the tangles of barbed wire that ran along the beach, with only two narrow channels left for fishing boats and for the lifeboat to come and go. But Burns seemed not to see the wire.

They stood together at the water's edge, two black shadows on the pale shingle, and small waves creamed over at their feet. Then the moon came out from behind a bank of dark cloud, and the fishermen's huts, the boats lined up in two short rows behind the wire, and the heaped nets, cast shadows behind them almost as sharply edged as day.

They returned to the path and began walking along the terrace of houses, which here and there had gaps. Many of the houses were shuttered and had sandbags piled against the front doors. 'The sea's been known to pay visits,' Burns said, following the direction of Rivers's gaze. 'I was here once when it flooded.' Evidently sandbags brought back no other memories.

'This is it,' he said a few minutes later, stopping in front of a tall but extremely narrow house. At this end of the foreshore the sea was much closer, turning and turning in the darkness. Rivers looked out and caught a glint of white. 'What's along there?'

'The marshes. More shingle. I'll show you tomorrow.'

They groped their way into the hall, closing the door carefully behind them before Burns switched on the light. His face, deeply shadowed from the unshaded bulb, peered anxiously at Rivers. 'I expect you'd like to go upstairs,' he said. 'I *think* I've given you a towel . . .' He looked like a child trying to remember what it was that grown-ups said to newly arrived guests. He also looked, for the first time, deranged.

Rivers followed him up the narrow stairs and into a small bedroom. Burns pointed out the bathroom and then went downstairs. Rivers put his bag down, bounced on the bed to test the mattress, and looked round. The walls were covered with paper of an indeterminate and confusing pattern, the background colour faded to the yellow of an old bruise. Everything smelled of the sea, as if the furniture had soaked it in. It reminded him of childhood holidays in Brighton. He splashed his face in the bowl, then, turning off the light, opened the shutters. His room overlooked the sea. The wind was rising, and with each gust the coils of wire twitched as if they were alive.

No sign of Burns's parents. Rivers had mistakenly assumed he was being invited to meet them, since a large part of Burns's letter had dealt with their anxieties about his future. But apparently not. This was probably their room. The house was so narrow there couldn't be more than one, or at the most, two small rooms on each floor.

The evening passed pleasantly enough. No mention of Burns's illness, no mention of the war. These were evidently taboo topics, but they talked about a great range of other things. Whatever else the war had done to Burns, it had certainly deepened his love for his native county. Suffolk flowers, birds, churches, he was knowledgeable about them all. More recently, he'd become interested in the preservation of country crafts. 'Old Clegg', who was apparently something of a local character, had promised to teach him flint-knapping, and he seemed to be looking forward to that. Even before the war he'd been very much a countryman in his interests, rather like Siegfried in a way, though without Siegfried's passion for hunting.

When the conversation turned to other matters, Burns was very much the bright sixth former, idealistic, intolerant, naïve, inclined to offer sweeping generalizations as fact, attractive in the freshness of his vision as such boys often are. Rivers thought how misleading it was to say that the war had 'matured' these young men. It wasn't true of his patients, and it certainly wasn't true of Burns, in whom a prematurely aged man and a fossilized schoolboy seemed to exist side by side. It did give him a curiously ageless quality, but 'maturity' was hardly the word. Still, he was better than he'd been at Craiglockhart, so perhaps his conviction that if he could only get back to Suffolk and forget the war he would be all right had been proved correct. But then why am I here? Rivers thought. Despite Burns's reluctance to mention his illness, Rivers didn't believe he'd been invited to Suffolk to talk about church architecture. But it would be quite wrong to force the pace. Whatever was bothering him, he would raise the matter in his own time.

Rivers woke the following morning to find the beach shrouded in mist. He leant on the window sill, and watched the fishing boats return. The pebbles on the beach were wet, though not from rain or tide. The mist clung to them like sweat, and the air tasted of iron. Everything was so quiet. When a gull flew in from the sea and passed immediately overhead, he heard the creak of its wings.

Burns was already up, in the kitchen by the sound of things, but not, Rivers thought, preparing breakfast. Nothing in the way of dinner or supper had appeared the night before, and Rivers had hesitated, on his first evening, to go into the kitchen and forage for food, though he suspected that might be the only way of getting any.

He washed, dressed, shaved, and went downstairs. By this time the mist on the beach had begun to thin, but it was cold for the time of year, and the sight of a fire in the first floor living room was welcome. He went down a further flight of stairs into the kitchen and found Burns at the kitchen table with a pot of tea.

'There's some cereal,' he said, pointing.

He sounded shy again, though last night he'd begun to talk quite freely by the end of the evening, just as Rivers, caught between the roar of the fire and the roar of the sea, had started nodding off to sleep. 'I'm sorry I had to go to bed so early,' Rivers said, reaching for the cereal packet.

''S all right.' Visibly, he remembered what it was he was supposed to ask next. 'Did you have a good night?'

'Fine.' Rivers bit the reciprocal question back. He'd heard part of Burns's night. Obviously, however hard Burns tried to thrust memories of the war behind him, the nightmare followed.

The doorbell rang, and Burns got up to answer it. 'This is Mrs Burril's day for sorting me out,' he said.

Mrs Burril was a remarkably silent person, but she managed, without words, to make it clear their presence was superfluous.

Burns said, 'I thought we might go for a walk.'

The mist had thinned but not cleared. It moved in slow, cold currents over the marshes, where drainage ditches and sump holes reflected a steely light at the sky. Reeds whispered, with a noise like the palms of hands being rubbed together. It was difficult to breathe, difficult even to move, and they spoke in low voices when they spoke at all.

They walked along a narrow raised path that divided the

marshes from the river. Small yachts rode at anchor, the breeze just strong enough to make their rigging rattle, not a loud sound, but persistent and rather disturbing, like an irregular heart beat. Nothing else here could disturb. The estuary lay flat and peaceful under a shrunken, silver sun, and nothing moved, except the reeds, until a flight of ducks whistled past.

Rivers had begun to realize how remarkable the area was. A strip of land, at times no more than a hundred yards wide, divided the estuary from the North Sea. Walking out along this strip, away from the town, into the bleached shingle distances, you became aware of two separate sounds: the roar and suck of waves on shingle, and the lulling sound of the river among its reeds. If you moved to the left, the crunch and chop of boots on shingle cut out the gentler river sounds. If to the right, the tapping of rigging and the lapping of water dominated, though you could still hear that the sea was there.

They turned and looked back at the huddled town. 'You know, I love this place,' Burns said. 'I wouldn't like you to think I'd left London just because of the raids. Actually it wasn't the raids, it was the regular meal-times. You know, everybody sitting down to eat. Waiting for food to be put in front of them. And father going on about the war. He's a great believer in the war, my father.'

'Will they be coming to Suffolk at all?'

'No, I shouldn't think so. They're both very busy in London.' They turned and walked on. 'It's best we don't see too much of each other at the moment. I am not a sight for sore eyes.'

A squat, circular building had begun to loom up out of the mist. It looked rather like a Martello tower, Rivers thought, but he hadn't known they'd been built as far north as this.

'This is the most northerly,' Burns said, slithering down the slope on to the beach. Rivers followed him across the shingle and down into the dank high moat that surrounded the tower. In its shadow, all water sounds, whether hissing waves or lapping water, abruptly ceased. Ferns grew from the high walls of the moat; and the tower, where the look-out turret had crumbled away, was thronged with bindweed, but the overall impression was of a dead place.

The sea must flood the moat at high tide, for all kinds of

debris had been washed up and left. Driftwood, the torn-off wing of a gull, bits of blue and green glass. A child would have loved it, picking over these pieces.

'We used to play here,' Burns said. 'Daring each other, you know. Who could go all the way up?'

There was a door, but it had planks nailed across it. Rivers peered through a crack and saw stone steps going down.

'Strictly forbidden. They were always afraid we'd get trapped in the cellars.'

'I suppose they flood, don't they? At high tide?'

'Yes. There's all kinds of stories told about it. People chained up and left to drown. I think we rather liked that. We used to sit down there and pretend we could see ghosts.'

'It feels like a place where people have died. I mean, violent deaths.'

'You feel that, do you? Yes. I expect that's why we liked it. Bloodthirsty little horrors, boys.'

Rivers wasn't sorry when they climbed the bank of shingle and stood on the beach in the strengthening sunlight again.

'Do you feel up to a longish walk?' Burns asked.

'Yes.'

'All right. We can follow that path.'

They walked four or five miles inland, and came out into a wood where great golden tongues of fungus lapped the trees, and a mulch of dead leaves squelched underfoot. Rather to Rivers's surprise they stopped at a pub on the way back, though no food was available. Burns could drink apparently, and did, becoming in the process quite flushed and talkative, though nothing was said about his illness.

They arrived back in the late afternoon with every bone and muscle aching. Mrs Burril had obviously built up the fire before she left, and it was rescuable, just about. Rivers knelt in front of it, sticking strips of cereal packet through the bars, and blowing when he got a flame. 'Have you any newspapers?'

'No,' Burns said.

No, Rivers thought, silly question. Once the fire was burning well, Rivers went out and bought cakes and biscuits for tea, which he served in front of the fire, tucking in himself and not looking to see whether Burns ate or not. He ate, sitting on the hearth rug, his wind-reddened arms clasped about his knees, and the firelight playing on his face.

After the plates were cleared away, Rivers asked if he might work for a couple of hours. He was writing a paper on the Repression of War Experience which he was due to give to the British Medical Association in December, and he knew, once he got back to Craiglockhart, there would be very little time. He worked at the table in the window, with his back to the room. He began by reading through what he'd written so far on the evil effects that followed from patients trying to suppress their memories of war experience, and was about to start writing when it occurred to him he was in the same room as a man who was doing just that.

Why do I go along with it? he thought. One answer, the easy answer, was that he was no longer Burns's doctor. It was up to Burns now how he chose to manage his illness. But then he'd gone along with the suppression in Craiglockhart too. Whenever he'd tried to apply to Burns the same methods of treatment he used with everybody else, and used, for the most part, successfully, his nerve had failed him. He'd told himself this was because of the peculiar nature of Burns's experience, the utter lack of any redeeming feature the mind could grasp and hold on to while it steadied itself to face the full horror. But was Burns's experience really worse than that of others? Worse than Jenkins's, crawling between the dismembered pieces of his friend's body to collect personal belongings to send back to the family? Worse than Prior's? *What shall I do with this gob-stopper?*

Corpses were everywhere in the trenches. Used to strengthen parapets, to prop up sagging doorways, to fill in gaps in the duckboards. Many of his patients treading on a dead body had been startled by the release of gas. Surely what had happened to Burns was merely an unusually disgusting version of a common experience. And I've let him, Rivers thought – no, that was unfair, that was *completely* unfair – I've let *myself* turn it into ... some kind of myth. And that was unforgivable. He wasn't dealing with Jonah in the belly of the whale, still less with Christ in the belly of the earth, he was dealing with David Burns, who'd got his head stuck in the belly of a dead German soldier, and somehow had to be helped to live with the memory.

He turned and looked at Burns, who was still sitting on the hearth rug, though now he'd found himself a book and was reading, his tongue protruding slightly between his teeth. As he felt Rivers's gaze, he looked up and smiled. Twenty-two. He should be worrying about the Tripos and screwing up his courage to ask a girl to the May ball. And yet even now Rivers was nervous of raising the subject of his illness. Burns's instinctive reaction had been to get back to this house, to forget. And there had been some improvement under this regime, by day at least, though evidently not by night. If he wants to talk, he'll talk, Rivers thought, and turned back to his paper.

That evening, rather to Rivers's surprise, they went to the pub. He was surprised because he'd been assuming Burns was isolated here, but apparently all the locals knew him. They'd watched him growing up, summer by summer. The family had been staying here when war broke out. Burns had joined up along with most of the local lads. They all remembered him in his uniform, in the first days and weeks of the war, and perhaps that mattered a great deal. In London, Burns said, on his first trip out in civilian clothes, he'd been handed two white feathers.

Here, as soon as they pushed the bar door open, he was hailed by several people, and by one man in particular: 'Old Clegg'. Clegg had rheumy blue eyes, whose overflow had dried to a scurfy crust at his temples; three brown but very strong teeth; unidentifiable stains on his abdomen, and other stains, only too identifiable, further down. His conversation was so encrusted with salty Suffolk sayings that Rivers suspected him of deliberate self-parody. That, or leg-pulling. Once he'd discovered Rivers was interested in folklore, he was well away. Rivers spent a thoroughly enjoyable evening being initiated into the folklore of rural Suffolk. By closing time, he was convinced Clegg was possibly the most unreliable informant he'd ever had. For sheer imaginative flights of fancy none of the Melanesians came anywhere near him. 'That man is a complete fraud,' he said as they left the pub.

But Burns disagreed. 'He's not a fraud, he's a rogue. Anyway as long as he teaches me flint-knapping, I don't care.'

*

Next morning the weather had changed. At dawn there was a strip of clear blue on the horizon, fading to yellow, but the sky darkened rapidly, until, by mid morning, the clouds humped, liver-coloured, and the sea was dark as iron. The wind had risen during the night, sweeping away the last remnants of mist. At first it came in little gusts, lifting the thin carpet in the hall, swirling dust in corners, then in blasts that made waves on the surface of the estuary, rocking the yachts until the rattle of their rigging became a frenzy, while on the beach great waves swelled like the muscles of an enormous animal, rising to crests that hung and seethed along their full length, before toppling over in thunder and bursts of spray.

Rivers worked on his paper all morning, looking up now and then to find the window mizzled with rain. Burns slept late, having had another bad and very noisy night. He appeared just before noon, pink eyed and twitching, and announced he was going to the White Horse to see Clegg and arrange a definite time for his flint-knapping session. Clegg was proving rather difficult to pin down.

'Git him up agin' a gorse bush, bor,' Rivers said, in a passable imitation of Clegg's voice. 'He ont back away then.'

'That's girls in kissing season, Rivers.'

'Is it? Well, I shouldn't go kissing Clegg. I doubt if flint-knapping's worth it.'

He was immersed in his paper again before Burns left the house.

He came back an hour later, looking rather pleased with himself. 'Thursday.'

'Good.'

'I thought we might go for a walk.'

Rivers looked at the rain-spattered glass.

'It's died down a bit,' Burns said, not altogether convincingly.

'All right, I could do with a break.'

The sea was racing in fast. The fishermen's huts were empty, the boats hauled up high above the last stretch of shingle, with the fishing nets in dark heaps behind them. Either they'd not been out today or they'd turned back early, for Rivers had seen none of them come in. Even the seabirds seemed to be grounded, huddled in the lee of the boats, watching the town with unblinking amber eyes.

Faced with this sea, the land seemed fragile. Was fragile. To the north, cliffs were scoured away, to the south, notice boards were buried up to their necks in shingle. And the little Moot Hall that had once stood at the centre of the town was now on the edge of the sea.

They walked as far as Thorpeness, then turned back, not talking much, since the wind snatched the breath from their mouths. The sea had covered the thin strip of sand, so they had to walk along the steep shelf of shingle, a lopsided business that set the back as well as the legs aching.

It took them two hours, there and back, and Rivers was looking forward to the fire and – if he could contrive it – toasted tea cakes for tea. Breakfast, lunch and dinner, he could do without, but afternoon tea *mattered*. His boot squelched on something soft. Looking down, he saw the place was littered with cods' heads, thirty or more, with blood-stained gills and staring eyes. It gave him no more than a slight *frisson*. Obviously the fishermen gutted their catch and threw the offal away. But Burns had stopped dead in his tracks and was staring at the heads, with his mouth working. As Rivers watched, he jerked his head back, the same movement that had been so common when he first arrived at Craiglockhart.

'It's all right,' he said, when Rivers went back for him. But it was obviously very far from all right.

They got back to the house. Rivers made tea, though Burns didn't manage to eat anything.

After tea they went out and piled sandbags against the doors, struggling with the heavy bags through driving rain and then struggling again to close the storm shutters. The air was full of spray and blown spume.

'We should've done that earlier,' Burns said, wiping the rain from his face and blinking in the firelight. He was very concerned to pretend everything was normal. He sat on the hearth rug, in his favourite position, while the wind buffeted and slogged the house, and talked about his drink with Clegg and various items of local gossip. But he jumped from topic to topic, assuming the connections would be obvious when very often they were not. His mood, once he'd got over the shock of seeing the cods' heads, seemed to be almost elated. He said more than once that he loved storms, and he seemed, at times, to be listening to something other than the roar of wind and sea.

Closing his eyes, Rivers could imagine the town entirely given over to the storm, bobbing on the tide of darkness like a blown eggshell, without substance or power to protect. Burns's conversation became more and more disconnected, the jerking of his head more pronounced. Piling up sandbags, followed by the nearest thing to a bombardment nature could contrive, was not what Rivers would have prescribed. He was prepared to sit up with Burns, if he wanted to stay up, but Burns started talking about bed rather earlier than usual. Probably he took bromides. Rivers would have liked to advise him to stop, since they certainly wouldn't help the nightmares, but he was determined to let Burns be the first to raise the subject of his illness.

The evening ended with nothing to the point having been said. Rivers went to bed and undressed in the darkness, listening to the wind howl, and imagined Burns in the room above, also listening. He read for a while, thinking he might be too tense to go to sleep, but the fresh air and the struggle with the wind along the beach to Thorpeness had tired him out. His eyelids started to droop and he switched off the light. The whole house creaked and groaned, riding the storm like a ship, but he enjoyed that. He'd always found it possible to sleep deeply on board ship, though on land sleep often eluded him.

He was woken by what he immediately took to be the explosion of a bomb. Less than a minute later, while he was still groping for the light switch, he heard a second boom and this time managed to identify it as the sound of a maroon. The lifeboat, no doubt. He was getting out of bed to go to the window when he remembered that he probably ought not to open the shutters, for he could hear from the whistling of wind and lashing of rain that the storm had by no means blown itself out. His heart was pounding, unreasonably, since there was nothing to be afraid of. He supposed it was having come straight from London with its incessant talk of air raids that had made him identify the sound so positively as a bomb.

He lay back and a moment or two later heard footsteps padding past the door of his room. Obviously Burns too had been woken up. Probably he was going downstairs to make himself a cup of tea, perhaps even to sit up the rest of the night.

The more Rivers thought about Burns sitting alone in the kitchen, the more he thought he ought to get up. The sounds of the storm had now been joined by running footsteps. He wouldn't find it easy to sleep again anyway.

The kitchen was empty, and didn't seem to have been disturbed since last night. He told himself that he'd been mistaken, and Burns was still in bed. By now rather anxious, perhaps unreasonably so, he went upstairs and peered into Burns's room. The bedclothes had been pushed back, and the bed was empty.

He had no idea what he should do. For all he knew midnight walks – or rather three am walks – were a habit of Burns's when the nights were particularly bad. Surely he wouldn't go out in this. Rivers heard shouts, followed by more running footsteps. Obviously other people were out in it. Quickly, he returned to his own room, pulled on socks, boots and coat, and went out into the storm.

A small group of figures had gathered round the lifeboat, three of them holding storm lanterns. The overlapping circles of light shone on yellow oilskins glistening with wet, as the men struggled to clear the shingle from the planks that were used to launch the boat. Silver rain slanted down into the lighted area, while beyond, pale banks of shingle faded into the darkness.

A knot of bystanders had gathered by the hut, separate from the labouring figures around the boat. Convinced that Burns must be among them, Rivers ran across to join them, but when he looked from face to face Burns was not there. A woman he thought to be familiar, but couldn't immediately identify, pointed to the marshes south of the town.

As he turned and began walking quickly towards the marshes, he was dimly aware of the boat hitting the sea, and of the waves surging up around her. He left the shelter of the last houses, and the wind, roaring across the marshes, almost knocked him off his feet. He dropped down from the path and walked along beside the river where he was slightly sheltered, though the wind still howled and the yacht rigging thrummed, a sound like no other he had ever heard. He could see fairly clearly most of the time. Once, the moon freed itself from the tatters of black cloud, and then his own shadow and the shadow of the tower were thrown across the gleaming mud.

Looking at the tower, Rivers thought again how squat and unimpressive it was, and yet how menacing. A resemblance that had merely nagged at him before returned to his mind with greater force. This waste of mud, these sump holes reflecting a dim light at the sky, even that tower. It was like France. Like the battlefields. A resemblance greater by night than by day, perhaps, because here, by day, you could see things grow, and there nothing grew.

– They were always afraid we'd get trapped in the cellars.

– I suppose they flood, don't they? At high tide?

Rivers climbed on to the path, trying to work out where the tide was and whether it was rising or falling, but he could hear only the crash of breaking waves and feel the drizzle of blown spume on his face. In spite of his mud-clogged boots and aching thighs, he started to run. As he neared the tower, a stronger blast of wind sent him staggering off the path. He was slithering and floundering through mud, calling Burns's name, though the sound was snatched from his mouth and carried off into the whistling darkness.

He slid down on to the beach. An outgoing wave sucked shingle after it, but the entrance to the moat was clear. He hesitated, peering into the darkness, afraid that an unusually powerful wave might trap him in there. He called 'David', but he knew he couldn't be heard and would have to go down, into the black darkness, if he were ever to find him.

He groped his way into the moat, steadying himself against the wall. It was so wet, so cold, so evil-smelling, that he thought perhaps the tide had already reached its height and was now falling. At first he could see nothing, but then the moon came out from behind a bank of cloud, and he saw Burns huddled against the moat wall. Rivers called 'David' and realized he was shouting when there was no need. Even the howl of the storm sounded subdued in the shelter of the moat. He touched Burns's arm. He neither moved nor blinked. He was staring up at the tower, which gleamed white, like the bones of a skull.

'Come on, David.'

His body felt like a stone. Rivers got hold of him and held him, coaxing, rocking. He looked up at the tower that loomed squat and menacing above them, and thought, *Nothing justifies this. Nothing nothing nothing.* Burns's body remained rigid in his arms. Rivers was aware that if it came to a fight he might not win. Burns was terribly emaciated, but he was also thirty years younger. His surrender, when it came, was almost shocking. Suddenly his body had the rag-doll floppiness of the newborn. He collapsed against Rivers and started to shake, and from there it was possible to half lead, half push him out of the moat and up on to the relative safety of the path.

At the kitchen table, wrapped in a blanket, Burns said, 'I couldn't seem to get out of the dream. I woke up, I *knew* I was awake, I could move and yet . . . it was still there. My face was dripping. I could taste it.' He tried to laugh. 'And then the bloody maroon went off.'

There were no electric lights. The power lines must be down. They were talking by the light of an oil lamp that smoked and smelled, and left wisps of black smoke like question marks on the air.

'I think we can do without this now,' Rivers said, walking across to the window and pulling the curtains back. He opened the windows and shutters. The storm had almost blown itself out. A weak light seeped into the room, falling on Burns's red eyes and exhausted face.

'Why don't you go to bed? I'll bring you a hot-water bottle if you've got such a thing.'

Rivers saw him settled into bed. Then he went out to the butchers in the High Street, which he'd already noticed was surprisingly well stocked, bought bacon, sausages, kidneys, eggs, took them home and fried them. As he was spooning hot fat over the eggs, he remembered his reaction when he was looking up at the tower. *Nothing can justify this*, he'd thought.

Nothing nothing nothing. He was rather glad not to be faced with the task of explaining that statement to Siegfried.

He sat down at the table and began to eat. He was still chasing the last dribble of egg yolk with a triangle of toast when Mrs Burril came in. She looked at the plates. 'Cracked, did you?' Two unpacked bags later she added, 'Thought you might.'

'Is the boat back?'

'Not yet. I keep busy.'

Rivers went upstairs to check on Burns and found him still asleep. The room was full of books, stacked up on tables and chairs, spilling over on to the floor. Church architecture, country crafts, ornithology, botany and – a slight surprise – theology. He wondered whether this was an expression of faith, or a quest for faith, or simply an obsession with the absence of God.

One of the reasons the books had to be stacked on tables and chairs was that the bookcase was already full of other books: boys' annuals, the adventure stories of Henty, Scouting for Boys. Games too: Ludo and Snakes and Ladders, a bat for beach cricket, collections of pebbles and shells, a strip of bladderwrack. All these things must have been brought here, or collected here, summer by summer, and then outgrown, but never thrown away, so that the room had become a sort of palimpsest of the young life it contained. He looked at Burns's sleeping face, and then tiptoed downstairs.

The lifeboat came back later that morning. Rivers looked out of the living room window and saw it beached at the water's edge, in that narrow space between the coils of tangled and rusting wire. He went out to watch.

The men were laying down the flat wooden skids over which the boat would be winched slowly back into place. A small group of villagers, mainly relatives of the crew, had gathered and were talking in low voices. The sea was choppy, but with none of the menace of the previous night. A light drizzle had begun to fall, matting the surface hairs on the men's jerseys and woollen caps.

When he got back, he found Burns stirring, though not yet up.

'Are they back?' he asked.

'Yes, they're hauling her up now.'

Burns got out of bed and came across to the window. The drizzle had become a downpour. The lifeboat, now halfway up the beach, was obscured by sheets of smoking rain.

'Be a load off Mrs Burril's mind. She's got two sons in the crew.'

'Yes. She said.'

'You mean she spoke?'

'We had quite a chat. I didn't know the lifeboat was such a family matter.'

'Oh, yes. You see it on the memorial in the church. Not a good idea, really. From the woman's point of view.' A long pause. Then Burns added, 'You get the same thing in a battalion. Brothers joining up together.'

Rivers went very still. This was the first time Burns had volunteered any information at all about France. Even in Craiglockhart, where he couldn't altogether avoid talking about it, the bare facts of his war service had had to be prised out of him.

'You know, you'll be writing letters and suddenly you realize you've written the same name twice.'

Rivers said carefully, 'That must be one of the worst jobs.'

'You get used to it. I did it for eighty per cent of the company once.'

A long silence. Rivers was beginning to think he'd dried up, but then he said, 'That was the day before the Somme. They got out there, and there was this bloody great dyke in the way. You couldn't see it from the trench because there were bramble bushes round it. And it wasn't on the map. Everybody bunched up, trying to get across it. German machine-gunners had a field day. And the few who did manage to get across were cut to pieces on the wire. General came round the following day. He said, "My God, did we really order men to attack across that?" Apparently we were intended to be a diversion from the main action. Further south.'

Slowly, Burns began to talk. He'd been promoted captain at the age of twenty-one, and this promotion coincided with the run-up to the Somme campaign. In addition to all the other strains, he'd been aware of a widespread, though unvoiced, opinion in the company that he was too young for the command, though in length of service he had been senior.

The story was one Rivers was well used to hearing: healthy fear had given way to indifference, and this in turn had given way to a constant, overwhelming fear, and the increasing realization that breakdown was imminent. 'I used to go out on patrol every night,' Burns said. 'You tell yourself you're *setting a good example*, or some such rubbish, but actually it's nothing of the kind. You can't let yourself know you want to be wounded, because officers aren't supposed to think like that. And, you see, next to a battle, a patrol is the best chance of getting a good wound. In the trenches, it's shrapnel or head injuries. On patrol, if you're lucky, it's a nice neat little hole in the arm or leg. I've seen men cry with a wound like that.' He laughed. 'Cry for joy. Anyway, it wasn't my luck. Bullets went round me, I swear they did.' A pause. 'It was going to happen anyway, wasn't it?'

'The breakdown? Oh yes. You mustn't attribute breaking down to that one incident.'

'I went on for three days afterwards.'

'Yes, I know.'

They talked for over an hour. Near the end, after they'd been sitting in silence for a while, Burns said quietly, 'Do you know what Christ died of?'

Rivers looked surprised, but answered readily enough. 'Suffocation. Ultimately the position makes it impossible to go on inflating the lungs. A terrible death.'

'That's what I find so horrifying. Somebody had to *imagine* that death. I mean, just in order to invent it as a method of execution. You know that thing in the Bible? "The imagination of man's heart is evil from his youth"? I used to wonder why pick on that? Why his *imagination*? But it's absolutely right.'

Rivers, going downstairs to make the tea, thought that a curious thing had happened during that conversation. For the first time, Burns had been able to put the decomposing corpse into some kind of perspective. True, he hadn't managed to talk about it, but at least it hadn't prevented him, as it so often had in the past, from talking about other, more bearable aspects of his war experience. Yet, at the same time, Rivers's own sense of the horror of the event seemed actually to have increased. It *was* different in kind from other such experiences, he thought, if only because of the complete disintegration of personality it had produced. He was very fond of Burns, but he could discern in him no trace of the qualities he must have possessed in order to be given that exceptionally early command. Not that one could despair of recovery. Rivers knew only too well how often the early stages of change or cure may mimic deterioration. Cut a chrysalis open, and you will find a rotting caterpillar. What you will never find is that mythical creature, half caterpillar, half butterfly, a fit emblem of the human soul, for those whose cast of mind leads them to seek such emblems. No, the process of transformation consists almost entirely of decay. Burns was young, after all. If today really marked a change, a willingness to face his experiences in France, then his condition might improve. In a few years' time it might even be possible to think of him resuming his education, perhaps pursuing that unexpected interest in theology. Though it was difficult to see him as an undergraduate. He had missed his chance of being ordinary.

16

Rivers arrived back at Craiglockhart in the late afternoon of yet
another stormy day. This autumn seemed to have a store of
such days, slapping them down remorselessly, one after the
other, like a fortune-teller with a deadly pack of cards. The trees
had already shed their leaves. They blew across the tennis courts
and, when Rivers pushed open the swing doors, accompanied
him into the hall.

Where a football match seemed to be in progress. A knot of
struggling backs and thighs gradually unravelled, as they became
aware of him standing there. On the black and white tiled floor
lay a mud-brown, pork-pie hat, evidently belonging to a visitor.
Rivers looked round the group and found Sassoon. 'Careful
with that hat, Sassoon,' he said, and passed through on his way
to his office.

Behind him, a much subdued Sassoon picked up the hat,
punched it into some semblance of its former shape, and restored
it to the peg. The other footballers slunk away.

Bryce was standing at the window of his room, looking out
over the leaf-littered tennis courts. Pausing in the doorway,
Rivers thought he looked older, but then he turned, and seemed
as full of energy as ever.

'Did you get my letter?' Rivers asked.

'I did.'

'I've said I'll wait and see how things turn out.'

'Take it, for God's sake. It's quite *obvious* how things are
going to turn out. I don't expect to be here next month.' He
smiled. 'Of course they might appoint *you*.'

Rivers shook his head. 'No, they won't do that. I'm too
identified with you.'

'*Will* you take it?'

'I don't know. Probably.'

More than probably, Rivers thought, returning to his own room. The thought of Craiglockhart without Bryce was intolerable. He sat behind his desk, and looked round the large, overfamiliar room. Whenever he'd come back before, he'd had an almost physical sense of the yoke settling on to his shoulders, beginning to chafe almost before he was into the building. Not this time. He looked at his crowded appointments book and actually managed to feel some affection for it. The offer of a job in London, with its prospect of more frequent contact with other anthropologists, had had the paradoxical effect of making him realize how much he *enjoyed* his work here. It had become of equal importance to him, and he'd begun to think of ways in which the two interests could combine. The condensation and displacement one encountered in the dreams of patients here – might not these mechanisms also be at work in the myth and ritual of primitive people? At any rate it was an idea worth exploring. But these new combinations only occurred because he no longer thought of his work here as an interruption of his 'real' work. Far from it, he thought, spreading his hands across his desk. The work he did in this room was the work he was meant to do, and, as always, this recognition brought peace.

'. . . we actually drove past your place.'

'You should've called in,' Sassoon said. 'Mother wouldn't't've stood on ceremony where *you* were concerned. She regards you as the Saviour of the Family Name. From the Disgrace of Pacifism.'

'Prematurely, perhaps?'

No answer.

'Have you been able to think . . . ?'

'I haven't been able to *think* at all. Look, Rivers, I've never asked you for anything. I've never asked or expected to be treated any differently from anybody else.'

'I should hope not,' Rivers said. 'I don't know what the grounds would be.'

Sassoon came to an abrupt halt. 'All right.'

'No, what were you going to say?'

'I was going to point out that the man in my room is driving me stark, staring mad, but it doesn't matter.'

'That could be grounds for a room change. If true. For *you* as for anybody else. What does he do? Does he sleep badly?'

'Snores like a newborn baby, if newborn babies snore.'

'So what *does* he do?'

'Preaches the consolations of Theosophy in his own inimitable brand of pseudo-medieval English.'

'I can see that might be irritating. Give me an example.'

'Friend of mine, Ralph Greaves. He's ... Is! *Was* a good pianist. He's just had one arm amputated, and the other's almost useless. Do you know what Fothersgill said? "It will assist his spiritual development."'

'Perhaps it would have been wiser not to tell him?'

Silence.

'After all, you must've had some idea of the *kind* of response you were likely to get?'

'I can't keep it in all the time.'

'Look, he's due to be boarded soon. Surely you can put up with the inconvenience for another ... what, *ten days*?'

'We had a row this morning. I pointed out the casualties for September were 102,000 – *official* figures. He said, "Yes, Sassoon, the Celestial Surgeon is at work upon humanity."'

Rivers sighed. He was thinking that Sassoon's insistence of hammering home the bitter reality was probably not doing Fothersgill much good either. 'What does *he* think about *you*? Do you know?'

'I have a disturbed aura. Apparently.'

'Really?'

'Indigo. I'm glad somebody finds it amusing.'

'I was just thinking how useful it would be. Instant diagnosis.'

'I've woken him up once or twice.'

'Nightmares?'

'Not exactly.'

Sassoon was avoiding his eye, but then he often did at the beginning of interviews. 'Do you want to tell me about it?'

'Oh, it was nothing. I just ... saw something I couldn't possibly have seen.'

He thinks I'll despise him for being irrational, Rivers thought. 'I did once see ... well, not see ... *hear* something I couldn't explain. It was on one of the Solomon Islands. On this particular island, the people believe the souls of the dead go to a bay at the other side – the spirits come up to the house in canoes and carry the dead person's soul away. So you have a kind of wake, and on this particular night we were all crowded together, gathered round the corpse, waiting for the sound of paddles. The whole village was there, all these dark brown intently listening faces. And we listened too and asked questions in whispers. The atmosphere was unbelievable. And then a moment came when *they* heard the paddles. You saw this expression of mingled joy and grief spread over all their faces, and of course we heard nothing. Until the moment when the spirits were actually in the room, taking the soul away, and then the whole house was suddenly filled with whistling sounds. I could see all the faces. Nobody was making those sounds, and yet we all heard them. You see, the *rational* explanation for that is that we'd allowed ourselves to be dragged into an experience of mass hypnosis, and I don't for a moment deny that that's possible. But what we'd been told to expect was the swish of paddles. Nobody'd said anything about whistling. That doesn't mean that there *isn't* a rational explanation. Only I don't think that particular rational explanation fits all the facts.'

After Rivers had finished there was a pause. Then Sassoon said, with great difficulty, 'What happened to me started with a noise.'

'What sort of noise?'

'Tapping. It started in Owen's room and then when I went back to my own room it started again. Owen didn't hear it. It didn't bother me particularly, I just went off to sleep and ... when I woke up, somebody was standing just inside the door. I knew who it was. I couldn't see the face, but I recognized his coat.' He paused. 'Orme. Nice lad. Died six months ago.'

'You said "once or twice". The same man?'

'No. Various people.' A long silence. 'I know this must sound like the the kind of thing I was seeing in London, but it isn't. It's ... nothing like that. In London they were clutching holes in their heads and waving their stumps around. These are ... very quiet. Very restrained.' He smiled. 'Obviously you get a better class of hallucination round here.'

188

'What do you feel when you see them?'

Sassoon shrugged. 'I don't feel anything. At the time.'

'You're not frightened?'

'No. That's why I said they weren't nightmares.'

'Afterwards?'

'Guilt.'

'Do they look reproachful?'

Sassoon thought about it. 'No. They just look puzzled. They can't understand why I'm here.'

A long silence. After a while, Sassoon roused himself. 'I wrote about it. I'm sorry, I know you hate this.'

Rivers took the sheet of paper: 'I don't hate it. I just feel inadequate.'

> When I'm asleep, dreaming and drowsed and warm,
> They come, the homeless ones, the noiseless dead.
> While the dim charging breakers of the storm
> Rumble and drone and bellow overhead,
> Out of the gloom they gather about my bed.
> They whisper to my heart; their thoughts are mine.
>
> 'Why are you here with all your watches ended?
> 'From Ypres to Frise we sought you in the line.'
> In bitter safety I awake, unfriended;
> And while the dawn begins with slashing rain
> I think of the Battalion in the mud.
> 'When are you going back to them again?
> 'Are they not still your brothers through our blood?'

Sassoon, who'd got up and walked across to the window, turned round when a movement from Rivers seemed to indicate he'd finished. 'It's all right,' he said. 'Don't feel you have to say something.'

But Rivers was not capable of saying anything. He'd taken off his glasses and was dabbing the skin round his eyes. Sassoon didn't know what to do. He pretended to look out of the window again. At last Rivers put his glasses on again and said, 'Does the question have an answer?'

'Oh, yes. I'm going back.'

A long indrawn breath. 'Have you told anybody else yet?'

'No, I wanted you to be the first.'

'Your pacifist friends won't be pleased.'

'No, I know. I'm not looking forward to that.' He was looking at Rivers with an extraordinary mixture of love and hostility. 'You are, though, aren't you? You're pleased.'

'Oh, yes. I'm pleased.'

Part 4

17

Ada Lumb arrived on the nine o'clock train. Sarah met her at the station, and they spent the morning looking round the shops. Or rather Sarah looked round the shops, while her mother, by a mixture of bullying, wheedling, cajoling, questions, speculations, wild surmises and sudden, bitter silences, extracted the whole story of Sarah's relationship with Billy Prior. By twelve, Sarah was glad to rest her feet, if not her ears, in a café, where they sat at a table for two by the window and ordered ham and chips. The alternative was steak and kidney pie, but Ada was having none of that. 'You can't trust anything with pastry wrapped round it,' she said. 'What they find to put in it, God knows. You've only got to look in the butchers to see there is nowt.'

Sarah was not deceived. She knew once the waitress was out of earshot she was in for a dollop of advice on rather more serious matters. She wiped a hole in the condensation on the window. Outside the people were moving shadows, the pavements of Princes Street jumped and streamed with rain. 'Just in time,' she said.

'I suppose you let him in?'

'*What?*'

'You don't say "what", Sarah. You say "pardon".'

'*What?*'

'I said, I suppose you let him in?'

'Isn't that my business, Mam?'

'Would be if *you* were gunna cope with the consequences.'

'There aren't going to *be* any consequences.'

'You think you know it all, don't you? Well, let me tell you something, something you don't know. In every one of them factories there's a bloke with a pin. Every tenth one gets a pin stuck in it. Not every other one, they know we're not fools. Every tenth.'

'Nice work, if you can get it.'

'Easier than bringing up the kid.' Ada speared a chip. 'The point *is* you gotta put a value on yourself. You don't, they won't. You're never gunna get engaged till you learn to keep your knees together. Yeh, you can laugh, but men don't value what's dished out free. Mebbe they shouldn't be like that, mebbe they should all be different. But they *are* like that and *your* not gunna change them.'

The waitress came to remove their plates. 'Anything else, madam?'

Ada switched to her genteel voice. 'Yes, we'd like to see the menu, please.' She waited till the waitress had gone, then leant forward to deliver the knock-out blow. 'No man likes to think he's sliding in on another man's leavings.'

Sarah collapsed in giggles. '*Mam.*'

'Aye, well, you can laugh.' She looked round the café, then down at the table, smoothing the white table cloth with brown-spotted hands. 'Nice, isn't it?'

Sarah stopped giggling. 'Yeh, Mam, it's nice.'

'I wish *you* worked somewhere like this.'

'Mam, the wages are rubbish. That girl didn't live at home, she wouldn't eat.'

'She's not bright yellow, though, is she?'

'She not bright anything. She looks anaemic to me.'

'But you meet nice people, Sarah. I mean I know some of the women you work with, and I'm not saying they're not good sorts – some of them – but you got to admit, Sarah, they're *rough.*'

'I'm rough.'

'You could've been a lady's maid if you'd stuck in. That's what gets me about you, you can put it on as well as anybody when you like, but it's too much bloody bother.'

The waitress returned with the menu.

'I don't think I could eat anything else, Mam.'

Ada looked disappointed. 'Aw, go on. It's not often I get a chance to spoil you.'

'All right, then. I'll have the tapioca, please.'

Sarah ate in silence for a while, aware of her mother watching her. At last, she said, 'Trouble is, Mam, the block chipped and you don't like it.'

Ada shook her head. It was true all the same, Sarah thought. Ada, ox-jawed, determined, ruthless, had struggled to bring up her two girls alone, and yet, when it came to *teaching* the girls, she'd tried to encourage all the opposite qualities. Prettiness, pliability – at least the appearance of it – all the arts of pleasing. This was how women got on in the world, and Ada had made sure her daughters knew it. As little girls, Cynthia and Sarah had gone to the tin-roofed chapel at the end of the road, but as soon as their bodices revealed curves rather than straight lines, Ada had called them to her and announced their conversion to Anglo-Catholicism. The Church of St Edmund, King and Martyr, served a very nice neighbourhood. There, Cynthia had obediently ogled the young men in the choir, while Sarah, missing the point completely, had fallen in love with the Virgin Mary. Ada's ambition was to see her daughters go down that aisle in white, on the arm of some young man with a steady income. If, subsequently, early widowhood left them with the income and not the man, then they were indeed blessed. Whether *Ada* was a widow or not, Sarah didn't know. It had never been made clear whether her father had departed this life, the town, or merely his marriage. Certainly black bombazine figured prominently in Ada's wardrobe, but then it was a material that conferred an air of awesome respectability at minimal cost. A dispiriting way to bring girls up, Sarah thought; to make marriage the sole end of female existence, and yet deny that love between men and women was possible. Ada *did* deny it. In *her* world, men loved women as the fox loves the hare. And women loved men as the tapeworm loves the gut. Nor did this view of life generate much sympathy for other women. Ada despised the hares, those who 'got caught'. If a girl came into the shop crying, she might sell her Dr Lawson's Cure, the Sovereign Remedy for Female Blockages and Obstructions (ninepence a bottle, and totally useless), but her sympathy ended there. The business of her life was scratching a living together; her recreation was reading romances, which she devoured three or four at a time, sitting in her rocking chair by the fire, sucking mint humbugs and laughing till her ribs ached.

'How's the tea hut going, Mam?' Sarah asked, pushing her plate away.

'Fine. I'm up there every day now.'

Ada had taken to selling tea to soldiers, young conscripts who did their six weeks' training in one of the local parks before being shipped out to France. The hut, which in peace time had been the boating lake ticket office, she'd turned into a small café.

'How much do you charge?'

'Fivepence.'

'My God.'

Ada shrugged. 'No competition.'

'You're a war profiteer you are, Mam. In a small way.'

'Wouldn't be small if I could get me hands on some money. You could do soup and all sorts, specially with the winter coming on. But it's the same old story. You need money to make money.'

Ada paid the bill, counting out the coppers with those thin, lined hands that Sarah could never see without pain.

'You know Billy?' Sarah asked suddenly.

'No, I don't, Sarah. I've not had the pleasure of an introduction.'

'Well if you'll just listen. If he gets slung out the hospital this time, he'll have a bit of leave, and we thought we might . . . We thought we might drop in on you.'

'Really?'

'Is that all you can say?'

'What am I supposed to say? Look, Sarah, he's an officer. What do you think he wants *you* for?'

'How should I know? Breath of fresh air, perhaps.'

'Bloody gale.'

'If he does come, you will be all right with him, won't you?'

'If he's all right with me, I'll be all right with him.' Ada slipped a penny under the saucer. 'But you're a bloody fool.'

'Why am I?'

'You know why. Next time he starts waving his old doo-lally around, you think about that pin.'

Sassoon arrived late to find Graves sitting by himself in the bar. 'Sorry I'm late.'

'That's all right. Owen was keeping me amused, but then he had to go. Somebody coming to see the printer.'

'Yes, that's right. I'd forgotten that.'

'Good game?'

'Not bad.' Sassoon detected, or thought he detected, a slight chill. 'It's the only thing that keeps me sane.'

'Last time you wrote you were complaining about playing golf with lunatics.'

'Ssh, keep your voice down. One of them's just behind you.'

Graves turned round. 'Seems fairly normal to me.'

'Oh, Anderson's all right. Throws a temper tantrum whenever he looks like losing half a crown.'

'You've been known to do *that* yourself.'

'Only because you were fooling around with a niblick instead of playing properly.' He raised a hand to summon the waiter. 'Have you had time to look at the menu?'

'I've had time to memorize it, Siegfried.'

At the table Graves said, 'What do you find to talk to Owen about? He says he doesn't play golf. And I don't suppose for a moment he hunts.'

'How acute your social perceptions are, Robert. No, I shouldn't think he'd been on a horse in his life before he joined the army. Poetry, mainly.'

'Oh, he *writes*, does he?'

'No need to say it like that. He's quite good. Matter of fact, I've got one here.' He tapped his breast pocket. 'I'll show you after lunch.'

'He struck me as being a bit shaky.'

'Did he? I don't think he is.'

'I'm just telling you how he struck me.'

'He can't be all that shaky. They're throwing him out at the end of the month. He was probably just overawed at meeting another Published Poet.'

A slight pause.

'Aren't you due to be boarded soon?'

'The end of the month.'

'Have you decided what you're going to do?'

'I've told Rivers I'll go back, *provided* the War Office gives me a written guarantee that I'll be sent back to France.'

'I wouldn't have thought you were in much of a position to *bargain*.'

'Rivers seems to think he can wangle it. He didn't say "wangle" of course.'

'So it's all over? Thank God.'

'I've told him I won't withdraw anything. And I've told him it's got to be France. I'm *not* going to let them put me behind a desk filling in forms for the rest of the war.'

'Yes, I think that's right.'

'Trouble is I don't trust them. Even Rivers. I mean, on the one hand he says there's nothing wrong with me and they'll pass me for general service overseas – there's nothing else they can do – and then in the next breath he tells me I've got a very powerful "anti-war complex". I don't even know what it means.'

'I'll tell you what it means. It means you're *obsessed*. Do you know, you never talk about the future any more? Yes, I know what you're going to say. How can you? Sass, we sat on a hill in France and we talked about the future. We *made plans*. The night before the Somme, we made plans. You couldn't do that now. A few shells, a few corpses, and you've lost heart.'

'How many corpses?'

'The point is . . .'

'The point is 102,000 last month *alone*. You're right, I am obsessed. I never forget it for a second, *and neither should you*. Robert, if you had any *real* courage you wouldn't acquiesce the way you do.'

Graves flushed with anger. 'I'm sorry you think that. I should hate to think I'm a coward. I believe in keeping my word. You agreed to serve, Siegfried. Nobody's asking you to change your opinions, or even to keep quiet about them, but you *agreed to serve*, and if you want the respect of the kind of people you're trying to influence – the Bobbies and the Tommies – you've got to be seen to *keep your word*. They won't understand if you turn round in the middle of the war and say "I'm sorry, I've changed my mind." To them, that's just bad form. They'll say you're not behaving like a gentleman – and that's the worst thing they can say about anybody.'

'Look, Robert, the people who're keeping this war going don't give a damn about the "Bobbies" and the "Tommies". And they don't let "gentlemanly behaviour" stand in the way either when it comes to feathering their own nests.' He made a gesture of despair. 'And as for "bad form" and "gentlemanly behaviour" – that's just suicidal stupidity.'

Over coffee, the conversation changed tack.

'There's something I didn't tell you in June,' Graves said. 'Do you remember Peter?'

'I never met him.'

'No, but you remember him? You remember *about* him? Well, he was arrested. Soliciting outside the local barracks. Actually not very far away from the school.'

'Oh, Robert, I'm sorry. Why didn't you *tell* me?'

'How could I? You were in no state to think about anybody else.'

'This was in July, was it?'

'Same post I got your Declaration in.' Graves smiled. 'It was quite a morning.'

'Yes, I can imagine.'

Graves hesitated. 'It's only fair to tell you that . . . since that happened my affections have been running in more normal channels. I've been writing to a girl called Nancy Nicholson. I really think you'll like her. She's great fun. The . . . the only reason I'm telling you this is . . . I'd hate you to have any misconceptions. About me. I'd hate you to think I was homosexual *even in thought*. Even if it went no further.'

It was difficult to know what to say. 'I'm very pleased for you, Robert. About Miss Nicholson, I mean.'

'Good, that's all right, then.'

'What happened to Peter?'

'You're not going to believe this. They're sending him to Rivers.'

This was a bigger, and nastier, shock than Sassoon knew how to account for. 'Why?'

'What do you mean, "Why?"? To be cured, of course.'

Sassoon smiled faintly. 'Yes. Of course.'

The munitions factory at night looked like hell, Sarah thought, as she toiled down the muddy lane towards it, and saw the red smouldering fires reflected from a bank of low cloud, like an artificial sunset. At the gate she fell in with the other girls all walking in the same direction, all subdued, with that clogged, dull look of people who'd just switched to night shift and hadn't yet managed to adjust.

In the cloakroom, donning ankle-length green overalls, pulling on caps, dragging at a final cigarette, were thirty or forty women. Smells of sweat, lily-of-the-valley, setting lotion. After a while conversations sprang up, the women appeared more normal, even jolly for a time, until the supervisor appeared in the doorway, jabbing her finger at the clock.

'Your mam get off all right, then?' Lizzie asked, as they were walking down the stairs to the basement workroom.

'Got the seven o'clock. She'll be back by midnight, so it's not so bad.'

'How did it go?'

Sarah pulled a face. 'All right. You know, I swore I wasn't gunna tell her about Billy, but she winkled it all out of me.'

'Well, she is your mam. She's bound to be worried.'

'Hm. All I could get out of her was: "What does he see in *you*?" 'S a nice thing to say to your daughter, isn't it? I says, "A breath of fresh air." As far as I can make out they're all disappearing up their own arseholes up there.'

'Long as it's only their own,' Lizzie said.

'They're not all like that,' Sarah said.

'Biggest part are,' said Madge. 'Place I used to work before the war, the son were like that. Oh, and when they found out you should've heard Missus. She *stomped* and she *shrieked*. Chandelier were going like that, I thought bugger were coming down. But you know he had no sisters, so he never met lasses that way. Goes to school, no lasses. Goes to university – no lasses. Time he finally claps eyes on me, it's too late, isn't it? It's *gelled*. And even the ones that aren't like that, they take one look at the Missus and bugger off round the Club.' Madge strutted along the basement corridor with a finger held be:o··· her nose, saying in a strangled, public school accent, '"I shall be dining at the Club tonight, m'dear. Don't bother to wait u··.' Then he staggers in at two o'clock and flops out on bed in dressing room. Beats me how they breed.'

Raucous laughter from the other women as they spilled into the work room and sat down at the benches. The supervisor, a round-faced, bespectacled, crop-haired lady in a severely tailored suit, bore down upon them. 'Do you girls ever intend to start work?'

They watched her walk away. 'Eeh, I hope a man never tries to shove anything up her flue,' Lizzie said. 'Be cruelty to moths.'

Sarah pulled the first belt towards her and started to work. No reason at all why they couldn't talk, since the task here required no concentration. It was intended as a break from the very demanding work on detonators, and from other jobs too, where masks had to be worn. Rather badly fitting masks. On more than one occasion Sarah had pulled hers away from her face and shaken out the yellow dust that had collected inside it. She remembered her mother's strictures on her appearance, the broad hints she'd dropped about handing in her notice and going home to help with the tea hut. But I like it here, Sarah thought. And then she corrected herself. You like it *now* because Billy's here. You mightn't be so keen when he's gone.

She turned, cautiously, to avoid attracting the supervisor's attention, and looked round. The women sat at small tables, each table forming a pool of light under a low-hanging bulb. Apart from the work surfaces, the room was badly lit and so vast that its far end disappeared into shadow. All the women were yellow-skinned, and all, whatever their colouring, had a frizz of ginger hair peeping out from under the green cap. We don't look human, Sarah thought, not knowing whether to be dismayed or amused. They looked like machines, whose sole function was to make other machines.

Sarah's eyes fell on the next table, where the girls were close enough to be identified. After a while she looked puzzled and leant across the table to whisper to Lizzie. 'Where's Betty?'

'You may well ask,' Lizzie said. She sniffed and remained silent, enjoying the moment of power.

'I am asking.'

Lizzie glanced round quickly. 'You know she's missed four times?'

All the girls nodded.

'Tried everything,' Lizzie said. 'She was supping Dr Lawson's Cure as if it was lemonade.'

'It is,' said Sarah.

'Well, she must've got desperate, because she stuck summat up herself to bring it on. You know them wire coat hangers?'

Nods all round.

'One of them. She straightened the curved bit and –'

'We get the picture,' Sarah said.

'Yeh, well it's worse than that. Silly little cow shoved it in her bladder.'

'*Aw no.*' Madge turned away as if she were going to vomit.

'She was in agony. And you know she kept begging them not to send her to the hospital, because like she knew she hadn't come all right. But anyway the girl she's lodging with got that frightened she went and fetched the landlady. Well of course she took one look. She more or less says, "Sorry, love, you're not dying here." Took her in. And the irony of it is she's still pregnant. She looks awful.'

'You mean you've been to see her?' Sarah asked.

'Why aye. Went last night. You know, her face is all . . .' Lizzie dragged her cheeks down. 'Oh, and she says the doctor didn't half railroad her. She was crying her eyes out, poor lass. He says, "You should be ashamed of yourself," he says. "It's not just an inconvenience you've got in there," he says. "It's a human being."'

Sarah and Madge were eager to know more, but the supervisor had noticed the pause in Lizzie's work and came striding towards them, though when she reached the table she found only silence and bowed heads and feverishly working fingers flicking machine-gun bullets into place inside the glittering belts.

On the night before a Board, Rivers took longer than usual over his rounds, since he knew the patients whose turn it was to be boarded would be feeling particularly tense. He was worried about Pugh, who had somehow managed to convince himself, in spite of repeated reassurances to the contrary, that he was to be sent back to France.

Sassoon, Rivers left till last, and found him lying on the bed in his new room, wrapped in his British warm coat. It was needed. The room was immediately beneath the tower and so cold that, in winter, patients who'd sweated their way through a succession of nightmares often woke to find the bedclothes stiff with frost. Siegfried seemed to like it, though, and at least now he had the privacy he needed to work. Rivers took the only available chair, and stretched out his legs towards the empty grate. 'Well, how do you feel about tomorrow?'

'All right. Still nothing from the War Office?'

'No, I'm afraid not. You'll just have to trust us.'

'*Us?* You're sure you don't mean "them"?'

'You know I'll go on doing anything I can for you.'

'Oh, I know *that*. But the *fact* is once they've got me out of here they can do what they like. Pen-pushing in Bognor, here I come.'

Rivers hesitated. 'You sound rather down.'

'No-o. Missing Robert. Don't know why, we came quite close to quarrelling.'

'About the war?'

'I don't know what about. Except he was in a peculiar mood.' Sassoon stopped, then visibly decided to continue. 'He had a bit of bad news recently.'

Rivers was aware of more going on in this conversation than he could identify. Sassoon had been distinctly reserved with him recently. He'd noticed it yesterday evening particularly, but he'd put it down to pre-Board nerves, and the worry of not hearing from the War Office. 'From France?'

'Oh, no, something quite different. I did *ask* if he'd mind my telling you, so I'm not breaking a confidence. Friend of his – a boy he knew at school and was very fond of – in an entirely honourable, platonic *Robert-like* way – got arrested for soliciting. Outside a barracks, actually not very far away from the school. As far as I can make out, Robert feels . . .' Sassoon came to a halt. '*Well*. Rather as you might feel if you were . . . walking down a pleasant country road and suddenly a precipice opened at your feet. That's how he sees it. Devastated. Because, you see, this . . . this *abominable* thing must've been there all the time, and *he didn't see it*. He's very anxious to make it clear that . . . *he* has no such disgusting feelings himself. We-ell.'

'So you were left feeling . . . ?'

'Like a precipice on a country road.'

'Yes.'

Sassoon looked straight at Rivers. 'Apparently he's being – the boy – sent to some psychiatrist or other.'

'Which school was this?'

'Charterhouse.'

'Ah.' Rivers looked up and found Sassoon's gaze on him.

'To be *cured*.' A slight pause. 'I suppose cured *is* the right word?'

Rivers said cautiously, 'Surely it's better for him to be sent to this psychiatrist than to go to prison?' In spite of himself he started to smile. 'Though I can see *you* might not think so.'

'He wouldn't have got prison!'

'Oh, I think he might. The number of custodial sentences is rising. I think any psychiatrist in London would tell you that.'

Sassoon looked downcast. 'I thought things were getting better.'

'I think they were. Before the war. *Slightly*. But it's not very likely, is it, that any movement towards greater tolerance would persist in wartime? After all, in war, you've got this *enormous* emphasis on love between men – comradeship – and everybody approves. But at the same time there's always this little niggle of anxiety. Is it the right *kind* of love? Well, one of the ways you make sure it's the right kind is to make it crystal clear what the penalties for the other kind are.' He looked at Sassoon. 'One of the reasons I'm so glad you've decided to go back. It's not just police activity. It's the whole atmosphere at the moment. There's an MP called Pemberton Billing. I don't know whether you've heard of him?'

Sassoon shook his head. 'I don't think so.'

'Well, he's going around London claiming to know of the existence of a German *Black Book* containing the names of 47,000 eminent people whose *private lives* make their loyalty to their country suspect.'

'Relax, Rivers. I'm not eminent.'

'No, but you're a friend of Robert Ross, and you've publicly advocated a negotiated peace. That's enough! You're *vulnerable*, Siegfried. There's no point pretending you're not.'

'And what am I supposed to do about it? Toe the line, tailor my opinions –'

'Not your opinions. I think you told me once that Robert Ross opposes the war? *In private.*'

'I wouldn't want to criticize Ross. I think I know him well enough to understand the impact those trials had on him. But what you're really saying is, if I *can't* conform in one area of life, then I *have* to conform in the others. Not just the surface things, *everything*. Even against my conscience. Well, I can't live like that.' He paused, then added, '*Nobody* should live like that.'

'You spend far too much time tilting at windmills, Siegfried. In ways which do *you* a great deal of damage — which I happen to care about — and don't do anybody else any good at all.' He hesitated, then said it anyway. 'It's time you grew up. Started living in the real world.'

18

Prior was not making a good impression. Getting a few simple facts out of him was like extracting wisdom teeth. At first Rivers thought Prior was simply being awkward – always a fairly safe assumption with Prior – but then he noted the tension in his jaw and realized the extent of the internal conflict that was going on. Prior had said he wanted nothing more than to get back to France as soon as possible, to get away from what he called 'the shame' of home service, and Rivers had no doubt that was true. But it was not the whole truth. He also wanted to save his life, and, in insisting on the importance of the asthmatic attacks, Rivers had, perhaps cruelly, held out the hope that he might be permitted to live. Small wonder, then, that Prior answered questions in monosyllables and finally, when asked whether he felt physically fit for service, said nothing at all, simply stared at Huntley, unable either to claim that he was ill or to deny it. Watching him, Rivers was filled with the most enormous compassion for his dilemma. Poor little blighter, he thought. Poor all of them.

Outside in the waiting room Sassoon looked at his watch. They were running almost an hour late and he wasn't even next. Pugh was next. Pugh was a Welshman with prominent green eyes and the worst twitch Sassoon had ever seen, even in Craiglockhart, that living museum of tics and twitches. Pugh's consisted of a violent sideways movement of the head, accompanied by a sound midway between a gasp and a scream. He did this approximately every thirty-five seconds. Like everybody else in the hospital, Sassoon's reflexes were conditioned by the facts of trench warfare. It was almost impossible for him not to dodge whatever it was Pugh was dodging. Something Owen had told him about Pugh was hovering round the fringes of his mind. Yes, that was it. Some kind of freak accident, a hand grenade bouncing off the wire. Pugh had been picking bits of his platoon off his gas cape for an hour.

Sassoon looked at his watch again. Even allowing for the fact that nobody in their right mind could take long to decide whether Pugh was fit for duty, he couldn't hope to be out of the place before six. He was supposed to have tea with the Sampsons at four thirty. Even if he left now and caught a tram immediately, he still wouldn't be on time. It was too bad. People who were prepared to die had at least the right not to be kept waiting. He closed his eyes again. He was so tired he really thought if it wasn't for Pugh and that dreadful jerking, he might have managed to nod off. He'd hardly slept at all last night.

In his breast pocket was a letter from Joe Cotterill, the Battalion Quartermaster. Sassoon knew it almost off by heart. Joe's journey to Polygon Wood with the rations, the ground as full of holes as a pepperpot lid, nothing but mud and dead trees as far as the eye could see. They'd spent the night in a shell-hole, lost, under heavy fire. Several of the ration party had been killed. But, said Joe, the battalion got their rations. Reading that, Sassoon had wanted to rush back to France at once, but then, right at the end of the letter, Joe had said: *Buck up and get out of there. Go to Parliament. Surely they can't keep you there against your will?* The trouble was, Sassoon thought, sighing and looking at his watch, that Joe's anonymous 'they' was his Rivers.

Thorpe arrived. 'D-d-d-do w-w-w-wwe kn-kn-know w-whwhat's t-t-t-taking s-s-so l-l-long?' he asked after a while.

Sassoon shook his head. Pugh shook his head too, though whether in answer to the question it was difficult to tell. And suddenly Sassoon had had enough. 'And I for one don't intend to stay and find out.'

He had a fleeting impression of Thorpe and Pugh with their mouths open, and then he was striding out of the room, down the corridor, through the swing doors and away.

'Pugh next, I think?' said Bryce.

'Hang on, old chap,' Huntley said. 'Got to pump ship.'

The door closed behind him. Bryce said, 'Where do you suppose he finds these nautical expressions?' Receiving no reply, he turned to Rivers.

'Why we had to take an hour over *that* I shall never know.'

'Prior didn't help himself much, did he?'

Rivers didn't answer.

'And at least you got what you wanted. In the end.'

The major came back, buttoning his breeches. 'All right, all right,' he said, as if *he*'d been waiting for *them*. 'Let's get on.'

Pugh was quick and distressing. Since the orderly had gone off to have dinner, Rivers himself went into the waiting room to summon Sassoon. Thorpe was sitting there alone. 'Have you seen Sassoon?'

'He's . . .' Thorpe went into one of his paroxysms. 'G-g-g-g-gone.'

'G-g-?' Deep breath. '*Where* has he gone?'

Thorpe economized with a shrug. Rivers walked along to the patients' common room and looked for Sassoon there, and instead found Prior, sitting at the piano picking out a few notes. Prior looked up. Rivers, thinking it was a long time to wait till the result was officially announced, stuck his thumb in the air and smiled.

'All right, Thorpe,' he said, going back to the ante-room. 'You'd better come in.'

Rivers came out of Thorpe's Board to find Sassoon still missing and Sister Duffy hovering in the corridor, wanting to talk about Prior. 'Crying his eyes out,' she said. 'I thought he'd *got* permanent home service?'

'He did.'

Rivers went up to Prior's room and found him sitting on the bed, not crying now, though rather swollen about the eyes.

'I suppose I'm expected to be grateful?'

'No.'

'Good. Because I'm not.'

Rivers tried to suppress a smile.

'I told you I *didn't want it*.'

'It's not a question of what you *want*, is it? It's a question of whether you're fit.'

'I was all right. It never stopped me doing anything the others did.'

'Now that's not quite true, is it? You told me yourself you were excused running through the gas huts, because on the one occasion you tried it, you collapsed. Your participation in gas-training exercises was restricted to listening to lectures. Wasn't it?'

No response.

'It's all very well to joke about being the battalion canary, but it's true, isn't it? You *would* be overcome by gas at much lower concentrations than most people, and that could be very dangerous. *And not just for you.*'

Prior turned away.

Rivers sighed. 'You realize the other man who got permanent home service is throwing a party tonight?'

'Good for him. I hope it's a good party.'

'Why do you hate it so much?'

Silence. After a while, Prior said, 'I suppose I'm not your patient any more, am I?'

'No.'

'So I don't have to put up with *this*?'

It was on the tip of Rivers's tongue to point out that the relief was mutual, but he looked at the swollen eyes and restrained himself. 'What don't you have to put up with?'

'The blank wall. The silences. The *pretending*.'

'Look. At the moment you hate me because I've been instrumental in getting you something you're ashamed of wanting. I can't do much about the hatred, but I do think you should look at the shame. Because it's not really anything to be ashamed *of*, is it? Wanting to stay alive? You'd be a very strange sort of animal if you didn't.'

Prior shook his head. 'You don't understand.'

'Tell me, then.'

'I'll never know now, will I? About myself . . .'

'But you do know. You were a perfectly satisfactory officer, until –'

'Until the strain got to me and I stopped being *a perfectly satisfactory officer*. Where does that leave me?'

'With the whole of your life ahead of you and other challenges to face.'

'If *you* were a patient here, don't you think you'd feel ashamed?'

'Probably. Because I've been brought up the same way as

209

everybody else. But I hope I'd have the *sense*, or – whatever it is – the *intelligence* to see how unjustified it was.'

Prior was shaking his head. 'Not possible. The hoop's there, you jump through it. If you question it, you've failed. If it's taken away from you, you've failed.'

'No, I don't see that. If it's taken away, it's out of your hands. You didn't *ask* for permanent home service. You were *given* it, on the basis of Eaglesham's report. *Not my report*. There's nothing in your psychological state to prevent your going back.'

Prior didn't answer. Rivers said gently, 'Everybody who survives feels guilty. Don't let it spoil everything.'

'It's not that. Well, partly. It's just that I've never let the asthma stop me. I was *ordered* to stay out of those gas huts, *I* was quite prepared to go through them. Even as a – a child I was *determined* it wasn't going to stop me. I could do anything the others did, and not only that, I could *beat* them. I'm not suggesting this is peculiar to me, I – I think most asthmatics are like that. My mother was always pulling the other way. Trying to keep me in. I shouldn't criticize the poor woman, I think she probably saved my life, but she did *use* it. She wanted me in the house away from all the *nasty rough boys*. And then suddenly here *you* are . . .' He raised his hands. 'Doing exactly the same thing.' He looked at Rivers, a cool, amused, mocking, affectionate, highly intelligent stare. 'Probably why I never wanted you to be *Daddy*. I'd got you lined up for a worse fate.'

Rivers, remembering the nanny goat, smiled. He was rather glad Prior didn't have access to his thoughts.

'Thanks for putting up with me.'

This was muttered so gracelessly Rivers wasn't sure he'd heard correctly.

'I was an absolute pig.'

'Never.'

Prior hesitated. 'Would you mind if I looked you up after the war?'

'*Mind?* I'd be delighted. Though I don't see why you have to wait till after the war. You can always write to me here. If – if I've moved on, they'll know where I am.'

'Thanks. I will write.'

At the door Rivers turned. 'If I don't see you again before you go, good luck.'

It was an effort to talk at dinner, partly tiredness, partly Sassoon's empty place. By now it was clear he'd deliberately skipped the Board. He'd left the Sampsons at six o'clock, but hadn't yet returned to the hospital. It was possible he was having dinner at the Club, putting off the moment when he'd have to face Rivers, but he was impetuous enough, and perhaps desperate enough, to take the train for London and launch himself into some further crackpot scheme to stop the war. Rivers knew the full extent of the dilemma that would face him if Sassoon *had* deserted and *did* make another public protest. He would be asked to take part in declaring him insane; they would never court-martial him. Not now. The casualty lists were too terrible to admit of any public debate on the continuation of the war.

Rivers roused himself to take part in the conversation to find Major Huntley riding one of his hobby horses again. Racial degeneration, this time. The falling birth rate. The need to keep up what he called 'the supply of heroes'. Did Rivers know that private soldiers were on average *five inches* shorter than their officers? And yet it was often the better type of woman who chose to limit the size of her family, while her feckless sisters bred the Empire to destruction. Rivers listened as politely as he could to the major's theories on how the women of Britain might be brought back to a proper sense of their duties, but it was a relief when dinner was over, and he could plead pressure of work and escape to his own room.

He'd left a message with Sister Duffy that Sassoon was to be sent to him as soon as he got back, no matter how late that might be. It was very late indeed. He came in, looking penitent and sheepish.

Rivers said, 'Sit down.'

Sassoon sat, folded his large hands in his lap, and waited. His demeanour was very much that of a keen, and basically decent, head boy who knows he's let the headmaster down rather badly, and is probably in for 'a bit of a wigging', but expects it to be all right in the end. Nothing could have been more calculated to drive Rivers to fury. 'I'm sure you have a perfectly satisfactory explanation.'

'I was late for tea with Sampson.'

Rivers closed his eyes. 'That's it?'

'Yes.'

'It would have been quite impossible for you to *telephone* Sampson, and *tell* him that you were going to be late?'

'It didn't seem . . . courteous. It –'

'And what about the courtesy due to Major Bryce? Major Huntley? Don't you think you at least owed them an *explanation* before you walked out?'

Silence.

'Why, Siegfried?'

'I couldn't face it.'

'Now that *does* surprise me. Juvenile behaviour I might have expected from you, but never cowardice.'

'I'm not offering excuses.'

'You're not offering anything. Certainly not *reasons*.'

'I'm not sure there are any. I was fed up with being kept waiting. I thought if I was going to *die*, at least other people could make the effort to be on time. It was . . .' A deep breath. 'Petulance.'

'So you can't suggest a reason?'

'I've told you, there aren't any.'

'I don't believe you.'

'Look, I'll apologize. I'll *grovel* if you like.'

'I'm not interested in your grovelling. I'd rather you told the truth.'

Sassoon wriggled in his chair. 'All right. I've had this idea floating around in my mind, for . . . oh, for five or six weeks. I thought if I could get myself passed fit and then go to London, I could see somebody like . . . Charles Mercier.'

'*Dr* Mercier?'

'Yes.'

'Why on earth would you want to see him?'

'For a second opinion. He's all right, isn't he?'

'Oh, yes, you couldn't do better. Except that . . . if you'd just been passed fit by the Board – why would you need to see Mercier?'

'So they couldn't say I'd had a relapse, if I went on with the protest.'

Rivers sat back in his chair. 'Oh, I see.'

Silence.

'And had you definitely decided to do that?'

'I hadn't definitely decided anything. If you want the *reason* I walked out, that's probably it. It suddenly struck me that in a few hours' time I'd be packing and I had no idea where I was going. And then at the back of my mind there was the idea that if I went to Mercier I'd be . . .'

Rivers waited.

'Doing the dirty on you.'

'You could've had a second opinion at any time. I'd no idea you wanted it. People whose psychiatrists tell them they're completely sane don't usually ask for second opinions.'

'That *is* what they'd do, though, isn't it? Say I'd had a relapse?'

'Yes. Probably. I take it you've definitely decided not to go back?'

'No, I want to go back.'

Rivers slumped in his chair. 'Thank God. I don't pretend to understand, but thank God.' After a while he added, 'You know the real irony in all this? This morning I had a letter from the War Office. Not exactly an undertaking to send you back, but . . . signs of progress.'

'And now I've gone and ruined it all by having tea with an astronomer.'

'Oh, I don't suppose you have. I'll write to them tonight.'

Sassoon looked at the clock.

'Well, we don't want him hearing it from Huntley, do we? By the way, late as it is, I think Major Bryce would still like to see you.'

Sassoon took the hint and stood up. 'What do you think he'll do?'

'No idea. *Roast* you, I hope.'

19

Prior had never broken into a house before. Not that he was exactly breaking into this one, he reminded himself, though it felt like it, standing cold and shivering in the back yard, in a recess between what must be, he supposed, the coalhouse and the shithouse. He wrapped his coat more tightly round him and craned his neck to see the sky. Light cloud, no moon, stars pricking through, a snap of frost.

He was waiting for the signal of the lamp at Sarah's window, but she was a long time coming, and there was a chill inside him that had nothing to do with the cold. The darkness, the nervousness, the repeated unnecessary swallowing . . . He was back in France, waiting to go out on patrol.

He remembered the *feel* of No Man's Land, the vast, unimaginable space. By day, seen through a periscope, this immensity shrank to a small, pock-marked stretch of ground, snarled with wire. You never got used to the discrepancy. Part of its power to compel the imagination lay precisely in that. It was the difference between *seeing* a mouth ulcer and probing it with your tongue. He told himself he was never going back, he was free, but the word 'free' rang hollow. *Hurry up, Sarah*, he thought.

He was beginning to wonder whether she'd met her landlady on the stairs, when a light appeared at the window. Immediately, he started to climb, clambering from the rusting washer on to the sloping roof of the scullery. Nothing difficult about the climb, the only hazard was the poor state of the tiles. He shuffled along, trying not to make too much noise, though if they did hear they'd probably think it was a cat.

Sarah's room was on the first floor. As he reached the main wall, he stood up, cautiously, and hooked his fingertips into the crack between two bricks. Sarah's window was perhaps three feet away, but there was a convenient drainpipe. He swung his left foot out, got a toe-hold on the drainpipe – fortunately in a better state of repair than the roof – and launched himself at the dark hole. He landed safely, though not quietly, colliding with Sarah, who'd come back to see why he was taking so long. They froze, listening for any response. When none came, they looked at each other, and smiled.

Sarah was carrying an oil lamp. She set it down on the table by the bed, and went to draw the curtains. He was glad to have the night shut out, with its memories of fear and worried sentries whispering. She turned back into the room.

They looked at each other, not finding anything to say. The bed, though only a single, seemed very big. Their imminent nakedness made them shy of each other. In all the weeks of love-making, they'd never once been able to undress. Prior was touched by Sarah's shyness, and a little ashamed of his own.

With an air of unconcern, he started to look round the room. Apart from the bed, there was a bedside table, a chair, a chest of drawers, and a washbasin, squeezed into the corner beside the window. A camisole hung from the back of the chair, and a pair of stays lay on the floor beside it. Sarah, seeing the direction of his gaze, kicked them under the chair.

'It's all right,' he said. 'I'm not tidy.'

The sound of his voice released them from nervousness. Prior sat on the bed, and patted it for her to come and sit beside him.

'We'd better not talk much,' she said. 'I told them I'd be late back, but if they hear voices they'll all be in.'

He couldn't have talked much anyway; his breath caught in his throat. They stared at each other. He reached up and unpinned her hair, shaking it out at the sides of her head. Then they lay down side by side, still gazing at each other. At this distance, her eyes merged into a single eye, fringed by lashes like prehistoric vegetation, a mysterious, scarcely human pool. They lay like that for ten or fifteen minutes, neither of them wanting to hurry, amazed at the time that lay ahead.

After a while Prior rolled over on to his back and looked at the photograph on the bedside table, moving the lamp so he could see better. A wedding group. Cynthia's wedding, he thought, and that rather fat, pasty-faced soldier, smiling sheepishly at the centre of the group, must now be dead. People in group photographs look either idiotic or insane, their faces frozen in anticipation of the flash. Not Sarah's mother. Even in sepia, her eyes jetted sparks. And that *jaw*. It would've been remarkable on a man. 'Your mother looks like my doctor,' he said. He looked at the photograph again. 'She's not smiling much, is she?'

'She was smiling at the memorial service.' She looked at the photograph. 'I love her, you know.'

'Of cou . . .' He stopped. Why 'of course'? He didn't love his father.

'I'm glad you're not going back.'

Without warning, Prior saw again the shovel, the sack, the scattered lime. The eyeball lay in the palm of his hand. 'Yes,' he said.

She would never know, because he would never tell her. Somehow if she'd known the worst parts, she couldn't have gone on being a haven for him. He was groping for an idea that he couldn't quite grasp. Men said they didn't tell their women about France because they didn't want to worry them. But it was more than that. He needed her ignorance to hide in. Yet, at the same time, he wanted to know and be known as deeply as possible. And the two desires were irreconcilable.

'Do you think your mam'll like me?'

They'd arranged to spend part of his leave together.

'Not as much as she would if you were going back.'

'Tell her about me lungs. That'll cheer her up.' He felt he knew Ada already.

Sarah rolled over and started to undress him. He pretended to struggle, but she pushed him back on to the bed, and he lay there, shaking with laughter, as she got into a tangle over his puttees. At last she gave up, rested her head on his knees, giggling. 'They're like *stays*.'

'Don't tell the War Office. You'll have a lot of worried men.'

They stopped laughing and looked at each other.

'I love you,' he said.

'Oh, there's no need to say *that*.'

'Yes, there is. It's true.'

She took her time thinking about it. At last she said on an indrawn breath, '*Good*. I love you too.'

*

Owen and Sassoon sat in a corner of the lounge at the Conservative Club. They had the room to themselves, except for one other member, and he was half hidden behind the *Scotsman*. After the waiter had served the brandies and departed, Sassoon produced a book from his pocket. 'I'd like to read you something. Do you mind?'

'No, go ahead. Anybody I know?'

'Alymer Strong. Given to me by the author. He brought me a copy of Lady Margaret's book and – er – happened to mention he wrote himself. Like a fool, I made encouraging noises.'

'Not *always* disastrous. Why am I being read it?'

'You'll see. There's a sort of dedication. In one of the poems.'

> Siegfried, thy fathers warr'd
> With many a kestrel, mimicking the dove.

Owen looked blank. 'What does it mean?'

'What a philistine question. I hope this isn't the future pig-keeper speaking. I believe it to be a reference to the persecution of the Jews.'

'But you're not a Jew.'

'I am, actually. Or rather my "fathers" were.'

'I didn't know that.' Owen contemplated the fact through a haze of burgundy. 'That's why you're called Siegfried?'

'No-o, I'm called Siegfried because my mother liked Wagner. And the only thing I have in common with orthodox Jews is that I do profoundly thank God I was born a man and not a woman. If I were a woman, I'd be called Brünnhilde.'

'This is our last evening and I feel as if I've just met you.'

'You know all the important things.'

They looked at each other. Then a rustling of the *Scotsman*'s pages returned their attention to the book. Sassoon began reading extracts, and Owen, who was drunk and afraid of becoming too serious, laughed till he choked. Sassoon had begun by declaiming the verse solemnly, but when he came to:

> Can it be I have become
> This gourd, this gothic vaccu-um?

he burst out laughing. 'Oh, I love that. *You* might like this better.'

> What cassock'd misanthrope,
> Hawking peace-canticles for glory-gain,
> Hymns from his rostrum'd height th' epopt of Hate?

'The *what* of hate?'

'E*popt*.'

'No such word.'

'There is, you know. It's the heroic form of epogee.'

'Can I see?' Owen read the poem. 'This man's against the war.'

'Oh, yes.' Sassoon's lips twitched. 'And particularly devastated by the role the Christian Church is playing in it. The parallels are worrying, Owen.'

'I'm worried.' He made to hand the book back. 'It's incredible, isn't it?'

'No, look inside.'

Owen looked at the flyleaf and read: *Owen. From S.S. Edinburgh. Oct. 26th 1917.* Underneath Sassoon had written:

> When Captain Cook first sniffed the wattle,
> And Love columbus'd Aristotle.

'That's absolutely typical,' Owen said.

'It does rather encapsulate his style, doesn't it?'

'You know what I mean. The only *slightly* demonstrative thing you've ever done and you do it in a way which makes it impossible to take seriously.'

'Do you think it's a good idea to be serious tonight?'

'For God's sake, I'm only going to Scarborough. *You'll* be in France before I will.'

'I hope so.'

'No news from the War Office?'

'No. And Rivers dropped a bombshell this morning. He's leaving.'

'Is he?'

'I don't look forward to Craiglockhart without either of you. I did mention you to Rivers, you know.'

'What did he say?'

'That you were an extremely gallant and conscientious young officer . . .'

'*Oooh.*'

'"*Oooh*". Who needed no one to teach him his duty. *Unlike* dot dot dot. And there were no grounds at all that he could see for keeping you at the hospital a moment longer. I think he was a bit put out about being asked to overrule Brock.'

'I'm not surprised. You shouldn't have done it. Look, I could do a lot with another month. I *hate* leaving. But the fact is I'd be taking up a bed some other poor blighter needs far more than I do.'

'As I shall be doing.'

'I didn't mean that.'

'No, but it's true.' He glanced at his watch. 'I'd better be off. Under the new regime I believe the penalty for staying out late is public crucifixion.'

In the hall Sassoon produced an envelope from his breast pocket. 'This is a letter of introduction to Robert Ross. It's sealed because there's something else inside, but that doesn't mean you can't read it.'

Owen tried to think of something to say and failed.

'Take care.'

'And you.'

Sassoon patted him on the shoulder, and was gone. Nothing else, not even 'goodbye'. Perhaps it was better that way, Owen thought, going back to the lounge. Better for Siegfried, anyway. Their empty brandy glasses stood together on the table, in the pool of light cast by the standard lamp, but the unseen listener had gone. The *Scotsman*, neatly folded, lay on a table by the door.

Owen sat down, got out the letter of introduction, but didn't immediately open it. The ticking of the clock was very loud in the empty room. He lay back in the chair and closed his eyes. He was afraid to measure his sense of loss.

20

Rivers was due to leave Craiglockhart on 14 November, having fulfilled his promise to Bryce to see the new CO in. He was leaving in what he considered a totally undeserved blaze of glory. Willard was walking at last. Rivers could understand the VADs, the orderlies, the secretaries and the kitchen staff regarding this 'cure' as a great medical feat, but it was a little dismaying to find that even some of the senior nursing staff seemed to agree.

Willard himself was exasperating. All Rivers's efforts to inculcate insight into his condition, to enable him to understand *why* he'd been in the wheelchair and how the same outcome might be avoided in future, were met with a stare of glassy-eyed, quivering respect. Whenever Rivers came anywhere near him, Willard positively leapt to the salute. He *knew* his spinal cord had been broken. He *knew* Rivers had reconnected the severed ends. Needless to say the other MOs were unimpressed. Indeed, after observing Rivers acknowledge one particularly sizzling salute, Brock was heard to murmur: '*And for my next trick I shall walk on water.*'

The last evening round was distressing both for Rivers and the patients. He left Sassoon till last and then, remembering that he'd spent the day with Lady Ottoline Morrell and had, presumably, been exposed to a great dose of pacifist propaganda, went along to his room.

Sassoon was sitting on the floor, hands clasped around his knees, staring into the fire.

'How was Lady Ottoline?' Rivers said, taking the only chair. 'In full cry?'

'Not really. The war was hardly mentioned.'

'Oh?'

'No, we talked about Carpenter mainly. Homosexuality. Or rather I talked. She listened.'

Poor Lady Ottoline. 'The war didn't come up at all?'

'Not today. Last night it did. I think we both knew there was no point going over that again. Do you know what she asked me? Did I realize that going back would involve killing Germans?' He brought his anger under control. 'Pacifists can be amazingly brutal.'

That brief flash of anger was the only emotion Sassoon had shown since skipping the Board. He seemed at times to be almost unaware of his surroundings, as if he could get through this interim period between one Board and the next only by shutting down all awareness of where he was or what was happening. And yet he was writing, and he seemed to think he was writing well. All the anger and grief now went into the poetry. He'd given up hope of influencing events. Or perhaps he'd just given up hope. At the back of Rivers's mind was the fear that Craiglockhart had done to Sassoon what the Somme and Arras had failed to do. And if that were so, he couldn't escape responsibility.

Sassoon roused himself. 'You're off first thing, aren't you?'

'Yes. The six o'clock.'

'So this is goodbye, then.'

'Only for a fortnight. I'll be back for the Board. Meanwhile . . .' He stood up. 'Keep your head down?'

Rivers stayed overnight with the Heads and then moved into his new lodgings in Holford Road, a short walk from the RFC hospital. The floor below was occupied by a family of Belgian refugees whose demands for better food and apparent indifference to rationing irritated the landlady, Mrs Irving, beyond measure. She was inclined to stop Rivers on the stairs and complain about them at considerable length. The other lodgers were apparently more easily satisfied, and gave no grounds for complaint.

The nights were disturbed by air raids, though less by German action than by the guns on the Heath that boomed out with a sound like bombs falling. Everybody congregated in the basement during these raids, the Belgian refugees, Mrs Irving, her unmarried daughter who worked at the hospital, all the other lodgers, and the two young girls who lived in the attics and between them did the whole work of the house. As far as he could make out, they sat around, or under, the table, venturing out to the kitchen to make endless cups of cocoa. He was invited to join these parties, but always declined, saying that the air raids didn't bother him much and he needed his sleep.

He managed to sleep through some of the raids, but on other nights, the guns made sleep impossible. He was not particularly well, but he didn't want to take more sick leave, and he had no routine leave due to him. He spent a lot of the time with the Heads, who turned up one night and swept him off to the theatre to see the Russian ballet. They came out, still dazed with swirling light and colour, to find another raid in progress. In Leicester Square they stopped and looked up at the sky, and there was a Zeppelin floating like a strange, silver fish. Rumour had it they were piloted by women. It seemed incredible to Rivers that anybody should believe this, but he soon discovered that most people did. Mrs Irving knew it for a fact.

As soon as he started work at the hospital he became busy and, as Head had predicted, fascinated by the differences in severity of breakdown between the different branches of the RFC. Pilots, though they did indeed break down, did so less frequently and usually less severely than the men who manned observation balloons. They, floating helplessly above the battle-fields, unable either to avoid attack or to defend themselves effectively against it, showed the highest incidence of breakdown of any service. Even including infantry officers. This reinforced Rivers's view that it was prolonged strain, immobility and helplessness that did the damage, and not the sudden shocks or bizarre horrors that the patients themselves were inclined to point to as the explanation for their condition. That would help to account for the greater prevalence of anxiety neuroses and hysterical disorders in women in peacetime, since their relatively more confined lives gave them fewer opportunities of reacting to stress in active and constructive ways. Any explanation of war neurosis must account for the fact that this apparently intensely masculine life of war and danger and hardship produced in men the same disorders that women suffered from in peace.

So he had plenty to think about, and before long it was clear he would have plenty to do. Many of his old Craiglockhart patients who were living in London or the south of England had already written to ask if they could come to see him. That, by itself, would supply him with a great deal of work.

He was due back at Craiglockhart on the 25th of November. On the 24th he'd accepted an invitation to visit Queen Square. The invitation had been issued several times before and he'd always found a reason for refusing, but now that he was one of the small number of physicians in London dealing with the psycho-neuroses of war, he judged it rather more expedient than pleasant that he should accept. And so, at half past nine on the 24th November, he walked up the steps of the National Hospital. His night had been even more disturbed by the guns than usual, and he was feeling distinctly unwell. If he'd been able to cancel or postpone this visit without giving offence, he would certainly have done so. He gave his name to the receptionist. Dr Yealland was expecting him, she said. Go up.

He took the lift to the third floor. He pushed through the swing doors on to a long, empty, shining corridor, which, as he began to walk down it, seemed to elongate. He began to be afraid he was really ill. This deserted corridor in a hospital he knew to be overcrowded had something eerie about it. Uncanny. Almost the feeling his patients described, talking about their experience of the front, of No Man's Land, that landscape apparently devoid of life that actually contained millions of men.

The swing doors at the far end of the corridor flapped open. At first Rivers was pleased, expecting to be received by some bustling nurse or VAD, but instead a creature – it hardly resembled a man – crawled through the door and began moving towards him. The figure made remarkably rapid progress for somebody so bent, so apparently deformed. His head was twisted to one side, and drawn back, the spine bent so that the chest was parallel with the legs, which themselves were bent at the knees. In addition one arm, the left, was pulled away from the body and contracted. The right hand clung to the rail, not sliding along it, but brought forward step by step, making repeated slapping sounds on the wood.

As they converged, the man turned his head, insofar as he was able to turn it, and stared up at Rivers. Probably this was dictated by no more than the curiosity patients always feel at the appearance of a doctor on wards where nothing else ever happens, but it seemed to Rivers that his expression was both sombre and malevolent. He had to drag his own gaze away. At that moment a VAD came out of a side ward and said in that bracingly jolly way of theirs, 'Nearly ten o'clock. Let's have you in bed.'

The morning round. Rivers wondered if he was in for that.

He was. Yealland came out of his room, flanked by two junior doctors, shook hands briskly and said that he thought the best general introduction was perhaps simply a ward round.

The party consisted of Yealland, the two junior doctors who were being put through their paces, a ward sister, who made no contribution and was invited to make none, and a couple of orderlies who hovered in the background in case they were required to lift. Yealland was an impressive figure. In conversation he did not merely meet your eye, but stared so intently that you felt your skull had become transparent. His speech was extremely precise. Something in this steady, unrelenting projection of authority made Rivers want to laugh, but he didn't think he'd have wanted to laugh if he'd been a junior doctor or a patient.

They did the post-treatment ward first. The bulk of the conversation was between Yealland and the two junior doctors, with occasional asides to Rivers. Contact with patients was restricted to a brisk, cheerful, authoritative greeting. No questions were asked about their psychological state. Many of them, Rivers thought, showed signs of depression, but in every case the removal of the physical symptom was described as a cure. Most of these patients would be out within a week, Yealland said. Rivers asked questions about the relapse rate, the suicide rate, and received the expected reply. Nobody knew.

The admissions ward was next. An immensely long ward, lined with white-covered beds packed close together. On both sides windows reached from floor to ceiling, and the room was flooded with cold northern light. The patients, many displaying bizarre contractures of their limbs, sat, if they were capable of sitting, upright in their beds, as near to attention as they could get. Rivers's corridor acquaintance was just inside the room, lying face down on his bed, buttocks in the air, presumably the only position he was capable of maintaining. It couldn't be said he added to the desired impression of tidiness, but the nurses had done their best. The little procession came to a halt by his bed.

Yealland's previous performance had been perfunctory. Rivers suspected he lost interest in the patients once the miracle had been worked. Now, though, he turned to Rivers with real zest. 'This one's fairly typical,' he said, and nodded to the ginger-haired doctor.

A shell had exploded close to the patient, who had been buried up to the neck and had remained in that position for some time under continued heavy fire. For two or three days after being dug out he'd been dazed, though he did have a vague recollection of the explosion. Six weeks later he'd been sent to England, to a hospital in Eastbourne where he'd been treated with physical exercises. During this time the abnormal flexure of the spine had grown worse.

The sheets were pulled back. It was not possible to bend the trunk passively, the doctor said, demonstrating. The patient couldn't eat from a table and, as they could all see, he couldn't lie straight in bed. He complained of considerable pain in the head, which was worse at night. And when he woke up there were coloured lights dancing in front of his eyes. Some right hemianalgesia was present. There was tenderness – probing – from the sixth dorsal spine down to the lumbar region. Free, but not excessive, perspiration of the feet. A mark made on the sole of the foot lasted an abnormally long time.

'*And?*' Yealland said.

The young man looked frightened, a fear Rivers remembered only too clearly. The missing fact came to him just in time. 'No sign of organic disease,' he finished triumphantly.

'Good. So at least we may be encouraged to believe the patient is in the right hospital?'

'Yes, sir.'

Yealland walked to the head of the bed. 'You will receive treatment this afternoon,' he said. 'I shall begin by making your back straight. This will be done by the application of electricity to your spine and back. You have power to raise your head, indeed you can even extend it. I am sure you understand the pain is due to the position you assume. The muscles are in too great a stretch and there is no relief, because even when you rest the same position is maintained. The electricity may be strong, but it will be the means of restoring your lost powers – the power to straighten your back.'

It was extraordinary. If Yealland had appeared authoritative before, it was nothing compared with the almost God-like tone he now assumed. The patient was looking distinctly alarmed. 'Will it hurt?' he asked.

Yealland said: 'I realize you did not intend to ask that question and so I will overlook it. I am sure you understand the principles of the treatment, which are . . .' He paused, as if expecting the patient to supply them. 'Attention, first and foremost; tongue, last and least; questions, never. I shall see you this afternoon.'

And so on round the ward. Yealland stopped in some triumph by the last bed. 'Now this *is* interesting.'

Rivers had been aware of this patient ever since they entered the ward. He sat up very straight in bed, and followed their progress with an air of brooding antagonism.

'Callan,' Yealland said. 'Mons, the Marne, Aisne, first and second Ypres, Hill 60, Neuve-Chapelle, Loos, Armentières, the Somme and Arras.' He looked at Callan. 'Have I missed any?'

Callan obviously heard the question, but made no response. His eyes flicked from Yealland to Rivers, whom he looked up and down dispassionately. Yealland leant closer to Rivers and murmured, 'Very negative attitude.' He nodded to the junior doctor to begin.

Callan had broken down in April. He'd been employed behind the lines on transport at the time, perhaps because his nervous state was already giving cause for concern. While feeding the horses, he had suddenly fallen down, and had remained unconscious for a period of five hours. When he came round, he was shaking all over and was unable to speak. He hadn't spoken at all since then. He attributed his loss of speech to heatstroke.

'Methods of treatment?' Yealland asked.

The patient had been strapped to a chair for periods of twenty minutes at a time, and very strong electric current applied to his neck and throat. Hot plates had been applied repeatedly to the back of the throat, and lighted cigarettes to the tongue.

'I'm sorry?' Rivers said. 'What was that?'

'Lighted cigarettes to the tongue. Sir.'

'None of it persevered with,' Yealland said. 'It's the worst possible basis for treatment because the electricity's been tried and he knows – or thinks he knows – that it doesn't work.' He walked to the head of the bed. 'Do you wish to be cured? Nod if you do.'

Callan smiled.

'You appear to me to be very indifferent to your condition, but indifference will not do in such times as these. I have seen many patients suffering from similar conditions, and not a few in whom the disorder has existed for a much longer time. It has been my experience with these cases to find two kinds of patients, those who want to recover and those who do not want to recover. I understand your condition thoroughly and it makes no difference to me which group you belong to. You must recover your speech at once.'

As they were leaving the ward, Yealland drew him aside. 'Do you have time to witness a treatment?'

'Yes. I'd very much like to.' Apart from anything else he was curious to know how strong 'strong' was when describing an electric current. It was a matter on which published papers were apt to be reticent. 'Would it be possible for me to see the man we've just left?'

'Yes. Though it won't be quick. And I can't interrupt the treatment.'

'That's all right. I've no afternoon appointments. I'd like to see *him* because of the the previous *failed* treatments.'

'Oh, quite right. *He's* the interesting one. The others are just routine.'

They were walking down to the MOs' dining room for lunch.

'You do only one session?' Rivers asked.

'Yes. The patient has to know when he enters the electrical room that there's no way out except by a full recovery.' Yealland hesitated. 'I normally do treatments alone.'

'I'll be as unobtrusive as I can.'

Yealland nodded. 'Good. The last thing these patients need is a sympathetic audience.'

21

After lunch they went straight to the electrical room. Rivers sat on a hard chair in the corner, prepared to stay as long as necessary. The only other furniture was a small desk under the tall window, with a stack of buff-coloured files on it, the battery and the patient's chair, rather like a dentist's chair, except for the straps on the arms and around the foot rest. Yealland, who'd been emptying his bladder in preparation for a long session, came in, rubbing his hands. He nodded cheerfully to Rivers, but didn't speak. Then, rather to Rivers's surprise, he began pulling down the blinds. The blinds were the thick, efficient blinds of wartime, and after he'd finished not a chink of light from the dank, November day could get into the room. Rivers now expected him to turn on the overhead lights, but he didn't. Instead, he left the room in darkness, except for a small circle of light round the battery. This light was reflected off his white coat and up on to his face.

Callan was brought in. He looked indifferent, or defiant, though once he was settled in the chair his eyes shifted from side to side in a way that suggested fear.

'I am going to lock the door,' Yealland said. He returned to stand before the patient, ostentatiously dropping the key into his top pocket. 'You must talk before you leave me.'

All very well, Rivers thought. But Yealland had locked himself in as well as the patient. There could be no backing down.

Yealland put the pad electrode on the lumbar spines and began attaching the long pharyngeal electrode. 'You will not leave me,' he said, 'until you are talking as well as you ever did. No, not a minute before.'

The straps on the chair were left unfastened. Yealland inserted a tongue depressor. Callan neither co-operated nor struggled, but simply sat with his mouth wide open and his head thrown back. Then the electrode was applied to the back of his throat. He was thrown back with such force that the leads were ripped out of the battery. Yealland removed the electrode. 'Remember you must behave as becomes the hero I expect you to be,' Yealland said. 'A man who has been through so many battles should have a better control of himself.' He fastened the straps round Callan's wrists and feet. 'Remember *you must talk before you leave me.*'

Callan was white and shaking, but it was impossible to tell how much pain he was in, since obviously he could no more scream than he could speak. Yealland applied the electrode again, continuously, but evidently with a weaker current since Callan was not thrown back. 'Nod to me when you are ready to attempt to speak.'

It took an hour. Rivers during all that time scarcely moved. His empathy with the man in the chair kept him still, since Callan himself never moved, except once to flex the fingers of his strapped hands. At last he nodded. Immediately the electrode was removed, and after a great deal of effort Callan managed to say 'ah' in a sort of breathy whisper.

Yealland said, 'Do you realize that there is already an improvement? Do you appreciate that a result has already been achieved? Small as it may seem to you, if you will consider rationally for yourself, you will believe me when I tell you that you will be talking before long.'

The electrode was applied again. Yealland started going through the sounds of the alphabet: ah, bah, cah, dah, etc., encouraging Callan to repeat the sounds after him, though only 'ah' was repeated. Whenever Callan said 'ah' on request, the electrode was momentarily removed. Whenever he substituted 'ah' for other sounds, the current was reapplied.

They had now been in the room an hour and a half. Callan was obviously exhausted. Despite the almost continuous application of the electric current he was actually beginning to drop off to sleep. Yealland evidently sensed he was losing his patient's attention and unstrapped him. 'Walk up and down,' he said.

Callan did as he was bid, and Yealland walked beside him, encouraging him to repeat the sounds of the alphabet, though, again, only 'ah' was produced and that in a hoarse whisper, very far back in the throat. Callan stumbled as he walked, and Yealland supported him. Up and down they went, up and down, in and out of the circle of light around the battery.

Rebellion came at last. Callan wrenched his arm out of Yealland's grasp and ran to the door. Evidently he'd forgotten it was locked, though he remembered at once and turned on Yealland.

Yealland said, 'Such an idea as leaving me now is most ridiculous. You cannot leave the room. The door is locked and the key is in my pocket. You will leave me when you are cured, remember, not before. I have no doubt you are tired and discouraged, but that is not my fault; the reason is that you do not understand your condition as I do, and the time you have already spent with me is not long in comparison with the time I am prepared to stay with you. Do you understand me?'

Callan looked at Yealland. For a second the thought of striking him was clearly visible, but then Callan seemed to admit defeat. He pointed to the battery and then to his mouth, miming: *Get on with it.*

'No,' Yealland said. 'The time for more electrical treatment has not yet come; if it had, I should give it to you. Suggestions are not wanted from you; they are not needed. When the time comes for more electricity, you will be given it whether you want it or not.' He paused. Then added with great emphasis: '*You must speak, but I shall not listen to anything you have to say.*'

They walked up and down again, Callan still repeating 'ah', but making no other sound. The 'ah' was produced by an almost superhuman effort, the muscles of the neck in spasm, the head raised in a series of jerks. Even the torso and the arms were involved in the immense effort of pushing this sound across his lips. Rivers had to stop himself trying to make the sound for him. He was himself very tense; all the worst memories of his stammer came crowding into his mind.

Yealland said, 'You are now ready for the next stage of treatment, which consists of the administration of strong shocks to the *outside* of the neck. These will be transmitted to your voice box and you will soon be able to say anything you like in a whisper.'

Callan was again placed in the chair and again strapped in.

The key electrode was applied in short bursts to his neck in the region of the larynx, Yealland repeating 'ah, bah, cah, dah', etc. in time with the shocks. On the third repetition of the alphabet, Callan suddenly said 'ba'. Instead of attempting the next sound, he went on repeating 'ba', not loudly, but venomously. 'Bah, bah', and then, unmistakably 'Baaaa! Baaaaa! Baaaaaa!'

Yealland actually looked gratified. He said, 'Are you not glad you have made such progress?'

Callan started to cry. For a while there was no other sound in the room than his sobbing. Then he wiped his eyes on the back of his hand and mimed a request for water.

'Yes, you will have water soon. Just as soon as you can utter a word.'

Callan pushed Yealland aside and ran to the door, rattling the handle, beating on the wood with his clenched fists. Rivers couldn't bear to go on watching. He looked down at the backs of his clasped hands.

Yealland said, 'You will leave this room when you are speaking normally. I know you do not want the treatment suspended now you are making such progress. You are a noble fellow and these ideas which come into your mind and make you want to leave me do not represent your true self. I know you are anxious to be cured and are happy to have recovered to such an extent; now you are tired and cannot think properly, but you must make every effort to think in the manner characteristic of your true self: *a hero of Mons.*'

Perhaps Callan remembered, as Yealland apparently did not, that Mons had been a defeat. At any rate he went back to the chair.

'You must utter a sound,' Yealland said. 'I do not care what the nature of the sound is. You will understand me when I say I shall be able to train any sound into the production of *vowel* sounds, then into *letter* sounds, and finally into *words* and *sentences*. Utter a sound when you take a deep breath, and as soon as I touch your throat.'

Callan, although he appeared to be co-operating, could make no expiratory sound.

Yealland appeared to lose patience. He clamped his hands down on to Callan's wrists and said, 'This has gone on long enough. I may have to use a stronger current. I do not want to hurt you, but if necessary I must.'

Rivers couldn't tell whether the anger was acted or real, but there was no doubt about the strength of the current being applied to the neck in shock after shock. But it worked. Soon Callan was repeating 'ah' at a normal pitch, then other sounds, then words. At this point Yealland stopped the use of electricity, and Callan sagged forward in the chair. He looked as if he were going to fall, but the straps held him in place. 'Go on repeating the days,' Yealland said.

'S-s-s-sunday. M-m-m-m-m-monday. T-t-t-tuesday . . .'

Saturday came at last.

Yealland said, 'Remember there is no way out, except by the return of your proper voice and by that door. I have one key, *you* have the other. When you can talk properly, I shall open the door and you can go back to the ward.'

And so it went on, through the alphabet, the days of the week, the months of the year – the shocks sometimes mild, sometimes extremely strong – until he was speaking normally. As soon as he could say words clearly at a normal pitch, he developed a spasm or tremor – not unlike paralysis agitans – in his left arm. Yealland applied a roller electrode to the arm. The tremor then reappeared in the right arm, then the left leg, and finally the right leg, each appearance being treated with the application of the electrode. Finally the cure was pronounced complete. Callan was permitted to stand up. 'Are you not pleased to be cured?' Yealland asked.

Callan smiled.

'I do not like your smile,' Yealland said. 'I find it most objectionable. Sit down.'

Callan sat.

'This will not take a moment,' Yealland said. 'Smile.'

Callan smiled and the key electrode was applied to the side of his mouth. When he was finally permitted to stand up again, he no longer smiled.

'Are you not pleased to be cured?' Yealland repeated.

'Yes, sir.'

'Nothing else?'

A fractional hesitation. Then Callan realized what was required and came smartly to the salute. 'Thank you, sir.'

22

That evening after dinner Rivers tried to work on a paper he was due to give to the Royal Society of Medicine in December. As he read through what he'd written, he became aware that he was being haunted by images. The man in the corridor at Queen Square, Yealland's hands, Callan's open mouth, the two figures, doctor and patient, walking up and down, in and out of the circle of light round the battery. It was unusual for Rivers to visualize as intensely as this, indeed to visualize at all, but then the whole experience, from beginning to end, had had something . . . hallucinatory about it.

Rivers left the typewriter and went to sit in his armchair by the fire. As soon as he abandoned the attempt to concentrate on the paper, he knew he was ill. He was sweating, his heart pounded, pulses all over his body throbbed, and he felt again that extraordinary sensation of blood squeezing through his veins. He thought he might have a slight temperature, but he never, as a matter of principle, took his own temperature or measured his pulse. There were depths of neuroticism to which he was not prepared to sink.

His confrontation with Yealland had exhausted him, for, however polite they had each been to each other, it *had* been a confrontation. He was too tired to go on working, but he knew if he went to bed in this state he wouldn't sleep, even if there was no disturbance from the guns. He decided to take a turn on the Heath, fetched his greatcoat from the peg and crept downstairs. Mrs Irving was a pleasant enough woman, but she was also a very lonely woman, and inclined to air her grievances about the excessive demands of Belgian refugees. He reached the bottom of the stairs, listened a moment, then quietly let himself out of the house.

He felt his way along the dark street. Shuttered windows, like blind eyes, watched from either side. It was something new this darkness, like the deep darkness of the countryside. Even on the Heath, where normally London was spread out before you in a blaze of light, there was only darkness, and again darkness. Starlight lay on the pond, waking a dull gleam, like metal. Nothing else. He started to walk round the edge, trying to empty his mind of Queen Square, but the images floated before him like specks in the eye. Again and again he saw Callan's face, heard his voice repeating simple words, a grotesque parody of Adam naming created things. He felt pursued. There they were, the two of them, Yealland and his patient, walking up and down inside his head. Uninvited. If this was what habitual visualizers experienced, he could only say he found it most unpleasant.

He stopped and looked at the pond. He was aware of rustling, dragging footsteps. Somebody bumped into him and muttered something, but he moved away. By the time he got back to his lodgings he felt much better, well enough to greet Mrs Irving in the hall and compliment her on a more than adequate dinner.

Back in his own rooms he went straight to bed. The sheets felt cold, so cold he again wondered if he was running a temperature, but at least the palpitations and the breathlessness had gone. He thought he might manage to sleep if the Zeppelins and the guns allowed it, and indeed he did fall asleep almost as soon as he turned off the light.

He was walking down the corridor at Queen Square, an immensely long corridor which elongated as he walked along it, like a strip of elastic at full stretch. The swing doors at the far end opened and shut, flap-flapping an unnaturally long time, like the wings of an ominous bird. Clinging to the rail, the deformed man watched him approach. The eyes swivelled to follow him. The mouth opened and out of it came the words: *I am making this protest on behalf of my fellow-soldiers because I believe the war is being deliberately prolonged by those who have the power to end it.*

The words echoed along the white corridor. Abruptly the dream changed. He was in the electrical room, a pharyngeal electrode in his hand, a man's open mouth in front of him. He saw the moist, pink interior, the delicately quivering uvula, the yellowish, grainy surface of the tongue, and the tonsils, like great swollen, blue-purple eggs. He slipped the tongue depressor in, and tried to apply the electrode, but the electrode, for some reason, wouldn't fit. He tried to force it. The man struggled and bucked beneath him, and, looking down, he saw that the object he was holding was a horse's bit. He'd already done a lot of damage. The corners of the man's mouth were raw, flecked with blood and foam, but still he went on, trying to force the bit into the mouth, until a cry from the patient woke him. He sat up, heart pounding, and realized he had himself cried out. For a second the dream was so real that he went on seeing the chair, the battery, the tortured mouth. Then, nothing. Gradually, his heart beat returned to normal, though when he got out of bed and went across to sit by the window the small effort made it pound again.

No raid tonight. It was ironic that on this one quiet night he should have woken himself up with a nightmare. As with all nightmares, the horror lingered. He was still inclined to accuse himself. That, he thought – self-reproach – had been the dominant affect. At first he was inclined to connect it with the quasi-sexual imagery of the dream, for the dream action had been both an accurate representation of Yealland's treatment and uncomfortably like an oral rape. He didn't feel, however, that the underlying conflict had been sexual.

The manifest content came from his visit to Queen Square, and was present with relatively little transformation. There was no doubt that the visit had been rife with opportunities for conflict. From the beginning he'd felt a tension between, on the one hand, his sympathy for the patients, his doubts about the quality of the treatment they were receiving, and on the other, the social and professional demands on him to be reasonably polite. As the day had gone on, this conflict had certainly deepened. Over lunch Yealland had told him about an officer patient of his who stammered badly, and whom Yealland had cured in – as usual – one session. Rivers – to his own amusement and exasperation – had responded to the story by beginning to stammer rather badly. And wherever he'd hesitated over a word, he'd sensed Yealland calculating the voltage. All nonsense of course. He'd been more amused by the situation than anything else, but nevertheless the worsening of his stammer did point to an underlying conflict that might well find expression in a dream.

The man in the corridor with the spinal contracture seemed to represent Sassoon, since he'd quoted the Declaration, though it was difficult to imagine anybody more physically unlike Sassoon than that deformed, pseudo-dwarf. And the expression of antagonism – that certainly didn't correspond with anything in the real Sassoon's attitude towards him. But then there was no reason why it should. The dream action is the creation of the dreamer. The mood of this dream, a mood so powerful he could still not shake it off, was one of the most painful self-accusation. The man's expression need reflect no more than *his* feeling that Sassoon, perhaps, had grounds for antagonism.

He hadn't been able to see the face of the second patient, and had no clear sense of who it was. The obvious candidate was Callan, since it was Callan he'd watched being treated. And Callan had been working with horses when he became mute, which might account for the bit. And yet he was fairly certain the dream patient had not been Callan.

On the wards he'd been struck by a slight facial resemblance between Callan and Prior, who had also been mute when he arrived at Craiglockhart. He remembered an incident shortly after Prior's arrival when he'd dragged a teaspoon across the back of his throat, hoping that the choking reflex would trigger the return of speech. This did sometimes happen. He'd seen more than one patient recover his voice in that way. But he'd tried it while in a state of acute irritation with Prior, and the choking had occasioned a momentary spasm of satisfaction. Very slight, but enough to make him feel, in retrospect, discontented with his own behaviour. Mute patients *did* arouse exasperation, particularly, as with both Prior and Callan, when their satisfaction with their condition was hardly at all disguised. Perhaps the dream patient was a composite figure, part Callan, part Prior, the combination suggested by his application of a teaspoon to Prior's throat and Yealland's application of an electrode to Callan's.

But there was no comparison in the amount of pain inflicted. On the face of it he seemed to be congratulating himself on dealing with patients more humanely than Yealland, but then why the mood of self-accusation? In the dream he stood in Yealland's place. The dream seemed to be saying, in dream language, don't flatter yourself. There *is* no distinction.

A horse's bit. Not an electrode, not a teaspoon. A bit. An instrument of control. Obviously he and Yealland were both in the business of controlling people. Each of them fitted young men back into the role of warrior, a role they had – however unconsciously – rejected. He'd found himself wondering once or twice recently what possible meaning the restoration of mental health could have in relation to his work. Normally a cure implies that the patient will no longer engage in behaviour that is clearly self-destructive. But in present circumstances, recovery meant the resumption of activities that were not merely self-destructive but positively suicidal. But then in a war nobody is a free agent. He and Yealland were both *locked in*, every bit as much as their patients were.

Bits. The scold's bridle used to silence recalcitrant women in the Middle Ages. More recently, on American slaves. And yet on the ward, listening to the list of Callan's battles, he'd felt that nothing Callan could say could have been more powerful than his silence. Later, in the electrical room, as Callan began slowly to repeat the alphabet, walking up and down with Yealland, in and out of the circle of light, Rivers had felt that he was witnessing the *silencing* of a human being. Indeed, Yealland had come very close to saying just that. 'You must speak, but I shall not listen to anything you have to say.'

Silencing, then. The task of silencing somebody, with himself in Yealland's place and an unidentified patient in the chair. It was possible to escape still, to pretend the dream accusation was general. Just as Yealland silenced the unconscious protest of *his* patients by removing the paralysis, the deafness, the blindness, the muteness that stood between them and the war, so, in an infinitely more gentle way, *he* silenced *his* patients; for the stammerings, the nightmares, the tremors, the memory lapses, of officers were just as much unwitting protest as the grosser maladies of the men.

But he didn't believe in the general accusation. He didn't believe this was what the dream was saying. Dreams were detailed, concrete, specific: the voice of the protopathic heard at last, as one by one the higher centres of the brain closed down. And he knew who the patient in the chair was. Not Callan, not Prior. Only one man was being silenced in the way the dream indicated. He told himself that the accusation was unjust. It was Sassoon's decision to abandon the protest, not his. But that didn't work. He knew the extent of his own influence.

He went on sitting by the window as dawn grew over the Heath, and felt that he was having to appeal against conviction in a courtroom where he himself had been both judge and jury.

23

Head's room was very quiet. The tall windows that overlooked the square were shrouded in white net. Outside was a day of moving clouds and fitful sunlight, and whenever the sun shone, the naked branches of plane trees patterned the floor. So Head's patients must sit, hour after hour, with those bright, rather prominent eyes fixed on them, while elsewhere in the house doors banged and a telephone started to ring. But there the normality of the 'consultation' ended, for Head would never, not even under the most extreme provocation, have told a *patient* that he was talking a load of self-indulgent rubbish. Rivers opened his mouth to protest and was waved into silence.

'All right,' Head swept on. 'He's muddle-headed, immature, liable to fits of enthusiasm, inconsistent. All of that. But . . . *And* he virtually had no father *and* he's put you in his father's place. *But*, he's also' – ticking off on his fingers – 'brave, capable of resisting any amount of pressure – the mere fact he protested at all in the present climate tells us that – and above all – no, let me finish – he has *integrity*. Everything you've told me about him suggests he was always going to go back, as soon as he knew the protest was useless, simply because there's no way he can *honourably* stay in Craiglockhart taking up a bed he doesn't need.'

Rivers smiled. 'What are friends for if not letting you off the hook?'

'Well, let me get you off the other hook while I'm about it. You and Yealland doing *essentially the same thing*. Good God, man, if you really believe that it's the first sign of dementia. I can't imagine anybody less like Yealland – methods, attitudes, values – everything. The whole attitude to the patient. And in spite of all this *self-laceration*, I can't help thinking you know that. Who would you rather be sent to if you were the patient?'

'You.'

Head smiled. 'No. I don't say I do a bad job, but I'm not as good with these particular patients as you are.'

'I suppose I'm worried about him.'

'Yes. Well . . .'

'I think what bothers me more than anything else is this total inability to think about after the war. You see, I think he's made up his mind to get killed.'

'All the more reason for you to get it clear whose decision it was that he went back.' A pause. 'You know after dinner the other night Ruth was saying how much she thought you'd changed.'

Rivers was looking out of the window.

'Do you think you have?'

'I'm probably the last person to know. I can't imagine going back to the same way of life. But . . .' He raised his hands. 'I've been there before. And . . .' A little, self-deprecating laugh. 'Nothing happened.'

'When was this?'

'After my second trip to the Solomons.'

Head waited.

'I don't know whether you've ever had the . . . the experience of having your life changed by a quite trivial incident. You know, nothing dramatic like the death of a parent, or the birth of a child. Something *so* trivial you almost can't see *why* it had the effect it had. It happened to me on that trip. I was on the *Southern Cross* – that's the mission boat – and there was a group of islanders there – recent converts. You can always tell if they're recent, because the women still have bare breasts. And I thought I'd go through my usual routine, so I started asking questions. The first question was, what would you do with it if you earned or found a guinea? Would you share it, and if so who would you share it *with*? It gets their attention because to them it's a lot of money, and you can uncover all kinds of things about kinship structure and economic arrangements, and so on. Anyway at the end of this – we were all sitting cross-legged on the deck, miles from anywhere – they decided they'd turn the tables on me, and ask me the same questions. Starting with: What would *I* do with a guinea? Who would I share it with? I explained I was unmarried and that I wouldn't necessarily feel obliged to share it with anybody. They were *incredulous.* How could anybody live *like that?* And so it went on, question after question. And it was one of those situations, you know, where one person starts laughing and everybody joins in and in the end the laughter just feeds off itself. They were rolling round the deck by the time I'd finished. And suddenly I realized that *anything* I told them would have got the same response. I could've talked about sex, repression, guilt, fear – the whole sorry caboodle – and it would've got exactly the same response. They wouldn't've felt a twinge of disgust or disapproval or . . . sympathy or anything, because it would all have been *too bizarre.* And I suddenly saw that their reactions to my society were neither more nor less valid than mine to theirs. And do you know that was a moment of the most *amazing* freedom. I lay back and I closed my eyes and I felt as if a ton weight had been lifted.'

'*Sexual* freedom?'

'That too. But it was it was more than that. It was . . . the *Great White God* de-throned, I suppose. Because we did, we quite unselfconsciously *assumed* we were the measure of all things. That was how we approached them. And suddenly I saw not only that we weren't the measure of all things, but that *there was no measure.*'

'And yet you say nothing changed?'

'Nothing changed *in England.* And I don't know why. I think partly just the sheer force of other people's expectations. *You* know you're walking around with a mask on, and you desperately want to take it off and you can't because everybody else thinks it's your face.'

'And now?'

'I don't know. I think perhaps the patients've . . . have done for me what I couldn't do for myself.' He smiled. 'You see healing *does* go on, even if not in the expected direction.'

Rivers's return to Craiglockhart on this occasion was quieter than any previous return had been. There were no boisterous young men playing football with a visitor's hat; indeed, the whole building seemed quieter, though Brock, whom Rivers sat next to at dinner, said that the change in regime had not been as striking as had been intended. The wearing of Sam Browne belts was strictly enjoined and offenders relentlessly pursued, but, aside from that, the attempt to run a psychiatric hospital on parade ground lines had been briefly and vociferously tried, then rapidly and quietly abandoned.

After dinner Rivers set out to see the patients who were due to be Boarded the following day. Anderson had at last received a visit from his wife, though it didn't seem to have cheered him up much. The conflict between himself and his family, as to whether he should return to medicine or not, was deepening as the time came for him to leave Craiglockhart. The nightmares were still very bad, but in any case the haemophobia alone prevented any hospital service whether in Britain or France. Rivers hoped that he would be given a desk job in London, which would also enable Rivers to go on seeing him. At the same time he was a little doubtful even about that. Anderson had moved from a position of being sceptical and even uncooperative to a state of deep attachment, in which there was a danger of dependency. He left Anderson's room shaking his head.

Sassoon was sitting by the fire in almost the same position he'd been in when Rivers left.

'What have you been doing with yourself?' Rivers asked.

'Trying to keep my head down.'

'Successfully?'

'I think so.'

'Have you managed to write?'

'Finished the book. It's called *Counter-Attack*.'

'Very appropriate.'

'You shall have the first copy.'

Rivers looked round the room, which seemed cold and bleak in spite of the small fire. 'Do you hear from Owen at all?'

'Constantly. He ... er ... writes distinctly effusive letters. You know ...' He hesitated. 'I knew about the hero-worship, but I'm beginning to think it was rather more than that.'

Rivers watched the firelight flicker on Sassoon's hair and face. He said, 'It happens.'

'I just hope I was kind enough.'

'I'm sure you were.'

'I don't suppose you've heard from the War Office?'

'On the contrary. I had dinner with Hope the other night, and I have an *informal* assurance that no obstacles will be put in your way. It's not a guarantee, but it's the best I can do.'

Sassoon took a deep breath. 'All right. Back to the sausage machine.'

'It doesn't mean you don't have to be careful with the Board.'

Sassoon smiled. 'I shall say as little as possible.'

The Board was chaired by the new CO, Colonel Balfour Graham. The previous evening Rivers and Brock had discussed the likely effects of this on the conduct of the Board, but had not been able to reach any firm conclusion. Balfour Graham hadn't had time to get to know most of the patients. Either he'd be content simply to move things along as smoothly as possible or, at worst, he might feel obliged to assert his authority by asking both patient and MO more questions than was usual. The third member of the Board was Major Huntley, still – if his conversation over breakfast was anything to go by – obsessed by rose growing and racial degeneracy.

Anderson came first. Balfour Graham expressed some surprise that Rivers was not recommending a general discharge.

'He still wants to serve his country,' Rivers said. 'And there's absolutely no reason why he shouldn't be able to do so. In an administrative capacity. I rather think he may be given a desk job in the War Office.'

'Are we doing the War Office or the patient a favour?' Balfour Graham asked.

'He's an able man. It might be quite good for them to have somebody with extensive experience of France.'

'Lord, *yes*,' said Huntley.

'It merely occurred to me that it might be convenient for Anderson to be able to postpone the moment when he has to face the prospect of civilian medicine.'

'That too,' said Rivers.

The actual interview with Anderson was reasonably quick. Indeed, the whole morning went quickly. They stopped for lunch – over which Rivers professed great interest in mildew and blackspot — and then sat down rather wearily but on time for the next ten. Rivers hardly knew at this stage whether he felt reassured or not. Balfour Graham was quick, courteous, efficient — and shrewd. Huntley's interventions, though rare, were rather unpredictable, and seemed to depend entirely on whether he liked the patient. He took to Willard at once, and was scandalized when Rivers made some comment deploring Willard's lack of insight. 'What's he want insight for? He's supposed to be killing the buggers, Rivers, not psychoanalysing them.'

Sassoon was last but one. 'A *slightly* unusual case,' Rivers began, dismissively. 'In the sense that I'm recommending him for general service overseas.'

'More than *slightly* unusual, surely?' Balfour Graham asked with a faint smile. 'I don't think it's ever been done before. Has it?'

'I couldn't make any other recommendation. He's completely fit, mentally and physically, he *wants* to go back to France, and . . . I have been given an assurance by the War Office that no obstacles will be placed in his way.'

'Why should they be?' asked Huntley.

Balfour Graham said, 'This is the young man who believes the war is being fought for the wrong reasons, and that we should explore Germany's offer of a negotiated peace. Do you think –'

'Those *were* his views,' Rivers said, 'while he was still suffering from exhaustion and the after-effects of a shoulder wound. Fortunately a brother officer intervened and he was sent here. Really no more was required than a brief period of rest and reflection. He now feels very strongly that it's his duty to go back.'

'He was dealt with very leniently, it seems to me,' Huntley said.

'He has a good record. MC. Recommended for the DSO.'

'Ah,' Huntley said.

'I do see what you mean by unusual,' Balfour Graham said.

'The point is he *wants* to go back.'

'Right, let's see him.'

Sassoon came in and saluted. Rivers watched the other two.

Balfour Graham acknowledged the salute pleasantly enough. Major Huntley positively beamed. Rivers took Sassoon through the recent past, framing his questions to require no more than a simple yes or no. Sassoon's manner was excellent. Exactly the right mixture of confidence and deference. Rivers turned to Balfour Graham.

Balfour Graham was shuffling about among his papers. Suddenly, he looked up. 'No nightmares?'

'No, sir.'

Sassoon's expression didn't change, but Rivers sensed he was lying.

'Never?'

'Not since I left the 4th London, sir.'

'That was in . . . April?'

'Yes, sir.'

Balfour Graham looked at Rivers. Rivers looked at the ceiling.

'Major Huntley?'

Major Huntley leaned forward. 'Rivers tells us you've changed your mind about the war. Is that right?'

A startled glance. 'No, sir.'

Balfour Graham and Huntley looked at each other.

'You *haven't* changed your views?' Balfour Graham asked.

'No, sir.' Sassoon's gaze was fixed unwaveringly on Rivers. 'I believe exactly what I believed in July. Only if possible more strongly.'

A tense silence.

'I see,' Balfour Graham said.

'Wasn't there something in *The Times*?' Huntley asked. 'I seem to . . .'

He reached across for the file. Rivers leant forward, pinning it to the table with his elbow. 'But you do now feel quite certain it's your duty to go back?'

'Yes, sir.'

'And you have no doubts about that?'

'None whatsoever.'

'*Well*,' Balfour Graham said as the door closed behind Sassoon, 'I suppose you are sure about this, Rivers? He's not going to go back and foment rebellion in the ranks?'

'No, he won't do that. He won't do anything to lower the morale of his men.'

'I hope you're right. He was lying about the nightmares, you know.'

'Yes, I gathered that.'

'I suppose he thinks that might be a reason for keeping him here. The point is do *we* see a reason for keeping him here? Huntley?'

Major Huntley seemed to return from a great distance. 'Spanish Jews.'

Balfour Graham looked blank.

'Father's side. Spanish Jews.'

'You know the family?' Rivers asked.

'Good lord, yes. Mother was a Thornycroft.' He shook his head. '*Ah well*. Hybrid vigour.'

Rivers was across the rose garden several paces ahead of Balfour Graham. 'So you think he's fit?'

''*Course he's fit*. Good God, man, how often do you see a physique like that, even in the so-called upper classes?'

They were back to eugenics again, but for once Rivers had no desire to interrupt.

After dinner Sassoon came to say goodbye. He'd been told the result of the Board and had spent the intervening time packing. Rivers hadn't expected him to linger. Apart from Owen, he'd made no friends at Craiglockhart, not even Anderson, though they'd spent a large part of every day together. And he'd never bothered to disguise his hatred of the place.

'What are you going to do?' Rivers asked.

'Oh, I'll have a couple of days in London, then go home, I suppose.'

'Time for a consultation with Dr Mercier? No, I mean it.'

'I know you mean it. You old fox. Then Garsington, try to explain myself to the pacifists.' He pulled a face. 'I don't look forward to that.'

'Blame me. They will.'

'I shall do no such thing.'

'It's a possible way of telling the story, you know.'

'Yes, I know. But it's not the way I'd tell it. Was it difficult, the Board?'

'No, surprisingly easy. Major Huntley thinks you have a great future as a rose bush. Hybrid vigour.'

'Ah, I see. Dad's lot.'

'I must say the sheer *force* of your refusal to recant came as rather a shock.'

Sassoon looked away. 'I couldn't lie.'

'You managed all right about the nightmares.'

Silence.

'How long has that been going on?'

'Since you left. I'll be all right once I'm out of this place.'

Sassoon didn't want to talk about the nightmares. He was feeling distinctly cheerful. Exactly the same feeling he had had on board ship going to France, watching England slide away into the mist. No doubts, no scruples, no agonizing, just a straightforward, headlong retreat towards the front.

Rivers seemed to read his thoughts. 'Don't take unnecessary risks.'

'No, of course not,' Sassoon said. Though he thought he might.

He stood up, visibly anxious to be off. Rivers followed him to the door and then out into the entrance hall. Balfour Graham and Huntley were there, deep in conversation. It was going to be a very public farewell.

'I'll keep in touch,' Sassoon said.

'Yes. Try and see me before you leave England.'

They shook hands. Then Sassoon, glancing sideways at the colonel and the major, smiled a distinctly conspiratorial smile and came smartly to the salute. 'Thank you, sir.'

For a moment, it was Callan standing there. Then the electrical room at Queen Square faded, and Rivers was back at Craiglockhart, on the black and white tiled floor, alone.

He returned to his desk, and drew a stack of files towards him. He was writing brief notes on the patients who'd been Boarded that day, but this he could do almost automatically. His thoughts wandered as he wrote. He wasted no time wondering how he would feel if Siegfried were to be maimed or killed, because this was a possibility with any patient who returned to France. He'd faced that already, many times. If anything, he was amused by the irony of the situation, that he, who was in the business of changing people, should himself have been changed and by somebody who was clearly unaware of having done it.

It was a far deeper change, though, than merely coming to believe that a negotiated peace might be possible, and desirable. That at least it ought to be explored. He remembered telling Head how he had tried to change his life when he came back from Melanesia for the second time and how that attempt had failed. He'd gone on being reticent, introverted, reclusive. Of course it had been a very introverted, self-conscious attempt, and perhaps that was why it hadn't worked. Here in this building, where he had no time to be introverted or self-conscious, where he hardly had a moment to himself at all, the changes had taken place without his knowing. That was not Siegfried. That was all of them. Burns and Prior and Pugh and a hundred others. As a young man he'd been both by temperament and conviction deeply conservative, and not merely in politics. Now, in middle age, the sheer extent of the *mess* seemed to be forcing him into conflict with the authorities over a very wide range of issues ... medical, military. Whatever. A society that devours its own young deserves no automatic or unquestioning allegiance. Perhaps the rebellion of the old might count for rather more than the rebellion of the young. Certainly poor Siegfried's rebellion hadn't counted for much, though he reminded himself that he couldn't *know* that. It had been a completely honest action and such actions are seeds carried on the wind. Nobody can tell where, or in what circumstances, they will bear fruit.

How on earth was Siegfried going to manage in France? His opposition to the war had not changed. If anything it had hardened. And to go back to fight, believing as he did, would be to encounter internal divisions far deeper than anything he'd experienced before. Siegfried's 'solution' was to tell himself that he was going back only to look after some men, but that formula would not survive the realities of France. However devoted to his men's welfare a platoon commander might be, in the end he is there to kill, and to train other people to kill. Poetry and pacifism are a strange preparation for that role. Though Siegfried had performed it before, and with conspicuous success. But then his hatred of the war had not been as fully fledged, as articulate, as it was now.

It was a dilemma with one very obvious way out. Rivers knew, though he had never voiced his knowledge, that Sassoon was going back with the intention of being killed. Partly, no doubt, this was youthful self-dramatization. *I'll show them. They'll be sorry.* But underneath that, Rivers felt there was a genuine and very deep desire for death.

And if death were to be denied? Then he might well break down. A real breakdown, this time.

Rivers saw that he had reached Sassoon's file. He read through the admission report and the notes that followed it. There was nothing more he wanted to say that he could say. He drew the final page towards him and wrote: *Nov. 26, 1917. Discharged to duty*.

Author's Note

Fact and fiction are so interwoven in this book that it may help the reader to know what is historical and what is not. Siegfried Sassoon (1886–1967) did, in July 1917, protest against the continuation of the war. Robert Graves persuaded him to attend a Medical Board and he was sent to Craiglockhart War Hospital, where he came under the care of Dr W. H. R. Rivers, FRS (1864–1922), the distinguished neurologist and social anthropologist, who then held the rank of captain in the RAMC. During Sassoon's stay he formed a friendship with one of Dr Brock's patients, Wilfred Owen (1893–1918), though it is probably fair to say that this friendship played a more central role in Owen's life, then and later, than it did in Sassoon's.

Rivers's methods of treating his patients are described in 'The Repression of War Experience' (*Lancet*, 2 Feb. 1918) and in his posthumously published book *Conflict and Dream* (London, Kegan Paul, 1923), in which Sassoon makes a brief appearance as 'Patient B'.

Dr Lewis Yealland's rather different methods of treating his patients are described in detail in his book: *Hysterical Disorders of Warfare* (London, Macmillan, 1918).

There is an interesting discussion of Rivers's pre-war work with Henry Head on nerve regeneration, and the concept of protopathic and epicritic innervation which evolved from it, in 'The Dog Beneath the Skin' by Jonathan Miller (*Listener*, 20 July 1972).

The amendments suggested by Sassoon to the early draft of 'Anthem for Doomed Youth' appear in Sassoon's handwriting on the MSS. See *Wilfred Owen: The Complete Poems and Fragments*, Vol. II, edited by Jon Stallworthy (Chatto & Windus, The Hogarth Press and Oxford University Press, 1983). Two modern texts which contain stimulating discussions of 'shell-shock' are *No Man's Land: Combat and Identity in World War I* by Eric Leed

(Cambridge University Press, 1979) and *The Female Malady* by Elaine Showalter (Virago Press, 1987).

Julian Dadd, whose psychiatric illness caused Sassoon some concern during his stay at Craiglockhart, subsequently went on to make a complete recovery.

I'm grateful for help received from the staff of the following libraries: Sheffield Public Library, Newcastle University Medical Library, Cambridge University Library, Napier Polytechnic Library, Edinburgh (formerly Craiglockhart War Hospital), The Oxford University English Faculty Library, the Imperial War Museum, and St John's College, Cambridge, where the Deputy Librarian M. Pratt did much to make my visit interesting and enjoyable.